WATER UNDER
THE BRIDGE

George Penroy

For Monica and John

Hope it makes you smile.

George Penroy.

THE KHARG PRESS

© George Penroy 2010
Water under the Bridge

ISBN 978-0-9565674-0-6

Published by Kharg Press
3 The Rosery
Gosport
Hampshire
PO12 2SD

A CIP catalogue record of this book
can be obtained from the British Library.

Book designed by Michael Walsh at
THE BETTER BOOK COMPANY

and printed by
ASHFORD COLOUR PRESS
Unit 600 Fareham Reach
Fareham Road
Gosport
Hants PO13 0FW

Pure water is the best of gifts that man to man can bring,
But who am I that I should have the best of anything?
Let princes revel at the pump, let peers with pools make free,
Whiskey, or wine, or even beer is good enough for me.

Unknown

Attributed to Lord Neaves 1800-1876
and also to G.W.E. Russell 1867 - ?

Author's note:

This work is fiction set in a background of actual ports in the Middle East. A consortium of oil companies operated in Iran during the second half of the twentieth century and many expatriates were employed there. Many of the events are based on fact. Nevertheless the characters portrayed and their names are imaginary and any resemblance to actual persons is unintended.

For Kay

THE PROLOGUE

George slowly surfaced into consciousness from a deep sleep, his head throbbing like an idling diesel motor. He dimly remembered struggling up from the depths some hours earlier, when the strident, high pitched, tenor call of '*Allah akhbar*' blasted from the electronic powered speaker system of the nearby mosque. The call was echoed by others, each lessening in decibels as the distance of the mosques from the hotel thankfully increased. He had sunk back into his alcohol-induced sleep gratefully, when the silence eventually returned. A gargle with the local Shams brew the night before had left him with a heavy head and a taste like a mouthful of the nearby, foetid Shatt al Arab River. He had rarely tried Shams beer before, and was completely unaware of the addition of glycerine to each sickly hued, green bottle to preserve the contents in hot weather. He soon became aware, however, that something in the drink was competing for supremacy with his last solid meal and headed for the toilet with all the speed of a greased whippet. He gazed around him, taking stock of the surroundings and feeling rather pleased that the facilities were well up to the familiar Western standards. He had somehow expected a lack of toilet paper, and having to squat over more basic plumbing.

A short while later, feeling rather better, he threw off his worn, blue, Marks and Sparks pyjama bottoms, and headed back to the bathroom for a shower. The room was already warming up, despite the air conditioning and he still had the unwashed, well travelled feeling that came from a long flight from Heathrow the day before. He stood under a steady piddle of tepid water, and slowly soaked some semblance of normality back into himself, pondering all the while on the way he had come to be in an Iranian hotel in an oil port that bordered neighbouring Iraq.

He towelled himself dry under the draught from the slowly revolving ceiling fan, and looked out of the window across the dusty, sun lit tops of gently waving palm trees. 'I wonder if they ever produce dates?' he asked himself, without bothering to ponder the reply. He had been to the port many times before but had always arrived by ship in the river. His trips ashore had been limited to the Seaman's Club; an American run haven where English films were shown on an outside screen at night, and where, for a few rials, one could get a passable hair cut. He thought of the ever-present geckos crawling across the cinema screen, usually across the most prominent parts of the female lead's anatomy and then remembered the date bugs that flew around the trees by the green tiled swimming pool every evening at dusk. Ugly beasts which took a delight in dive bombing the heads of the unsuspecting cinema-goers, especially those who weren't too keen on bugs that seemed the size of the Hindenburg. 'Better get used to them,' he thought, 'There's no turning back for at least three months.'

He had left England the day before. It had taken a long time to prepare everything for the journey and in a way he was glad. He had paid off from his last ship two months ago, pleased to be ending the part of life where he had to go to sea for month after dull, repetitive month with little hope of any respite. The daily monotony of the twelve to four watch, standing alone on the bridge of a rusting tanker from midnight to four in the morning and then repeating the performance from midday to four in the afternoon with only the ticking of the auto pilot for company was only relieved by chart correcting in the forenoon, repairs to the radar or gyro compass, or giving up sleep for arriving or sailing from another dreary port. A ship scudding across the horizon or sighting a distant headland hardly diminished the boredom and was far removed from the romantic ideas of visiting exotic countries that he had entertained in his early youth. It was not even remotely close to the vision of Noel Coward and the men of the merchant service from George's favourite wartime film 'In Which we Serve'. However, two months at home with his wife and two small children, and two weeks in front of the television watching the England football team unexpectedly defeating all comers in the World Cup, had gone some way to recharging the batteries for the new life to come.

For the first time in his life George possessed a passport instead of a battered green Seaman's Identity Card. The photograph showed his hollow cheeks with a day's growth of beard and the suspicion of thinning hair. It was a young face though and reflected a mischievous glint around the eyes. At twenty-seven years old the eyes had seen a fair proportion of the seamier side of foreign ports and spent a dozen years gazing at the empty oceans of the world. He had shown his shiny new passport to a turbaned Sikh at Heathrow airport before boarding an aeroplane for the first time in his life. After the first sudden swoop into the skies he had settled down, hoping that the popping in his ears would not last throughout the flight. He was pleasantly surprised with the meals, which were served on plastic trays and was tempted to pocket a teaspoon from the tray as a souvenir. Discretion, however, proved the better part of valour and the shiny silver teaspoon remained on the tray. Thoughts of being led away in an Islamic country, accused of stealing airline property, proved to be a formidable deterrent and caused an uncomfortable cutting sensation around the right wrist.

The flight touched down at Cairo to refuel and the ear popping business of flying then continued monotonously through the day. Darkness had fallen when the flight approached its final destination and the plane flew low over the desert and river delta, passing the occasional flare from an oil well before skimming the date palms and bumping unevenly onto the runway.

The plane trundled slowly off the runway, towards some drab, sandstone, single story buildings and at last came to a halt on the brightly lit airport apron. The engines whined down through the scales and finally stopped and the last gasp of air from the air conditioning louvres was replaced by faint piped music from hidden speakers. A steward threw open the door and a blast of hot air reached in from the desert. George felt the sweat start to pop out all over his body and his shirt immediately clung to his back. August in the Persian Gulf, and the night-time temperature was only a fraction less than the sweltering heat of day. He dripped his soggy way across the sticky tarmac into the airport building and took stock of the faded paintwork, the lazily turning fans that gave no respite from the heat and the faint smell of unwashed bodies. 'Welcome to the land of feet and sweaty socks,' he thought, quoting from an irreverent sailor's ditty and smiling to himself. 'Land of gonorrhoea and pox.' He remembered how quickly he'd learned such doggerel. A pity that he hadn't been so adept at memorising the Collision Regulations as an apprentice.

An open sided cart piled precariously high with luggage was wheeled in and an unseemly scramble of swarthy men struggled to extract their bundles and cases. He noticed how most of them wore shoes, but that they were trodden down at the back so that they could be slipped on and off quickly. George's two battered blue suitcases finally surfaced at the bottom of the cart. They contained just about all his worldly goods and chattels. He hadn't had a clue what he would need, so had packed everything from his serge uniform and sextant to a pack of cards and a harmonica. George was ready to face the world.

'Passport,' demanded the unshaven official in a sweat stained blue uniform at the Immigration desk. George handed it over and it was studied minutely before an oversized and regal looking stamp was produced, inked and placed on the empty first page from the back. An unintelligible note was added in Arabic script. He had no idea what would happen next and struggled with his bags through an open door, past a bored soldier who was propped up next to a rusty looking rifle against the wall. He followed behind the other passengers and amidst the crush of humanity outside stood a man waving a torn and greasy strip of cardboard. George recognised the spidery script on it as being his name and after introducing himself was greeted effusively as 'Capt'in Penroy', which put a smile on his face again. Promotion indeed from his most recent lowly rank of Second Mate. Although he held a Master Mariner's Certificate he had thought it would be another ten years before he would become Captain of his own ship. Dead men's boots governed the principles of promotion in the Merchant Navy and without the assistance afforded by some convenient war the boots of dead men were few and far between.

Captain George Penroy struggled with his cases across a road, narrowly avoiding two black and white cars labelled as taxis which both seemed to be trying to occupy the same few feet of space on the rough and potholed highway. A battered Volkswagen minibus stood waiting nearby and inside another passenger, complete with a preoccupied wife and two fretting children, waited. 'Hello,' said the passenger. 'I'm Dave.' 'I hear your joining us in the port' he continued. He introduced his wife, and then commented, 'We're in the Hotel tonight. Join us later for a drink in the bar, once the kids are asleep.' The minibus ground into gear before George had a chance to shut the door and careered alarmingly into a line of traffic, whilst the driver turned and called over his shoulder, 'Tight holding, please!'

'It's going to be a white knuckle ride,' thought George and wondered why none of the oncoming traffic bothered to dip its headlights. It worried him that the traffic kept to the right, but it troubled him even more that there seemed to be only two traffic speeds. Full ahead or stop.

The hotel had proved to be a pleasantly modern surprise, and after throwing a little cold water over his face and combing his thinning hair George sought out the bar. To his surprise there was a long table surrounded by Europeans, amongst whom he found the familiar, chubby face from the airport bus. 'Come and sit down,' said Dave. 'Beer?' he asked and without waiting for a reply called to a passing waiter in the local language. A large green bottle which would have looked more at home in a pharmacy promptly appeared and the waiter levered off the crown cork. He then gave the side of the bottle a smart rap with the opener and the pale yellow liquid frothed over the top and into the waiting glass. 'Strange procedure,' mused George, noticing that it was repeated at each subsequent serving. 'Must be some sort of local ritual,' he concluded and sipped cautiously at the ice-cold liquid that proved to have quite an acceptable tang despite its suspect appearance. After about two hours of idle chatter during which George was introduced to the other expatriates surrounding the table without really remembering any of their names, he was definitely feeling the effects of a long day and the unaccustomed brand of beer. He had to concentrate hard to get his tongue around saying goodnight without slurring the words. 'Wouldn't be a good start to be labelled as a lush,' he thought, as he fumbled with his room key. Sleep had come quickly.

Feeling slightly better after his morning shower, George again looked out of the window. He pulled back the net curtains, and discovered a balcony outside and still swathed only in a towel opened the door and went outside. He leaned over the balcony, and then to his horror heard the soft click of the door closing behind him. He swore loudly and tried the door, but to no avail. 'Pox rotten bloody thing's locked,' he thought. 'Just what I need and its only half an hour till the boss is due here to collect me for my first day in the new job.' He leaned over the balcony rail again, counting the floors. Three stories up and not a sign of anyone to shout to down below. 'Would it be any good to shout in English, anyway?' he wondered.

George took stock of the situation and concluded that it could have been rather better. Already the temperature was well into the nineties. He started to sweat and unconsciously dried his hands on the towel, which was tied around his waste. He leaned out over the balcony again, this time peering around the dividing wall and into the room next door. The curtains were pulled and door was tight shut. 'Try the other side' he thought, trying to dispel the feeling of desperation that was slowly building. 'Great!' The door of the room on the other side was open and with only the slightest feeling of fear, George swung his legs over the balcony. 'Blimey!' he thought, with a grin spreading over his face. 'They used to tell me at sea that I thought the sun shone out of my arse. If anyone looks up now they will think it's a second sunrise.' His towel flapped in the breeze as he clambered around the wall and onto the balcony next door. He cautiously knocked on the glass door and when there was no answer pushed his way into the room and headed towards the outer door. A figure in the bed opened one bleary eye but closed it again disbelievingly as George let himself out into the corridor. Luck, at last, as a white coated floor attendant appeared and after much gesticulation he let George back into his own room with a master key. 'What a hell of a beginning to the day,' said George to himself, heading back towards the shower to clean off a coating of sweat and sand from his mountaineering exploit. 'At least it can only get bloody better.'

BOOK 1

THE TRAINEE

1

It was half an hour later when George took the lift down to the ground floor. He dropped his room key into a polished copper box and then hovered near the Reception Desk. He had seen the Superintendent many times before in the port and at least should recognise him when he arrived. Another quarter of an hour passed, and despite the coolness of the air conditioning, George started to sweat again.

He pulled his letter of instruction out of his pocket once more. The paper was beginning to wilt and the creases would soon tear. The signature was already just a faint blue blob of ink. He thankfully read again that he would be met at the hotel and checked afresh with the large clock above the Porter's desk. There was no mistake. He hadn't mixed up the time zones and the Company's Superintendent was late.

He peered once more through the glass doors and was relieved to see a familiar, portly, bustling figure heading for the entrance. Captain Robinson pushed through the swing doors and his eyes homed in on George. 'You must be Penroy,' he said. 'Captain Penroy as far as the locals are concerned. We're all Captains here. Dozens of us!'

He shook George's damp hand and continued without pause, 'Got your passport?' he barked and when George nodded, 'Good. You'll need it at the Refinery.'

George hadn't the faintest idea what use his passport would be at a refinery, but went along with the idea on the grounds that the boss should know what he's talking about. Not that he'd always held that opinion, having argued with senior officers on a fairly regular basis. It rarely, if ever, did any good. According to the theories of George they still always seemed to go their own, ill-informed way.

The Superintendent and George thrust their way through a gaggle of giggling women who were dressed from head to toe in black veils and cloaks. 'Just like the ravens at the Tower of London,' thought George but then his opinion of Captain Robinson leapt upwards by several points when the Superintendent growled, 'Bloody Guinness bottles. Always getting in every buggers' way.'

'Neatest description I've heard since Adam was a cowboy,' smiled George to himself, crawling into the Super's scabrous looking Hillman Minx. It was a vague maroon colour, with patches of what looked suspiciously like ship's yellow oxide paint covering large, pustular bubbles of rust. They pulled away in a roar of exhaust and a cloud of acrid smelling smoke, and George found himself once more in the mayhem of Middle East traffic. Captain Robinson pounded the horn incessantly, especially at the black and white taxis which careered across the lanes to pick up ragged men and women in the ever-present black *chador*. 'Watch out if you're driving round here,' he said, 'There's a professional traffic diver around who waits for unsuspecting *farangis* to come along in their cars and then leaps head first under the wheels. He's an expert at just getting minor injuries but then he claims millions of rials in compensation. Makes a good living at it.'

It seemed a rather precarious way of earning a living to George but he filed away the information for future reference. He couldn't imagine owning a car in such a place, let alone driving it. The drivers seemed to aim their car and fire, rather than drive.

They drove down a tree-lined avenue with bungalows on either side. George could see gardens and water sprinklers, and marvelled that there were privet hedges and grass where he'd expected only sand and desert scrub. They navigated a roundabout, which was a bit scary, as they went around it contrary to the way of good old England. 'Suppose that's another thing I'll get used to,' George thought, clinging on to the arm rest in the car door. He thought, taking the state of the car into consideration, that there was a fair chance he'd be deposited in the road on the bones of his backside but the car creaked around the bends without the doors flying open and eventually ground to a halt outside an office building.

The building was rather grand, with a tiled dome in the middle and shady archways, but it backed on to the refinery boundary fence, which was made of red painted corrugated iron. It was difficult to tell ancient paintwork from large areas of rust. There were strands of barbed wire on top of the fence and they coiled into the distance around oil tanks, chimneys and long columns of catalytic crackers that belched out steam. Captain Robinson set course and sailed through a doorway under one of the archways, closely followed by a bewildered George, who was beginning to wonder if he would ever see the sea again.

The office appeared to be the security centre for the refinery and without further ado George was photographed, finger printed, had his passport inspected and was issued with a temporary pass, which he was told not to lose under any circumstances. It was printed on a sheet of paper large enough to wallpaper a small dining room and George folded it carefully before putting it into his wallet. They trailed back to the Hillman which was shimmering in the heat.

'Right,' said Captain Robinson, 'Let's get back to the hotel. You can pick up your luggage and we'll have you on board the tug by lunchtime.' He thought for a moment, and then added, 'Have you got any rials yet? You'll need a few.'

George shook his head and before he could add anything more Captain Robinson had viciously let in the clutch and swerved back onto the road. George wondered if he would suffer from whiplash as they roared back the way they had come. They jerked to a stop outside a line of what looked like shops and without explanation decamped into one that looked like a travel agency. George was introduced to a bulky, swarthy gentleman who actually wore a shirt with a collar and tie above creased pin striped trousers. 'This is Maroonian, our agent,' said Captain Robinson. 'Tell him how much you want and it will be deducted from your pay at the end of the month.'

George had absolutely no idea of how much he would need, or indeed of how much pay he would get after deductions. He took a wild guess and asked for fifty pounds, hoping he would still have enough to send home for his wife to pay the mortgage and eat. Maroonian counted out a fist full of grimy banknotes, took a signature from George and waved vaguely as the two Captains took their leave.

George was deposited on to the path in front of the hotel, with the instruction to be ready for the work bus to pick him up later that afternoon. He didn't like to ask for a specific time, so ended up sitting in the hotel foyer on top of his suitcases soon after midday, checking every vehicle that came through the ornate gateway. Three long hours later the battered Volkswagen minibus of the night before pulled into the driveway with tires squealing. George heaved his suitcases through the sliding door and followed them aboard. 'Where you go?' said the driver, and George realised, to his mortification, that he didn't know.

Taking a wild guess he said 'Jetties,' which seemed to satisfy the driver and the minibus plunged headlong into the afternoon traffic.

They soon passed the avenue of trees and the roundabout, followed by the refinery office and then the minibus swerved into a rutted alleyway with dingy, lock up shops on either side. 'Bazaar' grinned the driver. 'I take *chai*' he said, and stopped outside a nondescript opening in a wall, between two small shops.

'Come,' said the driver, and George followed him through

a doorway, silently hoping that the driver had locked the bus with his suitcases inside. They pushed their way through a beaded curtain and George found himself in a room lighted by a single, bare light bulb and with two wooden chairs and some dirty carpets in front of a counter. The driver pointed to a chair, and George sat down whilst the driver shouted something unintelligible towards the back of the room. An old man slowly appeared from the shadows, carrying a tray with glasses on it. He carefully filled the glasses with an evil looking, steaming brew. Beside the glasses was a small copper bowl containing sugar lumps. George accepted a glass, and following the lead of the driver popped a sugar lump into his mouth and loudly sucked the hot brew through the sugar. Surprisingly it tasted like tea and was fairly palatable as long as the sugar lump lasted. Taking courage, George took another lump of sugar and then drained his glass. It was immediately refilled and it took George three more glasses before he realised that if he left a little in the glass it didn't get refilled. He was acutely aware of a full bladder but couldn't even begin to think of enquiring where the nearest toilet was. 'Lord,' he thought, 'All I need now is to pee in my pants and the day will be complete.'

The driver threw a few coins on to the empty tray and they plunged back into the alleyway. George followed on, hoping against hope that it wouldn't be long until they reached somewhere with sanitation and privacy. They boarded the minibus, which surprisingly hadn't been looted of its contents and ground their way back towards what passed for a main road. They soon reached take off speed again, narrowly missing a donkey cart, driven by a small boy wielding an extremely large stick. The boy beat the donkey in time with every step it took and the donkey laboured to pull the load of what seemed to be horse manure and which certainly gave off an appropriately revolting smell.

They passed into another area of houses, once again with hedges and gardens and suddenly they passed a large gate that George recognised. 'At last,' he thought. 'We must be near the jetties. That's the entrance to the Seaman's Club.'

The minibus stopped, facing a security gate, and the driver leaned out of his window. An unshaven guard in a dirty blue uniform appeared and inspected the bus, idly scratching his groin. He shifted his belt, from which hung a holster and an extremely large pistol and threw open the passenger door. 'Pass' he demanded, still scratching and George fished in his wallet and withdrew his freshly folded sheet of paper. The guard inspected it minutely and walked into a nearby hut, still clutching the pass in a grimy hand. George crossed his legs, hoping that the guard would hurry. He was getting desperate and still clear in his mind was a stay in an Argentinian jail cell for a night for defiling the footpath. Caught short in a La Plata street with no sign of a public convenience and caught in the act of relieving himself in a shop doorway by a passing policeman.

The guard re-appeared and slowly opened the gate, waving the bus through. At last George was on home ground. He recognised the oiled sand bund and the oil jetties sprouting out into the muddy waters of the Shatt al Arab. Two tankers lay alongside the jetties and in the distance sat two ancient tugs at a smaller jetty, painted in familiar colours and with the funnel in the company's red, white and green, barber's pole stripes.

The minibus finally stopped at the tugs' jetty and with a gasp of relief George saw the portly figure of Dave, his fellow passenger from Heathrow, leaning over the bridge rail. Without bothering with his suitcases he leapt out of the bus and headed at speed for the rickety plank of wood that served as a gangplank. 'Where's the bog?' he asked a grinning Dave.

'Next deck down, port side,' replied Dave and George rushed headlong down the nearest ladder and gratefully found a minuscule toilet behind a stout wooden door. He didn't even bother to close the door before fumbling with his fly. A full two minutes later he breathed a contented sigh of relief. 'If a centipede a bucketful, how much could a precipice?' he muttered. He grinned thankfully to himself, his confidence finally restored.

He climbed back to the upper deck and to his surprise found his suitcases had been brought on board. He looked round and there stood a familiar figure. '*Salaam, sahib*' said Pedro, a Goanese Indian who had once been his steward at sea.

'*Wa aleikum salaam*, Pedro,' said George, 'Is this your ship now?'

'Yes, *sahib*,' he replied, 'I Captain's Tiger for tug nearly six month.'

'Great,' said George, happy to know that he could rely on being looked after in style whilst he was on board the tug. 'What about cigarettes, Pedro?' George asked.

'For you, ships price,' said Pedro. 'You want?'

'Certainly do,' agreed George, 'My supply from Heath-row won't last long.'

'OK, Captain *sahib*,' smiled Pedro, 'I take bags to cabin now'.

A pair of feet in sandals, followed by bare legs and shorts, appeared on the bridge ladder, followed by the grinning bulk of Dave. 'Welcome aboard,' he said, 'We wondered where you'd got to. Come and have a beer.'

'This is more like it,' thought George and followed Dave into a tiny cluttered cabin. Flowery curtains were drawn over the only porthole, and an icy blast came from the louvre in the deckhead. George took the offered chair, and felt thankful for the advent of air conditioning. He hadn't expected it on a tug that had started its working life in the Western Approaches during the Second World War.

The door burst open once again and Pedro re-appeared, smartly dressed in stewards mess jacket, and bearing a silver tray with two green bottles of Shams beer on it. 'Well,' thought George, 'Perhaps this tug job is going to turn out fine after all,' and with the knowledge gained from the night before opened his beer and smartly rapped the side of the bottle to make it foam over the top.

2

Two days had passed and very little had happened. This was rather fortunate for George, as regular intake of Shams containing the usual glycerine meant proximity to sanitary facilities was a must. George's body was beginning to adjust though and the laxative effects were lessening with every hour. The volume of Shams was due to a daily change of Captains and Engineers who worked the shift system, manning the tugs twenty-four hours a day. There were now three tugs lying alongside each other at the jetty and at any time two were on call.

The tugs were all of similar age and had started life belonging to the Admiralty. They had been built during World War Two and had been used to salvage ships that had been attacked in the Western Approaches. They had also formed part of the fleet of ships that towed Mulberry Harbours and had arrived in France on D-Day but thereafter they had enjoyed a much quieter career. At the end of hostilities they had been sold off to the highest bidder and twenty years later they were still giving sterling service. They had once been called the Empire Doreen, the Empire Jane and the Empire Jenny, cunningly identifying them as Empire Class tugs but they now had Iranian names to highlight the Company's origins in exploring for oil in Persia. Originally their triple expansion steam engines had been powered by coal and the old coaling doors amidships were still left open so that there was ventilation around the big new fire pumps that had been installed on the deck nearby. The boilers were now oil fired and supplied steam to the triple expansion engine that could push the tug along at a stately ten knots when required.

George was a deck man through and through but had succumbed to the wiles of one Chief Engineer and had stepped gingerly through the engine room door to survey the scene.

Polished brass pistons, jets of steam and a temperature well into the hundreds made George grateful to have chosen to spend his working life on the bridge rather than becoming a 'pig iron polisher'. The derogatory term typified the chasm between deck and engine room officers, reinforcing the old adage that 'oil and water don't mix'.

Each morning at nine a new Captain and Chief Engineer had boarded the duty tug, and George was introduced to the new men. It was difficult to tell them apart as they wore no uniforms. They boarded in casual shirts and slacks but then changed into shorts and sandals and settled in to wait for the call to work. An Indian Quartermaster manned the bridge and listened for a call from the tankers at the loading berths, whilst the Chief and Captain headed for the Officers Saloon and ordered breakfast from the Steward. George joined them and after answering the usual questions about his family and where he came from then joined in playing cards or reading the paper backed books which seemed to be in plentiful supply.

He now understood the shift system that the officers worked. One day on duty on the tug, one day on call at their home in the town, followed by two days off. Sounded like heaven to George, who was used to working every day for up to two years on the tankers. The Indian crew managed the maintenance of the tug and very little input was needed from the Captain. He would see the *Serang* in the morning and tell him what needed cleaning or painting and by the next morning the jobs would be done. The tugs shone in the sunshine so the system evidently worked well. Life seemed good to George who didn't mind at all getting paid for joining in the relaxed way of life on board.

In the two days that had passed the tugs had been called for work only twice. Both times were during daylight hours and George fully appreciated the opportunity to spend a full night in his bunk. Two tankers had finished loading and sounded the ship's whistle to call for a pilot. Strangely enough the river was not Iranian territory. Some long forgotten quirk of British diplomacy had decreed that the boundary with Iraq ran along the Iranian bank of the river. It was therefore an Iraqi pilot who came by boat from nearby Al Wassiliyah, about a mile down river from the jetties but on the Iraqi shore. It made little difference to the ships, apart from having to fly the Iraqi flag as a courtesy ensign on the foremast. The pilots all used the international seaman's language, English, when on board and gave instructions to the tugs by whistle.

The bustle on board the tug and the bridge telegraph ringing 'stand by' stirred George from his position under a fan in the saloon. He arrived on the bridge in time to watch the seaman casting off the moorings and Dave casually giving helm orders to the Quartermaster. Dave leaned over the bridge rail, with one hand on the telegraph and the tug swiftly responded to his orders for full speed. They headed up river, past a jumble of moored dhows and then on towards the loaded tanker. Dave manoeuvred the tug in towards the stern of the tanker and the bow fender landed softly against the stern of the ship. A heaving line came from the ship and ropes were sent up to be made fast on deck, while the second tug went to the bow and also made fast. All was ready and after answering a blast on the ship's whistle the tugs pushed and pulled the ship into the river with the help of the ebb tide. The tanker started on its way towards the sea and at a further signal the tugs cast of their ropes and headed back to their jetty to resume their waiting game.

'Nothing too difficult about that,' thought George to himself. 'Wonder how long it will be before I can have a go?'

'Looks easy, doesn't it' laughed Dave. 'Most of the time it is but don't be surprised when it all turns to rat shit. That's when it sorts the men from the boys.'

The next morning, when the new crew arrived in the minibus, a gaunt looking Captain called Brian told George that he was wanted at the office. 'We'll go in the tug,' said Brian. 'The office is at jetty number eight and we have to call there for some stores anyway.' He gave a wry sort of grin and added, 'Let's see what you can do on the way. It's time you started to do something yourself. We'll have some breakfast first, though.'

George was glad of the prospect of something to do and headed for the saloon to fuel up for the morning. Bacon and eggs had always seemed to him an appropriate way of starting a days work.

Brian and his engineer took their time over eating and after finishing ordered coffee. They were just starting their second cup when Brian turned to George and said, 'Better not keep the super waiting. Go and take the tug to number eight and don't bloody bounce it off anything on the way.'

'Sure,' said George. 'No problem,' and he headed casually for the bridge, trying to look a lot more confident than he felt.

'Okay, *Seacunny*?' he said to the Quartermaster. 'Stand by, please.'

'*Atcha, Sahib*' replied the Quartermaster, swinging the handle of the telegraph back and forth before stopping it on 'Stand-by'. He then skipped down the ladder calling to the *Serang* and Crew on the way, before returning to test the steering gear by turning the wheel hard over to port and then starboard.

'So far, so good,' thought George. 'Nothing unusual so far. Now we come to the bitter bit.'

The bridge telegraph rang out and the engine room confirmed that all was ready. 'Now or never,' mused George and he leaned over the bridge to call 'Let go for'd.' Unfortunately George's voice cracked when he said it and a knowing grin crossed the Quartermaster's face.

'Cheeky bastard,' thought George and cleared his throat before calling 'Let go aft'.

'Port ten,' George ordered and then tentatively rang for slow ahead on the engines. The tug drifted away from the berth on the tide as the engines started and, without showing any further signs of nerves, George steadied the tug on course and headed her up river. George thought carefully of what to do next and peered ahead towards number eight jetty where he had to berth again.

Strangely enough, during his twelve years at sea he had rarely had a chance to manoeuvre a ship. He had altered course many a time but manoeuvring a ship in confined areas, with engines, was always done either by the Master or a pilot. Of course he had studied the theory for his certificates but as he now realised, having a Master's ticket didn't mean he had the ability to move ships. In common with many Merchant Navy officers he had never been given the chance.

He gradually increased up to full speed but it wasn't for long. Well before arriving at number eight jetty he had reduced down to 'Dead Slow Ahead' and it was only fear of looking foolish that prevented him from stopping the engines altogether and letting the tug drift to a halt. He dredged his mind for characteristics of ship handling that he had learned at college and then tried to put them into practice as the tug approached the jetty. He stemmed the tide whilst still moving ahead and then put the engines astern, so that the bow of the tug canted in to starboard. George thought it went like a dream as the tug drifted slowly across the tide towards the jetty, landing with the slightest bump alongside. Two seamen leapt ashore, taking ropes with them and before George could do anything else the crew had heaved the tug close alongside. 'Finished with engines?' asked the Quartermaster and George nodded his agreement. He realised he was sweating profusely once the job was over and wondered if it was just the heat.

He went down the ladder to find Brian and the engineer sitting in deckchairs on the foredeck and it was evident that they had watched and listened for the whole performance.

'Think you did OK?' asked Brian.

'Not bad,' replied George hopefully.

'Took your time, didn't you?' said the engineer. 'Thought we were never going to arrive!'

George felt quite put out but his natural high spirits didn't let him worry for long. 'Wait till next time,' he thought, 'I'll do it like Sterling bloody Moss,' and he headed for the Superintendents office.

'Hello Captain Penroy,' said the Super, 'Come and meet Mr Morris the Engineer's Superintendent.' He led the way through a maze of corridors and barged into a nearby office without knocking.

'Mo, meet the latest recruit,' he said to a white haired, tall and aloof looking man who was sitting in a tilted back chair with his feet on the desk and smoking a cheroot. 'We're sending him down to Kharg on the new tug,' he continued.

'First I've bloody heard about it,' thought George, shaking hands with the boss of the engineers who didn't bother to take his feet off the desk. 'Didn't even know we had a new tug.'

They soon went back to the Super's office where George was briefed on what was to happen next. The new tug was due to arrive from England in the next few days and then George would sail to Kharg Island with it. He would finish off his training at the big export terminal where many more ships were handled each day and would return to the mainland after a couple of months, in time to fill in for Brian when he went on leave. Everyone agreed that by that time he should be a competent tug handler.

'That should see you through your first three months' the superintendent continued, 'And then I suppose you'll be wanting to move into a bungalow and bring your wife and children out?'

'That's right, sir.' Said George, who had been wondering how to bring up the subject. The whole point of the exercise was to have a job where the family could be together and this was the first time anyone had mentioned it.

'Well' said the super, 'We've got a house lined up for you but it's having a major maintenance at the moment. You'll be better off down on the happy isle for a while. Don't get into mischief while you're there,' he added.

George didn't have any idea of what mischief he could get into but thought he would check it out as soon as he could, as it might be fun.

3

An early morning haze softened the view Southward from the jetties at Bawarda. The sun was rising behind the refinery chimneys in Braim but fingers of mist still swirled over the river. George was learning the different areas of the town by constantly hearing references made by the other tug officers.

On the Iraqi side of the river the date palms came down to the water's edge in shady rows, whilst the Iranian side was clear of vegetation, showing the original mud flats of the Shatt al Arab delta. A few low, flat roofed mud huts showed up in the distance, marking the peasant village where water buffalo were led down to the river's edge each day. George was getting used to the scene as he had now been in the port for ten days. Today was the day though. The new tug was due to arrive on the morning tide.

Two tankers were due to arrive according to the typed schedule that was delivered each day from the shipping office and a note on the bottom of the schedule gave arrival time for the tug 'Zamand' as ten o'clock that morning. Only seven o'clock now, and George stood on the after deck relishing the last of the early morning's relative coolness before heading for the saloon and breakfast.

George had been ashore the previous night. He had been invited by one of the tug engineers to have dinner with him and his family in the bungalow they occupied in Bawarda. He had gone ashore in the minibus, dressed in slacks and a shirt and even wearing a tie, which was something he hated to do. George had always had a large neck and this caused problems when buying shirts. It was no problem when buying a short sleeved sports shirt to be worn without a tie but for a dressier occasion a shirt with a large collar size had to be bought Shirt makers took no account of people who had large necks but small bodies. Shirts with large necks had bodies that would wrap round George twice and the sleeves were so long that they looked like some kind of straight jacket. He compromised by tucking great wads of shirt into his trousers and always turning up long shirtsleeves.

Bob McKay, the engineer, was himself fairly new in town. He had only arrived six months previously, so had not long settled into his bungalow. His wife and family had only been in town for two months, and were finding their way in the new country that was now their home. Bob was watering the garden with a long rubber hose when the minibus arrived. It was already dark but the garden was lit by lights from the house and also by a lamp standard in the middle of the coarse grass lawn. Three children roared around the garden, shouting even louder when Bob sprayed them with the hose. A fourth child clung to its mother, a tall willowy lady with reddish hair, who looked rather preoccupied.

'Come in and have a bloody beer,' roared Bob, as the minibus turned in at the gateway. He turned and shouted at the small boy who was dripping water in the doorway. 'Get those sodding shoes off, and let's have two beers from the fridge,' he ordered, at the top of his voice. George was already used to Bob, a bluff Scot, who did everything at high speed and at maximum volume with little planning or forethought. He was also used to the sprinkling of swearwords that Bob constantly used when on the tug and was surprised that they didn't stop now that the family was around.

'Come on in,' he repeated. 'Make yourself at home. Spit on the deck and call the cat a bastard,' he added, aiming a lazy swipe at a passing child.

'Bloody kids!' moaned Bob. 'Be bleeding glad when they are back to school on Saturday. They're a pain in the arse during weekends.'

George was, by this time, aware that the Islamic working week was from Saturday to Wednesday and that all pretence of work stopped during the weekend on Thursday and Friday. He was also quite amused that all the expatriate children attended Sunday School on Fridays. Seemed rather a contradiction of terms to him.

They headed through the screen door into the bungalow. A low hum from the air conditioners in each room greeted them and ceiling fans whirred slowly round above them. The small boy arrived, precariously balancing two large Shams beer bottles and glasses on a tray and safely put them down on a round coffee table. He took the tops off and carefully went through the ceremonial of tapping the bottle, under the watchful eye of his father. 'Don't bloody break them,' said Bob, 'You just have to liven them up a bit, not bleedin' batter them to death.'

'Don't swear, Bob,' said his wife, Moira, in a soft voice which contrasted strangely with Bob's. But she might as well have been talking to the cream painted living room wall for all the notice her husband took. 'Do you want to see what the house is like?' she asked George, 'You'll need to know for when your own family come out.'

She led George, followed by Bob and a trail of children of diminishing size, around the bungalow. The walls were painted throughout with gloss paint and reminded George of the walls of the Shipping Office in Southampton where he had occasionally signed away his life for two more years on a tanker. Each room had its own air conditioning unit that jutted through a hole in the wall, humming quietly and each room had its own gecko on the ceiling, that waited patiently for flies and moths to land nearby. They were evidently quite successful, as they were larger and fatter than those George had seen out in the open. 'Better than fly paper or sprays,' commented Moira quietly.

The furniture was all made of tubular steel but the chairs looked as if they would be comfortable. 'You'll be issued with furniture like this when you get your own bungalow,' said Moira. 'There's not much choice but its quite easy to get the chairs re-covered in the bazaar if you can't stand the company's standard colour.' The house had three bedrooms, a living room, a dining room and kitchen, plus a large bathroom. They headed through the kitchen to the back door and on opening the outer screen door George found himself in a walled compound, with a further small house the other side of the paved courtyard.

'Servants' quarters,' announced Bob. 'You'll be needing either a house boy or a nanny and if they want to live in it will cost you less in wages. Everyone gets one or the other and it doesn't cost an arm and a leg.'

'Good thing,' said George, who was still very conscious that he had to keep up his mortgage payments at home in England, as well as live in Iran with his family once he had satisfactorily completed his three months probation period.

The evening had gone well for George. At an early stage he had thankfully discarded his tie and, after the first injection of Shams, he had relaxed enough to tell a few stories of his experiences at sea. Bob had joined in, and before long the two of them had started to tell jokes, which got progressively lower in tone, especially after the children were dispatched in the direction of their bedrooms. Off colour jokes and stories were one of George's specialities and the laughter went on late into the evening.

A halt was called when the stock of cold beer in the fridge had been exhausted and the company minibus was summoned by telephone to take George back to the jetty and his waiting bed on the tug. No such luck, however. He arrived at the jetty to find that the tugs had been called out, and he had to wait another hour before they came back from moving a couple of tankers. He sat on an oil pipeline, despite remembering the stories of how this could cause horrible haemorrhoids and watched the stars whilst wondering again what on earth was doing in a place like this.

George had been woken early the next morning by the noise of the Indian crew who were washing down the decks. It was amazing how much sand could accumulate in one day and he wondered what it would be like after a real sandstorm. He had opened his cabin door to find Pedro squatting outside. '*Cha, sahib*?' the Goanese asked, cheerfully, leaping to his feet. George grunted his assent and gratefully sipped his tea when it arrived, while Pedro whisked away George's dirty clothes from the day before. Pedro liked to get the *dhobi* done in the morning, so that he could finish all his duties and get away to the town bazaar in the evenings, where they showed Indian films at one of the local flea-pit cinemas. He had also taken away George's slacks, which had somehow got oil marks on the backside from his wait on the jetty the night before. 'Hope he can get the stains out,' thought George. 'It's the only decent pair of civvy trousers that I've got.' By agreement Pedro did all of George's washing for the princely sum of one pound per month. A godsend for George, who hated washing and ironing and a welcome extra for Pedro, whose wages were a miserly forty pounds a month. A pittance by European standards but a high wage for the subcontinent.

The Captain and Engineer had stirred themselves by this time. They were now getting shaved and cleaned up, ready to go home when their reliefs arrived at nine o'clock. The gaunt looking Brian and his sidekick Pat, the engineer, would be on duty again today and George wondered if he would get another chance to practice his ship-handling skills before he transferred to the new tug when it arrived. He had watched ever since his first try but didn't like to ask if he could have another go. 'I'll wait till I'm asked,' he thought to himself.

He was very wary of Brian who was the senior man in the port in terms of tug service. Brian had already been in the country for ten years and was accepted as an authority on all things maritime, Iranian and on life in general. George, with his natural self confidence, could see himself challenging

Brian's authority eventually and was taking care not to say, or do, anything out of place. He had also heard that Brian was not too popular with the resident Superintendent, Captain Robinson, but had kept that piece of information to the back of his mind. At this stage he just had to get on with everyone.

He liked Brian's engineer, Pat. Pat was a grizzled old Scot who spent a lot of his time sipping a glass of iced water in the officers saloon, gently feeding Brian with subjects to talk about. Pat was an expert at feeding bullets for Brian to fire. It was evident that there were many expatriate run clubs in the town and the running of them seemed to cause much interest amongst the tug officers and their families. There seemed to be a lot of rivalry between the clubs, and each one had its own group of devotees. Most people seemed to be members of just about every club, and George had already been asked about joining several of them.

There was an amateur theatre group, a golf club, a jockey club and a Go-kart club that George had heard of so far and he wondered how much it would cost to be a member of each one. He was sure that there would be fees to be paid and needed to keep a watch on his spending. His salary had nearly doubled when he joined the tug service but his expenditure back at home in England had to come first. He would like to visit some of the clubs before deciding if he could afford to join. Maybe it was a good idea that he was going to go to Kharg Island with the new tug, as it would delay any decisions till he was back on the mainland in a couple of months time.

Word had filtered down to George that he would return from the island at the end of October. He would then be slotted into the roster of tug captains, to cover for the taunt-ing Brian who was going on leave. He had to be proficient by then, so needed all the experience he could get in the meantime.

'No movements for us this morning,' said Brian to Pat, studying the shipping list that had just arrived. 'We'll go and see the new tug when it arrives at number eight jetty,' he added. 'Be interesting to see the latest addition to the fleet,' he said, and turning to George added, 'Give you a chance to do a bit more manoeuvring where you can't do too much damage, young George.'

George didn't appreciate being referred to as young but didn't reply. He looked forward to having another try at ship handling and hoped it would all go well again. Arriving at number eight jetty, with the Superintendents and all the shore staff watching from the office windows, meant extra care being taken. 'No place to make a fool of yourself,' thought George.

An hour later, they were still sitting in the saloon. The only movement had been when Pat added ice from the freezer compartment in the top of the fridge to his water glass. The conversation buzzed slowly from topic to topic when there was a knock at the door. In came the Butler, the Indian equivalent of the British Chief Steward, with pen and notepaper at the ready. 'What you want for lunch and dinner today, *sahib*,' he asked Brian.

'The usual, Pat?' asked Brian. 'Curry for lunch and then a roast tonight?'

'I won't eat much,' Pat replied, sipping at his glass, 'but what about the lad?' he asked, indicating towards George.

'That'll do for me,' said George. 'I'll eat anything, as long as its dead' he quipped.

'Comedian!' said Brian dryly and confirmed the menu for the Butler.

'OK, *sahib*' the Butler smiled. 'We are also definitely needing some supplies,' he said in the sing song tones of India, moving his head from side to side in time with the words.

'Right,' said Brian. 'Make up a list and we'll requisition some from the next company tanker that comes in.' It was the accepted way of getting fresh meat and tinned food without having to resort to the local ship chandler and the bazaar in town. The local Iranian customs officers frowned on the practice but as it was done in Iraqi waters they didn't have much choice in the matter. The fact that an illicit supply of English cigarettes and hard liquor was also transferred didn't help matters. These contraband stores were hidden away by the Indian crew until a quiet time when they were transferred ashore in the battered Volkswagen minibus.

The Butler left and a Quartermaster took his place in the doorway. 'New tug coming' he reported. Everyone got up and headed for the bridge to get a view of the new arrival. Binoculars were trained and the smart new tug puttered by, its diesel engine burbling quietly and a large bow wave pushing the usual floating river debris aside. The steam whistle was sounded in salute as the 'Zamand' passed by and the three officers went back to the saloon where Pat picked up his frosted glass and took another sip. 'Let's wait another hour, Brian,' he said, 'It'll give them a chance to get the run crew ashore before we get there.'

Brian agreed and called for Pedro. 'We'll have a beer while we're waiting,' he said.

'Not for me' said Pat. 'I'll stick to the water.' Pat glanced at Brian, and George noticed the knowing look that passed between them.

George didn't really want to start drinking that early in the morning but went along with Brian to show willing. 'Just the one,' he thought. 'Don't want to be smelling of beer when the Super is around.'

An hour later they got under way, with George by himself again on the bridge. He was getting to like being in command and quickly pushed the tug to full speed, remembering Pat's caustic comment from before. He'd get it done quickly this time.

The tug landed softly alongside number eight jetty, much to George's delight and George, Brian and Pat went down the gang plank as soon as it was readied by the crew. They walked along to the next berth where the 'Zamand' was now lying, rocking gently in the swell from a passing *dhow*. She had freshly painted sides and none of the car tires hanging over the sides like on the tug they had just left. A large rubber fender adorned the bow of the 'Zamand', not at all like the rope fender hanging over the bow of the old wartime tug they had just left. The 'Zamand' looked sleek and powerful by comparison.

They climbed the gangway and went aboard to be met by a diminutive engineer who was dressed in an oily boiler suit and who Brian and Pat evidently recognised. He greeted the visitors with a casual 'What do you lot want?' in a Scots accent.

'Not another Scot' thought George. 'The place is awash with them.'

The engineer was introduced to him as 'Wee Al', and it was evident that he had come out from England with the tug. He had overseen the building in the shipyard and was now returning to take up his job in Kharg Island again. He had also brought out large stocks of food, clothing and furniture for various people who lived on the island, and this was crated and stored on the tugs after deck for delivery later.

Wee Al looked George up and down, and with a glance at Brian said, 'I hear you're joining us to go and train on the happy isle. Big Mike, the captain, will be down later, along with his wife and kids. You'd better stick around and meet them.'

This seemed to be agreed by everyone and, at Brian's suggestion, they went into the accommodation in search of whatever alcohol Wee Al had brought from UK. Al had a stash of canned lager that was quickly unearthed and passed around. 'Sorry, Pat,' he said. 'No vodka left. The run crew polished it off one night in the Red Sea. Ended up steering the damn tug myself as they were all under the weather.'

Pat nodded his acceptance and then wandered off to see the engine room. Brian, can in hand, followed him, leaving

George to decipher Al's broad Fife accent. 'How're ye gettin' on wi' the boys?' he asked. 'Is Pat still sipping vodka and ice all day?'

It slowly dawned on George that Pat wasn't drinking water all the time he was on duty. 'Christ!' he thought, 'I must be in with a bunch of real pissheads.' He'd seen drinkers before and heard of the fabled few that polished off whole bottles in a day but had never actually come across an expert such as Pat. 'Thought the old boy was just a bit unsteady on his pins,' he remarked to Al, who chuckled quietly.

'Old and unsteady,' said Al scornfully. 'He's only forty-five and permanently pickled.'

George took leave of Wee Al, promising to be back on board to meet Big Mike that night and headed for the bridge. He wanted to have a look at the latest equipment on the new tug. It was all very clean and bright on the bridge and George was fascinated by the three sets of engine controls, one in the centre of the bridge and one on each side. This was a new concept for George. Direct control of the engines without a telegraph to ring and no engineer to reply from the engine room. He would like to have tried the controls but didn't know what would happen if he pushed one of the levers. 'Better keep my fingers off until I know a bit more about it,' he thought, and headed down the ladder to find Brian and Pat. He knew they would want to be back at the tug jetty in time for lunch and would follow their meal with a short siesta as long as there were no tanker movements. It had been a busy morning.

4

During that afternoon, whilst Brian and Pat slept off the effects of the morning's hard work, George got out his trusty blue suitcases and started to pack. There were one or two things he could leave in Pedro's tender care until he got back so the cases were a little lighter than when he had arrived. George's promise that Pedro would still receive a full month's *dhobi* money brought the smile back to Pedro's face and a slice of cake along with his afternoon tea. 'A little bribery keeps the world turning,' thought George, who was already getting conditioned to the eternal demand of the East for '*baksheesh*'.

Soon after dinner that evening George summoned the minibus and struggled with his cases on to the jetty. The driver opened the doors for him, and they heaved the cases inside. He turned and shouted back to Brian and Pat who were casually leaning over the tug rails, 'See you in a couple of months.'

'Make sure you get a couple of trips with Robbie Roberts,' Brian shouted back. 'He'll really show you how it's done.' George filed the name away in the back of his mind and then told the driver to head for number eight jetty where the 'Zamand' and his further training lay. He no longer worried about the frantic speed of the journey or the demands of the guards on the gates for his pass. The pass was actually becoming worn at the edges, and was now reinforced along the folds with clear sticky tape. However, it was still happily accepted by the guards, who no longer seemed so intimidating. Indeed, if George went through the gate during the guard's meal times they waved him through with just a cursory glance. They were too busy with their hand in the communal eating dish to bother with any check. This was also filed away in George's memory for later use, as it could prove useful when smuggling cigarettes and spirits ashore.

'No stopping in the bazaar for *chai*, Ali,' ordered the more confident George as they hurtled along the main road towards Braim.

'OK, sir,' replied Ali, with his head turned round to face George, '*Imruz no chai*'.

George wasn't quite sure what that meant and was more interested in getting Ali to face the way the minibus was travelling. They veered steadily towards the oncoming traffic until the hooting of horns finally caught Ali's attention and he swerved the bus back on course, gaily shouting insults at the passing drivers. He was displaying the fatalistic approach of all Middle Eastern drivers who believe implicitly in the '*Inshallah* Syndrome'. They would get to their destination if God willed it so, regardless of how badly they were driving.

They quickly reached number eight jetty and George checked his watch. 'Record time,' he thought as he jumped down from the bus. He dragged out his cases, carried them up the narrow wooden plank that served as a gangway and then headed off in search of Wee Al. He found him in a horizontal position on the settee in the officer's saloon and made enough noise to ensure that at least one eye opened.

'Och, it's you,' slurred Wee Al, 'What d'ye want?'

'Not you, that's for sure,' George thought, before replying 'A key for a cabin wouldn't go amiss.' Al reluctantly heaved himself to his feet and headed out of the saloon, muttering something unintelligible under his breath in a broad Scots accent. Al went up the ladder to the Captain's cabin and after fumbling for a while with a bunch of keys let himself in. George followed and then waited while Al searched through a glass fronted key cupboard until he found what he wanted.

'There ye go,' he said, brandishing a key. 'The Mate's cabin.'

George took the key and headed to the next door along the deck which bore the label 'First Officer' He let himself in and found himself faced with box upon box of stores. It was evident that someone had cleaned out the local super market before leaving the bountiful shores of the UK.

'Shit!' said Al in a doleful voice. 'I'd forgotten Big Mike's stock of food. It's sometimes difficult to get supplies on Kharg,' he explained. 'We'd better put you in the Second Engineer's cabin for now, till we can get this place cleared out.'

The Second Engineer's cabin turned out to be leading off from the saloon, and was equipped with brand new furniture and clean bedding. 'This will do me,' said George, and heaved his cases over the step.

'Bloody have to,' agreed Al who was rummaging about under the saloon dining table as if he'd lost something. He came up with two cans of lager and put them on the table. 'They're a bit warm,' said Al, 'But we had a few visitors today and they finished off the cold ones.' He pulled the ring pull on the top of the first can and beer foamed out on to the deck. 'At least you don't have to bash these to prove they are good,' he commented, licking lager from his fingers.

George really didn't want to get into a drinking session with Al. He would rather settle down, unpack and then write a letter home. He was finding it difficult to get the time for writing and wanted to tell his wife the latest news before going to Kharg Island. He also had to tell her the Kharg Island address so that any incoming mail would still get through to him.

He didn't have to talk to Al for long though. Half way through drinking his can of beer Al stretched out on the settee again, and in mid sentence he dozed off. George was grateful for small mercies and headed quietly for his cabin. He unpacked a few necessities, pushed his cases under the bunk, and then settled down to write. He got half way through the letter before a sudden thought stopped him. 'Who's going to supply and cook the breakfast?' he wondered. He had just realised that the Indian crew was not joining till the next day and he hadn't the faintest idea of where the galley was and even less idea of where to find food to cook.

George went out through the saloon, past the dormant, snoring body of Al, and walked round the alleyway. There were several doors, all neatly labelled with brass plaques. He stopped outside the one marked 'Certified for use as Pantry' and tried the door. It opened, and on switching on the light George was delighted to find a large fridge which was purring gently to itself. On investigation the fridge proved to have a milk jug inside, and further examination of the nearby shelves uncovered corn flakes, sugar and two large cockroaches. 'Great!' thought George, flicking the roaches on to the deck and under his boot, happy now that his breakfast was ensured. He would just have to be up before Al as there wasn't much milk in the jug. He went back to his cabin and finished the letter. He'd have to get someone to take it ashore for him as soon as possible.

An hour later and George headed for his bunk. He'd found a couple of well thumbed magazines in the saloon sticking out from under the prone Al and had picked them up without waking him. The magazines were six weeks old but George hadn't seen them before. He scanned the pages slowly and after gazing at the pictures of scantily dressed girls started to read an improbable article about the life and times of a guard on a railway train. If it was to be believed then the happenings on the London to Scotland train in the sleeping compartments weren't quite what was offered in the British Rail timetable. George wasn't too convinced and thought that it would take an acrobat to perform in one of those bunks on a sleeper. He drifted off to sleep, pondering the problem.

He wondered where he was when he awoke, but soon remembered. Sunshine was streaming in through the porthole, and he could smell food. Bacon if he wasn't mistaken.

He threw on a pair of shorts and headed for the bathroom for a shower. 'Good morning,' called Al, as George headed through the saloon. 'Breakfast in five minutes,' he continued, evidently none the worse for his night on the saloon settee.

'Don't know where Big Mike got to last night,' said Al as they ate their breakfast. 'He'll be on board soon though, as the crew should arrive in an hour.'

Al went on to describe Big Mike as a bit of a character and something of a hard case. He was married to an equally bizarre lady called April who was evidently quite unstable. Known for her erratic driving and her erotic habits, according to local folk law, the mainland residents were quite glad she was about to depart for the island. According to Al, Mike was a good tug handler but hopeless when it came to handling people, especially April.

George didn't have long to wait. He had just mopped up the remaining egg from his plate with a slice of bread when the door burst open. In came a figure in khaki shirt and slacks. About the same height as George but stocky and heavily muscled, he sported a jet black beard and moustache. Red rimmed eyes peered over the top of the beard as he said quietly, 'For Christ sake don't make too much noise. April insisted we went to the night club last night and we're not long home.'

'Who the hell are you?' he continued, turning his bleary eye on George. George introduced himself, assuming that this apparition was Big Mike. He was evidently right, as Mike continued, 'Do you think you can sign the crew on and issue them with their uniforms and gear? I'm going to get a couple of hours kip while I can.' He beckoned George to follow him and went up the ladder to the Captain's Cabin and let himself in. Without further to do he handed George a large sheaf of official papers for the signing of the crew and a key to the stores. 'You know what to give them,' he grunted. 'Al will give you a hand.' He then arranged himself horizontally on the settee and closed his reddened eyes.

'Good job he closed them,' thought George, 'It looked as if he could easily bleed to death.' Once again the question flicked through George's mind. 'What am I doing here with this bunch of artists?' He quietly left the cabin and went back down to the saloon. He was grateful that he at least knew what he was doing when signing on crew and issuing uniforms. Always assuming that it was the same on tugs as it was on tankers!

Within the hour the crew arrived, shepherded on board by the senior crewman, the *Serang*. The *Serang* was fairly fluent with seaman's English and one by one he introduced the men who would make up the crew. They seemed a fairly motley bunch to George but he was glad to see one or two familiar faces amongst them and knew that they would all be good seamen. Many of them were unable to read or write, so the *Serang* confirmed their rating and pay scale to them before organising them to place their thumb on an ink pad and then putting a thumb print in the space labelled 'signature'.

There were over thirty crewmen to be signed on, and George wondered where they would all find space to live. They disappeared down a ladder to the lower deck though, and later appeared outside the store to be kitted out with uniforms. Once again the *Serang* organised the men into an orderly queue and assisted George to issue them with everything from Long Johns to balaclavas. It was evident that the company issue didn't take much notice of the fact that the tug would remain in the Middle East throughout and the need for winter clothing was hardly relevant.

George thoroughly enjoyed the morning, especially when issuing boots. 'What size?' he would enquire from the *Serang*. After a muffled conversation in Urdu the *Serang's* reply would boom out, loud and clear.

'Half past ten, *sahib*.' It was a job for George to keep a straight face as he handed out the size ten and a half boots.

The new Butler took stock of the food stores and presented George with a list of requirements. The crew had to be fed that day and there was little that was suitable. There was enough in tins to feed Big Mike, Al and George but nothing with which to serve up the staple crew diet of curry. George sought out Al, who wasn't able to help, so he then tried Big Mike. Here he totally failed. Big Mike remained dead to the world on his settee, not even breaking the rhythm of his snoring. George wondered what to do next.

He didn't have any idea where such food stores would come from, so he then made the smartest move he could have done and phoned Brian. It was evident that Brian had been sleeping late that morning but with fairly good grace gave George the phone number of the local ship chandler and told him to give the chandler a list of immediate requirements. George muttered his thanks and then sped back aboard to consult the *Serang* and the Butler. Between them they concocted a list and with his fingers crossed George telephoned the chandler.

It was evident that the chandler was used to such requests and within the hour arrived at the jetty in a filthy open truck which was filled to overflowing with George's stores. The crew happily unloaded them and warily, George put his signature on the bottom of the receipt, hoping against hope that Brian had given him the correct information. There was no way he could afford to pay the bill himself and it wasn't unknown for all sorts of tricks to be played on any new boy.

The *Serang* reported to George after lunch and asked what work he should start the crew on. George didn't have a clue and as Mike was still virtually unconscious he gave the men the afternoon off so that they could settle in. A broad grin crossed the *Serang's* face as he hurried off to pass the good news to the crew as he knew that time off would be hard to come by in the next twelve months. George had made a friend.

5

Two more days passed and George was happy to be working each day along with the crew. They were preparing the tug for work by hanging fenders all around the hull. This hadn't been done before, as tires hanging over the side would have created a drag in the water when the tug was making the passage from the builders' yard in England. More stores and food were also coming aboard and towing ropes and wires were supplied from the company store at number eight jetty. The crew then had to splice the wires and ropes together to make up the towing spring and turning springs, that the tug would need for working ships when it got to Kharg Island.

These were jobs that were familiar to George. Once Mike had given him the lengths for each component of a towrope he could pass the information to the crew and then oversee the splicing. He was getting impatient to be under way again and to see how the new tug compared to the old ones.

Big Mike had proved to be much less intimidating than George first thought and together with Wee Al they were forming a team. Mike liked to head for his bungalow in the town at regular intervals, leaving George to see to the details of the days work on deck, while Al headed for the engine room where the engine ratings were polishing and oiling and getting to know the new ship. The engine room was still a mystery to George. As long as the engines answered to the call when required and the fire pumps sent water to the fire monitors on the upper deck he was happy. He had no intention of passing through the engine room door unless in dire emergency. 'Leave it to Al and the other ginger beers,' was George's motto.

Captain Robinson, the Superintendent, had visited the new tug just once. He had asked Mike how long before the tug would be ready to sail for Kharg Island and then headed back ashore with several large parcels, all carried by the crew. Evidently he had also taken advantage of the free transport of supplies from England. 'Great,' thought George. 'Just about everyone seems to be fiddling something.' He kept his thoughts to himself though, as it probably wouldn't be popular to raise the subject with Mike or Al and certainly not with the Super.

George had been ashore each evening and had met up with several of the other tug men and their wives. It seemed that most of them got together in the evening for whatever entertainment was going on. They congregated at whatever club was open that day, or went to the cinema in town if it was English night. Films were shown twice; one night in English and the next night dubbed into Farsi. It seemed that most of the local oil company staff preferred to watch the films in English too, as the dubbing left a lot to be desired.

These runs ashore and the people George met were all noted in his letters home. His wife would have to join in with the other expatriates when she arrived and it was good to know something about them in advance. He wondered how she would fit in with the others and how she would manage in the new country. She had lived in South Africa as a child but that was rather different to living in a Middle Eastern country as an adult, with two young children to care for. The wives were a pretty normal lot. They were harassed by small children who required feeding and by husbands who were more used to being at sea than at home. It seemed to George that most of the couples had been married for a long time but they were only just getting used to living together. They were kind enough to George though and quite freely offered advice on how to live as an expatriate. They differed widely in the way they lived, some sticking rigorously to other British friends and others integrating with the locals to varying degrees. Many of the Iranians spoke excellent English and would invite the expatriates into their homes. It was as well to learn some of the language and customs though, as things could get rather embarrassing.

There was a well known story that was circulated around town about one new arrival that went into an Iranian home with someone he had met at the Oil Company Club. Thinking that he should compliment his host, he commented on the beautiful home and was especially impressed by the Kashan carpet that was strewn casually on the living room floor. 'That is a beautiful carpet,' he said to his Iranian host.

At that the host started rolling up the carpet, saying, 'It's yours. Please accept it with my sincere best wishes.'

It took all of the guest's tact and diplomacy to get out of the house without having to accept a gift worth thousands of rials. It was a long time before he accepted any invitations after that and he could only wonder what would have happened if he had complimented the man's wife.

Armed with folklore such as this George was wary wherever he went. He had bought a book on colloquial Farsi and was hoping to be able to learn enough to get by. It was proving more difficult than he had first thought and he was struggling with the first phrase in the book which was 'Father gave bread. *Baba naan daad.*' Little did he realise that the book was based on what an Iranian child would learn when first going to school, as the characters in Arabic type script were the easiest ones. 'Where is the nearest public convenience?' might have been of more use to George but since such an item was virtually non-existent anywhere in the Middle East it didn't figure in the few pages that he had studied so carefully.

The Thursday and Friday of weekend passed and it was evident that Big Mike was more interested in packing up his bungalow than getting the tug ready. The contents of his house would be crated and then sent to the island ready for his family to move in. Meanwhile they would stay in the hotel at the company expense, something that Mike intended to make full use of. However, first thing on Saturday morning the Superintendent was back on board and after a cursory inspection decreed that the tug would sail for Kharg the next day. Mike was not aboard and it took George an hour of telephone calls to find him. Mike was none too pleased at the news but George was more than satisfied. He was tired of life in port and wanted to be on the move and to resume his training. It was time to move on again.

Things on board started to buzz. Al was also happy to be on the move. His wife and family were already on the island and it was some time since he'd seen them. They had been in England whilst the tug was being built, but now they had returned to Iran and Al was looking forward to some home comforts.

The crew was also coming alive. They had settled in on board and were now anxious to start working. Working meant the opportunity to go alongside ships and that meant a resumption of the Indians' favourite sport, commerce. They had all saved their money for some time, and had now converted it into American dollars, the common currency of the smuggling fraternity. All they needed now was an accommodating Greek with something to sell at a bargain price and they would be happy to do business.

Mike finally appeared on board during the afternoon but after collecting the ships documents departed to visit the local customs office. Before the tug could sail it had to be signed out of the port. The tankers coming to load oil would have their local agents to do this for them but Mike hoped to get it done without assistance. George also suspected that he would not be seen again till sailing time, but after a couple of hours Mike turned up again with the papers signed and sealed. 'We'll get away early in the morning,' he announced. 'Pilot will be on board at seven so I'll stay aboard tonight.'

'April's kicked him out,' Al commented to George when they were alone. 'She won't want him disturbing her beauty sleep that early in the morning.' Al grinned and then added, 'She sure as hell needs it. She's no oil painting.'

They ate an early dinner that evening and Mike headed for the Seaman's Club to watch the latest film. George went along to post his latest letter home but then headed back for the tug as he'd seen the film before. He sat on deck with Al and was grateful for the cooling breeze that blew along the river. He was surprised when Al refused a beer and went instead to make up a jug of orange juice. The run crew had stuck to alcohol and had left a supply of concentrated orange untouched. 'I want my wits about me when we sail,' said Al. 'A new crew and a new tug, so I'll be watching what happens pretty closely.'

They headed for bed at around eleven and shortly after, George heard the Captain's door open and then thud closed. Mike was back aboard. Everything was quiet, and George dozed off peacefully wondering what his wife and children were doing at home. 'Wonder if they're thinking about me?' he dreamed.

It only seemed to be a few minutes later and George was fully awake. 'What the bloody hell's that noise,' he thought. He threw his legs over the side of the bunk and pulled on a pair of shorts as he went out through the saloon and headed for the upper deck. Mike and Al were already there and the wailing noise from the refinery was even louder. 'Look at that,' croaked Mike, brushing sleep from his eyes and pointing down river.

George turned and immediately saw what Mike was pointing at. A red sheet of flame and a pall of black smoke were shooting up into the sky and at the base of the flame was something that George had dreaded since his first day at sea. A tanker was on fire alongside an oil jetty.

Mike was shouting again and Al rushed past George and down the ladder towards the engine room. 'Get the crew on stand by,' Mike roared at the wide eyed Quartermaster who had appeared on deck, and then added, 'Lets go, George. I'm going to need your help. Go and make sure the radio is on channel 10 so we can hear what the other tugs are doing.'

George went up to the bridge, and found he was sweating, even in the cool night air. He tuned in the radio, and a crackle of static and excited voices boomed out. The radio had been left on full volume. He adjusted it, and then felt a throb under his feet as the engines started. Big Mike arrived on the bridge and the crew came tumbling out onto the deck. 'Soon as we get under way go and get the *Serang*,' he ordered. 'I'll want you up on the flying bridge with the *Serang* and a couple of sailors to direct the fire monitors.

The Quartermaster took the wheel and the mooring lines were quickly thrown off. Mike turned the 'Zamand' slowly off the jetty and headed down river. 'Steady now,' he called and the Quartermaster kept the tug on course towards the fire. Mike turned to the radio. He picked up the handset and called for instructions whilst the wailing of the fire siren droned on.

The three old tugs that worked the port were already heading for the fire. 'Pity I don't have a camera,' thought George, as one by one they started to shoot water from their fire monitors, but the thought was soon lost. A roar of engines came from beneath his feet as Al started the fire pumps and George headed for the flying bridge calling for the *Serang* as he went. He was glad now that he'd been all over the tug and knew how to operate the fire monitors. He quickly turned the monitors to face down wind, and then opened the valves to start the water. 'Monitors open,' he called down to Mike, and then watched as the full power of the pumps was opened up.

Four jets of water spurted out of the fire monitors and curved in a lazy arc down into the river a hundred feet away. The muddy river foamed like a good bottle of Shams beer and suddenly sparkled with phosphorescence. George grinned at the *Serang*. 'Everything's getting lit up tonight,' he called above the rush of water.

The tug was now getting closer to the burning tanker and George strained his eyes against the glare of the flames. 'Oh, no,' he thought, 'It's not one ship but two that are in trouble.' The ship on the next berth down river was also alight and so was the water between the two of them. George scuttled down the ladder and reported to Mike.

The radio crackled to life. 'Zamand, this is fire control.' Mike quickly replied and received orders to proceed to the downstream ship, whilst the three local tugs dealt with the major fire on the other one.

'Will do, control,' he answered, and told George what the plan would be. 'We'll tackle the river first, and lay down a carpet of foam between the two ships. If that works and isolates each fire we'll then put foam on the downstream ship for as long as the supply lasts. After that it will have to be water.'

'OK,' said George, 'I'll give you a shout as soon as we are in range with the monitors.' He went back up the ladder, barking his shins on the tread on his way. He hardly noticed, and passed the orders on to the *Serang* who translated them for the sailors.

They skirted the first tanker that was blazing from stem to stern and George called the range down to Mike who then signalled to Al on the main deck. Al quickly opened a valve and foam started to pour from the monitors. It spread on top of the river waters like a carpet of frothy whipped cream and as it spread the flames on the surface of the river guttered, hissed and died. The 'Zamand' slowly drifted on the tide towards the downstream tanker and as they came near the monitors were directed upwards, shooting a milky white spray of foam on to the flaming amidships accommodation and then onto the main deck.

Very quickly the supply of foam was gone, and only river water came from the monitors. Clouds of sizzling steam rose as the water touched the flames but gradually the water was winning. The flames were getting smaller and smaller.

By now Mike had landed the tug alongside the ship and was holding it in position by pushing against the side with the bow. The new rubber fender left a greasy black mark along the hot side of the ship, but gradually the heat was leaving the metal and the ships crew were rolling out their own fire hoses to help quell the fire.

George heard a shout and looked round. Mike's head stuck up above the deck at the top of the ladder. He was smoke blackened except for two patches around his eyes and with his black beard reminded George of the Black and White Minstrel Show on television at home. 'We're going to leave this one,' said Mike. 'The shore firemen and the ship's crew can handle it now. We've got to go alongside the stern of the other one. There's a group of people trapped there by the fire and we're going to take them off. Get the *Serang* to find a ladder if we have one,' he ordered.

'OK,' said George, dripping water from head to toe.

'What the hell have you done to yourself?' asked Mike, pointing at George's legs.

He looked down to find his shins covered in blood. 'Must have been the bloody ladder,' said George running a finger down one shin and then sucking his finger. 'Could have been worse,' he said, 'We could have been flaming fried!' A shiver ran down his spine at the thought but it was quickly forgotten. There was still work to do.

He left the monitors to be directed by the two sailors and headed below with the *Serang*. He couldn't remember seeing a ladder amongst the stores. He ran down to the main deck where he found Al with some of the engine crew.

'Fine night,' greeted Al rubbing a filthy oily rag over his face. 'You'll be wanting something as usual'

'Have we got a ladder?' asked George and was pleased when Al pointed to a bracket on the nearby bulkhead.

'Trouble with deckies,' said Al, 'Never look further than the end of their big noses.'

George and the *Serang* were too hurried to bother with an insult in reply and they headed for the foredeck with the ladder between them. George swore loudly as the ladder got stuck. They freed it with a stout kick and heaved it on to the foredeck. 'Get a couple of lashings,' said George to a nearby sailor and ran back up to the bridge.

He stood watching as Mike manoeuvred the tug with the bow right on to the stern of the ship and shouted to the men huddled on the deck of the ship. 'Put a heaving line down to the tug,' he called, 'And we'll send a line up.'

A smoke stained sailor detached himself from the group and tossed a line down to the tug and then shouted at the others to lend him a hand. A ragged smoke stained Greek flag hung from the stern of the ship and fluttered in the breeze. A pall of black smoke still poured up from the forward end of the ship and a roaring and crackling noise made George feel sure that the fire was still blazing. The tug was quickly secured to the bollards on the stern of the ship and the tug crew leaned the ladder against the stern just below the ship's rail. The Greek crewmen pushed towards the rail and the sailor who had thrown down the line screamed at them in a torrent of mixed Greek and foul English. It seemed to calm them and instead of pushing they lined up and, one by one, climbed over the rail and down the ladder to the tug.

They milled around on the tug foredeck so George left the bridge once more and called to them to follow him. He took them aft to the main deck, which was now relatively quiet and handed them over to Al. 'What the hell am I supposed to do with them?' asked Al.'

'Buggered if I know,' replied George, 'But don't turn your back on them. You know what Greeks are like.'

He pushed his way past them and went back to the bridge. 'We're going to take the tanker crew to number eight jetty,' said Mike. 'They can be looked after there until the authorities decide what to do with them.'

They let go from the tanker, leaving their ropes dangling over the stern and headed back upstream. The three port tugs were making headway with the fire which was now confined to the midships accommodation only. The 'Zamand', with a bow wave like a bone in her teeth, sped upriver. 'Wish they'd shut that poxy fire siren off,' shouted Mike, and George realised that it had been wailing its accompaniment since the start of the emergency. He just hadn't noticed it while he was busy.

They docked shortly afterwards and the Greek crewmen shuffled ashore. They stood on the dock peering around them and looking rather forlorn. 'Poor bastards,' said Mike to no one in particular. 'Probably lost everything they own and they wouldn't have had much to start with'

The radio burst into life again just as the fire siren from the refinery finally tailed off into silence. 'Zamand, control,' it squawked.

George picked up the handset. 'Zamand here,' he replied.

'Zamand, thank you very much. You are no longer required.'

'Thank you,' replied George and turned to Mike.

'Bollocks!' said Mike explosively.

'What's wrong?' asked George.

Mike sighed. 'What's wrong?' he echoed. 'What's bloody wrong is that we only fought the fire on one ship. You know what that means?'

George confessed that he didn't have a clue what that meant.

'Means we'll only get a salvage claim on one ship,' he said. If we hadn't bothered with rescuing people we would have been able to fight the fire on both of the ships. Double the money!'

George pondered the morality of Mike's thoughts for a fleeting second before wondering if he would be included in the salvage payout. 'Hope they count trainees when it comes to sharing out the folding green,' he thought.

A look of satisfaction suddenly crossed Mike's face. Something good had occurred to him. 'Well,' he beamed, 'At least we won't be able to sail tomorrow. We'll have to stay and top up our foam tanks again. Reckon it will take a day or so to organise it and we can get the tug cleaned up in the meantime. She's looking a bit black.'

They headed for the saloon and cracked open three more of Al's supply of cans. 'Better clean the blood off your legs, young George,' cackled Al. 'Looks like it's your time of the month.'

6

It took a long time for George to drop off to sleep after the excitement of the fire and even longer to wake up in the morning. Ignatius, the officers' Goanese steward, brought him tea at seven o'clock, as usual, but the tea just got cold when George dozed off again. George finally dragged himself out of his bunk at half past eight and after rooting out some clothes that didn't smell of smoke went in search of breakfast.

In the saloon Ignatius was hovering, waiting to serve anyone who came in. It was evident that Al and Mike had also slept in, so George had Ignatius all to himself. This was okay for service but not so good otherwise. Ignatius lived on a staple diet of garlic and his breath was strong enough to strip paintwork. George and Mike had re-christened him Hal, which Ignatius now answered to. He was proud to have a nickname from the *sahibs* but didn't realise it was short for halitosis.

'Bacon and eggs please, Hal' said George, helping himself to the hot toast that had already appeared on the table. George had little need for watching his diet. He weighed in at just over ten stone when soaking wet and twenty cigarettes a day suppressed any real urge to over eat. The saloon door cracked open and the *Serang* peered in.

'Any jobs, *sahib*?' he asked.

'Just clean everything from the top to the bottom,' mumbled George around a mouthful of toast.

'Already started, *sahib*,' replied the *Serang*, opening the door wider. George looked up from his plate and guessed what was coming.

'We get salvage money?' the *Serang* asked.

'Sure,' George replied, although he was totally unsure. All he knew was that it would take months or years to be paid rather than days or weeks, if it happened at all. The *Serang* departed happily to tell the rest of the crew that they could start planning what to do with a small fortune and George went back to demolishing his toast.

The saloon door opened again, and the round face of Captain Robertson appeared. He heaved his bulk over the sill and sat down heavily in a spare chair. 'Cup of coffee, please,' he ordered and George called for Hal who sped off in the direction of the pantry to oblige.

The coffee came and Captain Robertson looked up at George and said, 'Well done last night.'

'Thanks,' said George. 'The crew have been asking about salvage money already,' he continued. 'What can I tell them?'

'Tell them it will all get sorted out in a few months time, and hope that will keep them quiet,' he replied, taking a long swallow from the cup.

'Bloody hell,' he exploded. 'A couple of tiny fires during the night and they forget to put sugar in my coffee in the morning. Tell them to get their priorities right or they won't last long enough to claim salvage. Where's Mike?' he asked.

'Gone to see about getting the foam tank topped up,' lied George, knowing full well that Mike was still in his pit and crossing his fingers that Mike wouldn't arrive in the saloon in pyjamas.

'Too late,' said the Super, 'I've already got it arranged. They'll supply you from a fire truck this afternoon and then you have to sail for Kharg. One of the other tugs needs to come for dry docking so you're required on the island yesterday if not sooner.'

He finished his coffee and heaved himself to his feet. Fixing George with a malevolent stare he added, 'Tell Mike I was here, when he gets up.' He then grinned and said, ' Not a bad try, Penroy, but you'll have to get up earlier in the day to fool a cunning old bastard like me.'

The door closed behind him and George heaved a sigh of relief. 'Nearly dropped myself in the brown stuff then,' he thought. 'Crafty old sod didn't let on that he knew what was going on all the time.'

George finished his breakfast and about an hour later Mike and Al surfaced. Mike didn't react well to the news that they had to sail that day and headed for the hotel to report in to April. 'She'll be wondering what happened during the night,' he said as he beat a hasty retreat.

The morning passed quickly and just after Al and George finished lunch Mike appeared back on board. The fire truck had already refilled the tug's tank with foam so all was ready for the voyage to Kharg. An Iraqi pilot boat bumped alongside a few minutes later and with very little fuss the tug was under way and heading down the river.

'Leave the pilot to it,' said Mike. 'Whilst he's on board you can get a couple of hours rest to make up for last night. Later on we'll sort out some watches for tonight. We should be down at the happy isle early in the morning.'

George needed no further urging and headed for his bunk. He was glad to be moving again and was looking forward to arriving in Kharg. He had never been to the island before but knew a lot about it. It was the latest in oil terminals with the most modern of systems. It had been purpose built for the export of crude oil and was currently the biggest crude export port in the world. There was going to be plenty to learn.

Several hours later the pilot left and the gentle pitching and rolling motion of the tug confirmed that they were out of the river and at sea. George was back in familiar territory. Mike said he would take the first watch and it immediately dawned on George that he was the fall guy as usual. He would have to take over at midnight and do the graveyard watch.

'Charming, bloody charming,' he muttered to himself as soon as he was out of Mike's earshot.

He went back to his cabin as there was absolutely nothing to see apart from the horizon. He started to write a letter home but couldn't settle to it and eventually he lay on the saloon settee and dozed off. About an hour later he woke up, feeling stiff from lying in the draught from the air conditioning vent. He went through to his cabin and started to read but the lack of sleep from the night before caught up with him once more, so he threw off his clothes and climbed into his bunk. Might as well make the most of his chances as he would be awake during the night again.

The Quartermaster woke him just before midnight. 'One bell, *sahib*' called the old Indian, softly. George scratched his groin, rubbed the sleep from his eyes and climbed out of his bunk. He threw on a pair of shorts and a shirt and headed for the bridge. He expected to see Big Mike but the bridge was deserted apart from the Quartermaster who was steering the tug and an Indian seaman who was boiling an electric kettle on the end of the chart table.

'Where's the Captain?' asked George.

'Gone sleeping,' replied the seaman, 'Maybe two hour before.'

'Great,' thought George. 'The idle sod has left the crew to do the work and me to take over for the difficult bit.'

He looked at the compass course and checked it on the chart that lay on the table and was pleased to see that they were at least headed in the right direction. The tug had little navigation equipment other than the standard compass so they were working on dead reckoning. At least Mike had noted on the chart when the pilot had left so George quickly made a calculation based on the course and distance since that time. He marked the probable position on the chart with a cross and the time and then measured the distance remaining to Kharg Island. He looked around the horizon, taking into account the direction of the wind and sea. It was coming from astern, so he estimated that they must have made about twelve knots.

He checked the chart again, this time to see the height of the land they were heading for. The chart showed several flares on the top of the island and George knew that he would see them well before the tug arrived.

His estimations told him that if the weather remained clear he should see the flares in the next hour when they were still forty miles from the island. He would then see the loom of the South Light an hour after that. By the time the dawn came they would be able to see the island and he should be able to adjust the course as necessary to round the western tip of Kharg. George installed himself in the large wooden pilot chair and settled down to drink coffee and keep a lookout. 'Coffee every half hour,' he told the sailor on watch, and he put his feet up on the wheelhouse window sill to get more comfortable.

Twice during the hour he stirred himself from his chair. Lights on the horizon demanded a closer look. He took the binoculars from the box by the chart table and focussed them on the lights. He quickly identified the lights of tankers heading north and also saw that they weren't going to pass near to the tug. He went back to his chair, closely watching the lights to see that their bearing changed. Sure enough the bearing changed and they passed slowly until they were astern of the tug and out of George's view. A short while later a vague red smudge appeared on the horizon ahead. This time George remained seated, as he had kept the binoculars in reach by hanging them from the back of the chair. The smudge looked a little like the first light of dawn but it was definitely wasn't in the east. It was the reflection of oil installation flares on the night time clouds. George settled back again, clutching the latest cup of coffee in both hands. It was getting cold.

Another hour passed and slowly, almost imperceptibly at first, the glow of dawn started to light the eastern sky. Southwards there was a dark mark on the horizon; it was not yet the hills of Kharg but it was the smoke from the flares where the excess gas was burnt off. George stirred himself and glanced at the compass. He ordered a slight alteration of course to leave the smoke on the port bow and wished that the company had thought it worthwhile to install a radar. On maximum range a radar would have picked up the rocky island easily, making navigation that much easier. George thought moodily on the miserly ways of shipping companies for a while, concluding, as usual, that they suffered from short arms and long pockets.

Gradually the outline of the island crept over the horizon and eventually George got to his feet. They were now in sight of the anchorage and it seemed to be crammed with tankers. He counted nine or ten, all of around the hundred thousand ton size, all heading into the morning breeze. No wonder the place seemed crowded. He set a new course to pass around the western end of the island and went below to wake Mike. 'About five miles to go,' he told Mike , cheerfully, and passed him a freshly brewed cup of coffee. Mike grunted and sat up in his bunk.

'I'll be there in five minutes,' he said, and George headed back for the bridge.

Fifteen minutes later the tug had rounded the tip of the island and the oil terminal was in full view. One great jetty nearly a mile long, with every berth occupied by a ship loading crude oil. George was getting jumpy. He headed below again and knocked on Mike's door. Mike was sitting in his chair, gazing into the half-finished cup of coffee with a glazed look on his face. He looked up as George came in. 'What's up,' he asked.

'Just making sure you're up,' George replied, 'We're getting a bit close now.'

Mike looked out of the porthole. 'Don't get your knickers in a twist,' he said, sharply, and George went back to the bridge.

'Sod him,' he thought. 'If he doesn't turn up I'll take the damn tug into the boat harbour by myself.' He checked the position against the chart again, and then studied the large scale chart of the small boat harbour that lay inside the oil jetty, protected from any poor weather. It looked a bit small but he thought he would give it a go.

They rounded the end of the oil jetty and the boat harbour came into view. George eased the engine control back until it showed slow ahead and the tug immediately responded. 'Great,' thought George easing the control back further to dead slow. The tug crept towards the harbour and George jumped when Mike's voice behind him said, 'I'll take her now.'

They turned into the tiny harbour and headed for a small empty jetty. 'Home, sweet home,' said Mike as he gently laid the tug alongside and stopped the engines. Crew men leapt ashore carrying ropes and within a few minutes they were made fast. A smart minibus raced along the unpaved white coral sand road around the harbour and skidded to a halt at the jetty. Several people climbed out and headed for the tug. 'Here come the vultures,' said Mike, 'They're all coming to see if we've brought them their stores from the UK.'

They left the bridge and headed for the saloon. 'Sod them,' said Mike. 'We'll get our priorities right and have our breakfast first.'

7

A busy month had passed and George was well into the life of the island. Most days and some nights he would go aboard whatever tug was on duty and observe what was happening. More and more frequently he was allowed to handle the tug for himself, under the watchful eye of the duty Captain. He had started off with Mike and Al, but soon realised that Mike himself was only just getting to know the new tug and would not often let George handle it.

Kharg Island Terminal was far removed from the quiet life of the mainland and the river. Immense quantities of crude oil were pumped to the island from the many wells in the interior of the country. It was stored at the tank farm on top of the island and from there was piped downhill at a fantastic rate into the waiting tankers. George had never heard of such loading rates for the ships. Twenty thousand tons an hour could be delivered to each of the ten berths. A hundred thousand ton tanker could discharge her ballast and be loaded with crude oil and on its way again within eight hours.

At such rates the turn-round of ships was phenomenal. The three tugs on duty would be constantly either attending the berthing or sailing of a ship and it was rare that they could anchor for more than an hour's rest. Quite often the tug master and engineer would be on their feet for twenty-four hours continuously, taking a real toll of their strength and energy. They would then have two days off in which to recover.

George would join a tug at nine in the morning when the shifts changed and would then generally stay on board until early evening. He would then get a lift back to the harbour in a passing pilot boat and head for the bright lights of the Seaman's Club. The Club was at the end of the oil jetty and each night would show a film. George would usually watch the movie and then head back for the boat harbour where he would board whatever tug was off duty and find a bed in one of the spare cabins.

He had also been invited ashore several times. The captains and engineers all lived in modern bungalows on the island where there was a considerable social life. Apart from the standard oil company club there was a beach club on the north side of the island and there was the golf club. The golf club was the favourite haunt of the expatriates and was the social centre of the island. A single story building in the middle of desert scrub, it was approached by a winding tarmac road that was set with deep potholes. On one side the sandy fairway and oiled greens were bordered by the rocky slopes of the hill and on the other side was the fence that surrounded the local airport. The clubhouse was, however, something of an oasis. The cupboards in the clubroom were stocked with every sort of drink imaginable and the bar was open continuously throughout the day. Shams beer was delivered on a daily basis from the company liquor store, as were soft drinks and the spirits were the product of an active contraband system that operated through the tugs. If there was ever a shortage of liquid at the club it was invariably caused by a leak in the single pipeline that snaked across the desert and brought pure fresh water.

The clientele of the club was, to George's delight, mostly expatriates in their thirties. Kharg was a place for young people. There were a dozen tug masters and a dozen more engineers working in the port, plus twenty or so pilots. Each had a wife and family living on the island and these were the mainstays of the club. There was also a shifting population of contractors who were building more oil installations and a team of helicopter pilots who serviced the offshore oil rigs and production platforms. On any day, at any time there were people in the bar and on most days there were dedicated golfers hacking their way around the course.

George had looked at the course both from the road and from the clubhouse window. He had never played golf before and looked on in wonder at the apparitions who sweated and swore their way round nine holes and then started round again if they wanted to do eighteen. The fairways looked as if they had been prepared by a road grader and were full of stones and small rocks. The ground was covered in coral sand, which showed that originally the island had been under the sea, probably some thousands of years ago. If the players tried to undercut the ball and take a divot the club struck coral rock. Something then had to give. Either the club bent or the player felt the shock waves right up through his bones. Players were allowed to move their ball up to two club lengths to get a better lie, as long as they moved away from the hole but most times they didn't bother as there was no better lie anywhere.

'I'll have to have a go at it,' thought George, wondering from whom he could borrow a set of clubs. In his youth, before going to sea, he had tried any sport requiring a ball, and some that didn't as well. He counted chancing his arm with the young ladies of the fifties as a sport, but had always found less success at that than some of the other games.

George had also been to the beach club along with a couple of families. Men, wives, children, a portable barbecue and several dogs had completed the party. They had arrived during the late afternoon when the waters of the Gulf were at their most sparkling clear. Snorkels and masks were a favourite and George joined with the others in floating face down and watching the fish. He had never seen such a variety before, nor known water so warm. At first he had looked over his shoulder at regular intervals in case something large with sharp teeth sneaked up on him. He made discreet enquiries later from the children, who shrieked with amusement because he was worried about sharks. 'Better safe than sorry,' thought George, who had no wish to disagree with something that ate him.

As darkness fell the men had lit the barbecue. It seemed a bit dangerous to George when they disconnected the fuel pipe of one of the cars and got a cup full of petrol to speed things up, but they evidently knew their oil products. After an initial furious blaze the charcoal soon settled to a red-hot glow and steaks, sausages and potatoes were piled on to the grill in quick succession. The cooking was rudimentary and seemed to be based on the maxim 'When it's brown it's done and when it's black it's buggered,' but none of the food lasted long. It was washed down with beer for the men and a variety of soft drinks for those who didn't want beer. Several of the women and one or two children seemed to be keeping pace with the men on the beer but in general life was very relaxed and the time soon passed.

No one wanted to finish the night off early, so after a while they headed for the cars and back to a bungalow in the housing area. George's eyes lit up when he saw the inside of a Kharg Island bungalow for the first time. It was more modern than anything he had previously seen and he was astounded by the size. At a conservative estimate you could have fitted the whole ground floor of George's house in England, *khaz*i and all, into the bungalow's living room. The furniture was modern and the whole place was cool and comfortable as there was a central air conditioning unit. Even in the kitchen cool air prevailed.

Long into the night the bungalow reverberated to the sounds of rock and roll which blasted out from the latest in tape recorders. The big reels on the deck went on for hours and the sounds boomed on. Everyone was dancing and George soon joined in. It seemed that parties like this were a regular occurrence and you could dance with any of the ladies you liked. Since half of them were still in bikinis from the beach George quite liked them all and with several Shams beers under his belt he quickly lost any inhibitions that he might have started with.

Some time after three in the morning everyone went home. 'You don't want to head back to the tug now, do you George?' said the bungalow owner and shortly afterwards George was stretched out in a bed in a spare bedroom contemplating life in general and his navel in particular. 'I could get used to this,' he thought and decided that his wife and family might just get to like it too. 'Beats hell out of going to sea,' was his last conscious thought before drifting into a beer soddened sleep.

He was woken early the next morning by the owner of the house. 'Want a cup of coffee before we head for the tugs?' he was asked. He accepted gratefully and swung his legs over the side of the bed. His head buzzed from last night's beer and he wondered if he would manage to keep the coffee down. The words 'Never again' sprung into mind but he didn't utter them. He'd done that too many times before and still hadn't learned yet. The coffee settled him down though and he headed for the minibus when it stopped at the front gate, calling his thanks back to a lady in a night-dress who appeared in the doorway as they left. 'Don't remember her,' he thought, idly wondering if she would remember him for any reason. 'Can't remember doing anything I should regret,' he concluded.

That afternoon there was a lull in shipping movements and George headed for the nearest empty bunk to catch up on sleep. Three hours later he felt much refreshed, and decided that instead of heading for the bright lights that evening he would stay aboard and get in a little night work. He was getting used to landing the tugs alongside moving ships in daylight but needed more practice when the only light came from a single searchlight mounted above the bridge. He scanned the rota of tug masters and found that Robbie Roberts was on duty on the 'Farahdast'. He remembered Brian telling him to learn what he could from Robbie, so caught a passing pilot boat and got a lift to the 'Farahdast' just as it was getting dark.

He jumped on board the tug as the pilot boat was riding the top of a wave, falling into the arms of an Indian crewman. It took time to get used to small boats and transferring from one to the other. He brushed himself down and headed for the Captain's cabin where he knocked before going in. Robbie Roberts was a dumpy Scot who was in his sixties and had been on tugs forever and a day. George introduced himself to Robbie and to the engineer who was sitting on the settee smoking. The engineer was Olwyn and George had heard all about him. His liking for Iranian women was exceeded only by his attraction to young men and his reputation as someone to avoid was legend. He was someone that George felt he should avoid socially at all costs.

He was invited to take a seat and took care to take one as far from Olwyn as possible. Robbie and Olwyn were drinking Shams direct from bottles and, for a change, they didn't offer one to George. They were arguing about the tug's engine controls and seemed to George to be near coming to blows. He was just wondering if it had been wise to come on board the 'Farahdast' when the door opened again and a Quartermaster announced 'Stand by, *Sahib*,' before going to call the crew.

'I'll see everything is ready,' said George and headed for the door, taking care not to turn his back on Olwyn. He thankfully went up the bridge ladder and watched as the crew tumbled out onto the foredeck and started heaving up the anchor. The tug's engine rumbled into life, making the deck vibrate under George's feet and the VHF radio crackled into life.

'Farahdast from pilot,' came over the airwaves.

'Farahdast,' confirmed George.

'Ship berthing at number one jetty. Make fast for'd, please.'

'Will do,' replied George and headed down for the Captain's cabin.

Robbie and Olwyn were still arguing. 'Ship for number one,' interrupted George.

Robbie looked up. 'Get the anchor up and head for the ship,' he said, 'I'll be up in a minute.'

George went back to the bridge. He could see the ship heading towards the jetty and another tug already making its way towards it. The bell on the foredeck clanged, telling George the anchor was aweigh, so he pushed the engine control gingerly to dead slow ahead and turned the Farahdast towards the ship. He increased speed a little and waited for Robbie to appear.

Five minutes passed and they were getting close to the berthing tanker. 'Keep her steady,' said George to the Quartermaster and clattered quickly down the bridge ladder again. Robbie and Olwyn were still hard at it, getting rather red faced and heated. 'We're close to the ship now,' said George interrupting them in full flow.

'Well, go alongside the bloody thing then,' said Robbie, turning back to Olwyn and the argument.

George left them to it. He felt a quiver in his stomach as he headed back to the bridge and hoped it was just a mild attack of flatulence brought on by nerves. Couldn't afford to follow through at this stage of the game. He took stock of the position again.

The Quartermaster seemed to understand the situation and left the wheel, turning towards the switchboard behind him. He threw a switch and the floodlight beamed out, shining on the side of the docking tanker. 'Thanks,' said George. He'd forgotten the searchlight in his preoccupation with getting the tug alongside. Gradually he inched the tug into position, landing gently along the flat sides of the tanker. He breathed a sigh of relief as the crew sent up the ropes for making fast. The difficult bit was over.

The pilot's orders came over the radio, loud and clear and George made the Farahdast push and pull as required until the tanker was alongside the berth. The order to let go was given after an hour of manoeuvring and George was heading the tug back towards the anchorage when the next call came. He headed back down to Robbie's cabin again. 'We've got another call,' he told Robbie, who barely looked up from his beer and argument.

'Go do it,' he replied.

'Where's the log book?' asked George, who knew he should be recording the ship's names and what was happening.

'Just scribble some notes on scrap paper,' replied Robbie, ' And I'll fill it in properly tomorrow.'

'OK,' said George and went back to the bridge with a lot more confidence. He did two more jobs before getting a chance to anchor again and in the lull between ships went down to the saloon and made himself a sandwich. It was near midnight and he was hungry as well as getting tired.

He had just finished his sandwich when there was the sound of feet in the alleyway and the Quartermaster appeared. 'Pilot calling, *sahib*,' he reported. 'Ship sailing.'

George went back to the bridge, apprehensive once more. There was no sign of Robbie so he got the tug under way again and headed in for the jetty and the ship requiring assistance to sail. This time he would have to work 'on the hook', and he had only watched it done before. For most of the time the tug made fast to ships from the bow and then pushed or pulled back as required. This time she would make fast and tow from the stern, a different and more difficult operation in many ways.

George took his time getting the tug into position with her stern under the bow of the ship. He then held the position whilst the heavy wire towrope was sent up from the after deck. There was a mark on the tow rope which told George when there was enough wire on board the ship to allow it to be made fast, and as the mark passed through the fairleads George called to the ship's crew .

'Make fast,' he shouted and crossed his arms over his head, giving the internationally recognised signal. So far, so good!

Once the crew had made fast George reported to the pilot who then went about his business and got the ship ready to sail. One by one the ship's lines were cast off and the pilot then called for the tug to move out on the bow, ready to tow. Cautiously, George took up the slack on the towline and eased the tug into position.

'Take her off,' called the pilot over the radio, and George increased the weight on the towing wire. The wash from the tug's propeller boiled out from under the counter of the stern and the ship's bow started to move away from the quay.

'Great,' said George under his breath and eased the tug round more on the bow. He knew that the ship would start to move ahead soon and didn't want to get the tug aft of the ship's beam. He'd been warned about that over and over by all the tug captains.

'Thanks, Farahdast,' called the pilot over the radio. 'Stop and let go.'

'Let go,' echoed George and swung the tug sharply round ahead of the ship before stopping the engines. The towline slacked and George shouted back to the crew to let go. The wire slithered through the tanker's bow fairlead and splashed into the water and as it did so George put the engines ahead again to clear from out of the tanker's path. Once clear he stopped the engines again, and the tug crew went through the process of recovering the wire. George found that he was sweating, even though it was now quite cool. 'Another job under my belt,' he thought, wondering if Robbie and Olwyn were still awake.

There was no respite for George though. No sooner had the wire been brought dripping over the stern than there was a call to attend another ship. He headed the tug into the anchorage, gaining confidence with every minute that passed.

They were at full speed when George heard a commotion on the bridge ladder and Robbie and Olwyn swayed onto the bridge. George could smell the beer on them and they were still arguing heatedly. They took no notice of George whatsoever and headed towards the engine controls.

'Look,' said Robbie, heaving the engine control to full astern, 'The engine doesn't cut out.' He was right. The tug shook and rattled furiously as the engine went astern and the tug swung wildly off course.

'You didn't do it fast enough,' yelped Olwyn, accusingly and viciously swung the control back to full ahead. Once again the tug shook itself and then it gathered speed again whilst the Quartermaster struggled to bring it back on course.

'See,' squawked Robbie, ' You don't bloody know everything. I told you I'd done it before.'

'It'll cut out eventually,' shouted Olwyn, going red in the face as he swung the control back again. This time the engine struggled to go astern and the noise abruptly ceased as it finally cut out. Robbie and Olwyn glared at each other for a minute and then started for the ladder again. 'Lets call it quits,' said Robbie as they disappeared from sight.

'Farahdast,' came the call over the radio from the pilot, 'Are you coming to the ship this week?'

'Cheeky bastard,' thought George and then replied, 'Just had a little engine trouble,' as the engine rumbled back into life. 'We're on our way now.'

The rest of the night passed without further incident and a tired George gratefully headed the tug towards the boat harbour the next morning. Brian had been right to suggest he went along with Robbie to learn how it was done. He'd learned more in one night than in the previous month but not quite in the way he'd expected. As they came alongside in the harbour Robbie appeared on the bridge. He looked around and then studied all the notes on scraps of paper that George had left under a paperweight.

'Christ,' said Robbie, 'Don't they teach you blokes to write in Log Books these days?

George grinned to himself. 'Silly old fart,' he thought as he started to collect up the papers. 'Where is the Log Book?' he asked.

'Top drawer of the chart table, where it always is.' muttered Robbie, leaving George to write up the nights exploits.

8

One experience with Robbie and Olwyn was quite enough for George and he kept away from the 'Farahdast' whenever they were on board. There were plenty of others who would teach him the tricks of the trade, including one captain who even preferred to let George work the tug while he watched. At first George thought he was a good teacher but he gradually came to see that the man had little or no confidence whatsoever in his own ability and was scaring himself into an early breakdown. He would allow George to work the tug but he answered the radio himself to give anyone who listened the idea that he was alone on the bridge.

This situation suited George, who was gradually getting much more confidence in his own ability. He was familiar with all the routine duties of the tug and was looking forward to the day when he would take over a shift on his own. He was also becoming known around the island, especially as a purveyor of jokes at parties, and was generally accepted as one of the gang. Several people had suggested that he should request to stay in the island but George already knew his time was getting short. The mainland bunch would want their leave and George was needed as a relief. Besides, his bungalow in the town must be ready by now and he could do with getting his wife and family out.

George was also aware by now that there was an undercurrent of musical bungalows going on at Kharg. Rumour and stories abounded about wives who were taking advantage of husbands who were away for twenty-four hours on duty and there were always stories of single contractors who weren't averse to chancing their arm or anything else at the parties. This worried George a little and though accommodation on the mainland was not as good as on the island he thought he would be better off away from the free and easy habits of some of the islanders. The suspected antics of April, who now lived on the island, were alone enough to frighten George back to the mainland.

George was now into the golfing fraternity and had found someone who was as bad at it as he was. Wee Al regularly got up early in the morning, when the weather was at its coolest and would then hack his way around the course, thrashing clubs around in the style of a demented windmill. He had suggested to George that he came out and had even borrowed a set of clubs for him. They evidently belonged to Vi, Al's wife and, as she was nearly a foot taller than Al, they suited George quite well. The putter was something out of the Ark and it's leather grip was parting company with the shaft but if George wound the loose bits of leather around his hand they didn't upset his wayward putting too much.

Al and George weren't averse to a little creative counting when adding up their scores but since neither would ever bother the professionals at the Royal and Ancient it really didn't matter. What did count was their participation and the rest of the golfing fraternity heartily approved of their commitment to the sport. They also appreciated a new face in the bar to listen to their tall golfing stories and a new pocket to buy a round of drinks. They also appreciated George's ability to mimic the voices of other Kharg personalities and would roar their approval of his stories of tug training. His description of his experience with Robbie and Olwyn was growing with every telling and was fast becoming part of the island folklore. George was getting a bit worried that the story might reach back to the mainland and the attention of the Marine Superintendent but the glory of telling the story outweighed the worries. Wherever a few Shams were gathered together the call went up for the story and George's standing in the community grew. He liked that.

George was sitting aboard a tug one morning, waiting for the duty men to board, when Olwyn sought him out. 'Christ,' thought George,' He's heard the stories.' However that wasn't the case. Olwyn had been past the oil company main office and had picked up the mail. There were two letters from George's wife, and an official communication from the Superintendent. The gist of the message from the mainland was that George was booked on a flight at the end of the next week and should report to the Super's office on arrival.

'Sounds as if things are happening,' mused George, happy that he would be getting to work by himself at last. 'Might be news about the arrival of the family too,' he thought.

'It's going to cost you a few rials for the party,' said Olwyn with a sly smile.

'What party?' asked George.

'Your farewell to the island,' replied Olwyn. 'Reckon there's a lot of wives who might miss you when you're gone,' he leered.

'Oh well,' said George, 'That's better than being missed by the blokes,' and Olwyn departed, scowling to himself. 'Blasted greasy poofter,' George added when Olwyn was safely out of earshot.

The news spread quickly and by the time George was ashore that night he was met by Al who had been busy. 'You can have the do at my place,' said Al, 'Vi won't mind.' It had also been settled that George would pay for the beer, whilst the spirits and mixers would come from the guests. 'We'll have Abdul from the Golf Club as bar man,' Al continued. 'There won't be anyone at the club that night so he can help out. Feed him a swift few beers and he'll do it for free.'

'Thank the Lord for that,' thought George, who was mentally adding up how much he had to his name. He had the distinct feeling that this party was going to be expensive.

'You won't have to supply food,' said Al. 'Couple of the wives have said they'll bring stuff. We'll pass the word round and they'll all come up with something. Won't cost you anything. They've wanted an excuse for a big do for a long time and you've provided it. Watch out for April though,' he warned, 'If she wants to thank you personally just run.'

The next few days passed in a blur. George was in demand most evenings in the bungalow area and most of the demands were in connection with the party. Everyone wanted an invite and to be sure of getting one they were inviting George for a few drinks in advance. George had actually left all the arrangements to Al and Vi but the only thing he hadn't done was to ask about numbers. How many could a bungalow reasonably hold? How many would Vi permit?

George sought out Al as soon as he could. Al was in the engine room of the Zamand even though it was his morning off. He was checking over valves and pipes, pumps and separators, suctions and discharges and generally getting more familiar with the ins and outs of the Zamand's inner workings. Such engineering mysteries still left George cold and he had the deckies blinkered faith in the Almighty where engines were concerned. Engines were instruments of torture for Scotsmen in George's opinion and if he hadn't needed to see Al he wouldn't have stepped over the engine room sill.

'And what can I do for you, bugger lugs?' enquired Al, wiping his hands on a terminally greasy piece of cotton waste.

George ignored the insult and asked his question. 'How many people are we expecting at this party?'

'About half the island,' grinned Al, 'And that's only because the other half is local employees.'

George had expected something like that. He was familiar with several of the local inhabitants who worked for the oil company but was already aware that they usually kept to themselves. He had supposed that it was the booze that kept them away, as they were nominally Muslim but according to most of the ex-pats it was because they couldn't understand the expatriate women. The women appeared to dance and fraternise with men other than their husbands, leading the local men to think they were fair game. Trouble was always on the cards when the nationalities mixed, especially once the expatriate men had downed a few stiff drinks.

'What about the contractors?' asked George.

'They'll arrive whether you ask them or not, so you might as well invite them. That way they may bring some booze with them.'

Al opened a valve and oily black water trickled into the bilges.

'What are you doing that for?' asked George. He knew the dirty oil would eventually end up in the clear waters of the Gulf.

'Counteracts the smell of the crew,' explained Al, 'The tired sods always pee in the bilges instead of heading for the bog.'

George laughed. It was always the deckies' opinion that it was the engineers and not the crew who were too lazy to climb the ladders.

He left Al to his work and headed for the Seaman's Club. He had found that this was the best place for posting mail and during the day it was usually free of tug men and pilots. That meant he could write a few lines in peace and without fear of disturbance. He could also get a hamburger and chips for lunch. The meal would be cooked over an open grill by a fat cook, whose one notable achievement was to smoke a whole cigarette without removing it from the corner of his mouth. The ash on the cigarette would get longer and longer but never in human memory had it dropped onto the hamburgers. Fat Ali was famous throughout the Persian Gulf and also a large proportion of the maritime world. He was also a consummate misery and it was rarely known for his face to crack into a smile. When asked the reason by the curious seamen he would reply, 'I've got four wives. Two are ugly and the other two are even worse. What I got to smile for?'

George finished his letter and mailed it. He had told his wife about the move back to the mainland and about the party. He hadn't worried her with the small detail of who was paying for the beer and with any luck she wouldn't think to ask. He had promised to see Captain Robinson as soon as he got back to town to get a firm date for her to travel out and join him. He was hoping that at least his bungalow would be ready.

On the day before the party George collected up all his belongings and packed them in his suitcases. The cases were getting a bit worse for wear but they would have to do for now. His gear was strewn around various tugs so it took some time to collect it all. Some of it was none too clean either and George was looking forward to getting Pedro back into harness with his dhoby. Trying to keep smart when leapfrogging from tug to tug wasn't the easiest of jobs. He called for the minibus from the phone on the jetty and when it arrived he heaved his cases on board. He was staying at Al's after the party and would have to be at the airport by nine the next morning. If he kept his best slacks and shirt for the party he would just have to put them on again in the morning for the flight back to the mainland. He had already decided that he was rather short of clothes. One didn't get done up in Merchant Navy uniform under any circumstances. The judge in Southampton who had once solemnly intoned, 'Fit for pigs and Merchant Seamen,' may have been censured but the standing of MN personnel ashore was none too high, nevertheless.

George arrived at Al's bungalow to find the front door wide open. He shouted a greeting and staggered in with his cases, only to be met by Vi in her underwear coming out of a bedroom. George could feel his face going red but it didn't seem to bother Vi.

'Hi, George,' she said, heading for the kitchen. 'I'm just making a cup of tea. Do you want one?'

'Thanks,' said George. 'I could do with one. Where shall I put my bags?'

'Throw them in the end bedroom,' replied Vi. 'There's a bed there for you. Make yourself at home.'

George made for the bedroom, hoping Vi would find some clothes before the tea was ready and hung around putting out his best gear in order to waste a few moments. He headed hesitantly for the lounge and found both Al and Vi there. Vi was shrugging on a housecoat but Al was in his Y-fronts, looking like something out of a prison camp. You could count his ribs and his arms and legs looked like matchsticks. George had never seen him without a boiler suit or his golfing gear before and was quite shocked.

Al saw George looking and grinned. He bent up one arm to show a scraggy bicep and said, 'Dear Mister Atlas, I've finished half of your course. You too can have a body like mine young George. If you're not careful.'

George started to blush again.

'Don't worry about it,' said Wee Al, 'Comes of having TB when I was a kid. At least it's all in working order. Ask Vi.'

'Perhaps I'll take your word for it,' said George, fully aware that his hosts had two children. He didn't want to think about the mechanics of the matter but wondered how Al could be such a heavy smoker after having such an ailment.

They served up tea from a silver service and for the first time George saw that there might be a normal side to life on the island. A life of families and children and mundane things like shopping and housework. Not that anyone did much housework as they all had servants, some permanently living in the quarters attached to the bungalow, others arriving on a daily basis from the nearby bazaar. Many of the servants spoke English and all could usually understand what their *ferangi* employers wanted. A little English, a little Farsi and a lot of hand waving seemed to serve the general purpose.

'You won't be going to work tomorrow, will you?' said Vi. 'We'll need someone here to arrange the delivery of the beer and to run errands to the Commissary for food.'

That sounded a good idea to George and he fully intended to catch a few hours sleep in the afternoon if he could. It would set him up for what promised to be a rather busy night.

'I'm going round to the school later,' said Vi. 'Have to see the teachers about the kids' progress. You might as well come too, George. You can invite the teachers to the party.'

It sounded like a good idea to George, as the teachers were the only two unattached expatriate females on the island. They were always the objects of attention for the contractors, even though rumour had it that they were more interested in each other than in men. They were decorative anyway and liked to dance, so would be an asset to the gathering.

The day passed quickly and George enjoyed a meal at the oil company club with Al's family. They dined on *chelo kebab*, an Iranian favourite, washed down with Shams for the men, gin and tonic for Vi and the inevitable Coke for the children. There were several other families at the club so while the children played together after the meal the adults joined forces for coffee and drinks. It was only a short walk back to the house afterwards and George was glad to be able to retire to his room at a reasonable hour. 'Might as well get some kip in advance,' he thought as he drifted off.

The next day dawned as bright and clear as usual. The summer season usually lasted from April to the end of October and there was rarely a cloud to be seen in the sky during that time. George knew that the end of the summer was near though, as the humidity was extremely high. The winds in the Gulf were influenced by the monsoon out in the Indian Ocean and when the South West monsoon started the southerly winds blew into the Gulf. They brought the warm moist air with them; a very necessary thing for ripening the dates on the trees but a highly uncomfortable time for humans. The slightest exercise produced a bath of sweat and leaving an air conditioned house meant instant fogging up of sunglasses. It was going to be pretty sweaty for the party.

The daylight hours passed slowly in a welter of work. And George was a willing gofer. He went for beer, he went for ice and he went for soft drinks, crisps, nuts and anything else that Vi could dream up. He also collected the children from school and took them to the swimming pool to keep them out of Vi's kitchen, where several wives were preparing snacks for the evening. An hour or so later he took the children to the Seaman's' Club for hamburgers, using Al's battered old car. The children happily ate on the hoof, playing around the legs of the sailors who sat drinking beer at the bar. In theory each sailor was limited to three beers in order to avoid drunkenness. They bought their issue of three beer tickets on board their ship but in practice they then bartered for the beer tickets of anyone who didn't want to go ashore. The system was therefore doomed to failure. Every so often a fight would break out in the bar but the protagonists were usually so inebriated that they rarely did any damage to themselves. Their language was always highly colourful and descriptive and the children would listen carefully. They soon learned to swear in several different languages, a habit they found useful when out of backhand range of their parents.

George had to bribe the children with one last drink to get them back in the car. He was taking them to a friend's house for the night. They would then be safely out of harms way so that the adults at Al's could make fools of themselves without fear of the children waking and watching. George checked his watch for the tenth time. It was time he was back at Al's and getting cleaned up. He finally got back to Al's but needn't have worried. The lights were on all over the house and music blared from the tape recorder at full power. No one had arrived though and Al and Vi were just warming up with the first drink of the night.

'Get your backside in gear, George,' called Al as George headed for the shower. If April comes in and catches you in just a towel you'll regret it.'

George took the wise precaution of bolting the shower room door before he turned on the cold water. It came out tepid but it was as cold as you could get in the Kharg cauldron. He wasted no time in showering, drying himself and throwing on his clothes for the evening. He wondered why he had bothered drying himself as the sweat immediately burst from every pore but then he settled down with his first ice cold beer to wait for the first arrivals. He didn't have long to wait.

A noisy group of contractors in a battered Land Rovers drew up in front of the bungalow and piled in through the front door bearing crates and bottles. 'Where's the party?' they demanded.

'Right here,' answered Al 'But you're the first to arrive.'

'Hell, let's not waste any time,' the leader shouted. 'Let's get to the wine, even if we have to wait for the women and song.'

He threw himself into a seat and opened the offered Shams and the rest of his mates followed suit. It wasn't long before the rest of the guests started arriving and before long there was a continuous hum of conversation to back up the insistent thump of music from the sound system. Bodies gyrated across the floor, deftly avoiding the furniture and the feet of the bystanders and booze started to disappear down gaping necks at an alarming rate.

A screech of brakes and cloud of dust heralded the arrival of April, dressed fit to kill in a long evening dress. 'Where's Mike?' asked Al.

'Don't know and don't bloody care,' came the answer and April swept regally up to the bar. 'What's available,' she asked, 'And I don't mean the sodding contractors,' she continued. She selected gin from the available stock and poured herself a tot large enough to floor a fair sized horse. 'Tonic, madam?' asked Abdul, the barman.

'Hell, no! I need a real drink – one not like watered down gnats pee' screeched April. She was obviously going to enjoy herself.

She navigated her way to the dance floor, grabbing the nearest man as she passed and, still with glass in hand, started to leap about wildly. Gin splattered the nearby dancers but April was oblivious. 'Must have had quite a few before she came,' thought George from a safe distance. He then saw April's partner as they whirled past and realised it was the Catholic Priest from the mainland. He was evidently enjoying himself thoroughly and appeared to be trying to grope various parts of April's anatomy whenever he got close enough. It amused April no end and more gin slopped from her glass.

'Thank goodness Vi had the forethought to take up her carpets before the guests arrived,' thought George

By ten-thirty the party was really starting to swing. The guests filled up nearly every room and had demolished a fearsome amount of hard booze. The table, which had groaned under the weight of food, was looking like a disaster area. Suddenly there was an exodus of men. The night shift of pilots, tug men and jetty operators was leaving for work. They were hoping for a quiet night during which to recover but if not they would muddle through regardless. The celebrations quietened for a while and then the men who had been on afternoon duty arrived, straight from work. More food was loaded on to the table for the newcomers and the momentum increased again as fresh legs started to dance.

George wandered happily from room to room, chatting to everyone on the way. He tried the door of his bedroom to get a change of shirt. He had attracted a large proportion of April's gin and the smell was getting to him. The door refused to open so he went in search of Al. He found him lying across a sofa, snoring gently, so he looked for Vi. He found her trying to prop Father McDougal on a dining chair without having much success. He kept sliding to the floor muttering, 'Ah, McDougal, may the good Lord forgive you.' Vi gave up and left him slumped in a shapeless heap on the floor.

'How's life, George?' she asked gaily.

'Be OK if I could get into my room,' said George.

'Bloody hell,' exploded Vi. 'That'll be April in there with one of the contractors. We shouldn't let them perform on your bed, 'she added. 'Come and help me get her out.'

They thumped on the door of the bedroom and shouted to be let in. Nothing happened. 'April, if you don't get out here now I'm going to get Mike,' Vi shouted. The door inched open and Vi gave it a violent push. A surprised contractor fell backwards and the open door revealed a scantily dressed April, smiling happily. 'Useless!' said April, dreamily, 'Reckon the bugger's got a bad attack of brewers droop.'

'Stay out of my bedrooms, or we'll throw you out,' Vi threatened, while George thanked providence that they had got there in time.

'Ah, keep your hair on. I've been thrown out of better bedrooms than this,' retorted April and started back for the bar for her next gin whilst shrugging her way back into her dress.

By three in the morning they were down to the hard core partygoers and the volume and speed of the party had diminished. George was fighting to keep his eyes open but wouldn't head for his bedroom whilst April was still on the loose. He started another beer, although he knew he had already had more than enough. 'How the hell am I going to make the nine o'clock plane,' he wondered.

Relief was not long coming though when Mike burst into the room. He took one look at April and grabbed her by the hand. 'You're leaving,' he said quietly and, like a large misshapen lost sheep, April followed him meekly out of the door. The party broke up.

George locked the front door and headed back into the living room, deftly avoiding the odd bottles and dropped food on the floor. Al still lay comatose on the settee and Vi was surveying the wreckage of the night.

'What are we going to do about Al?' asked George.

'Don't you worry about him,' came the reply and Vi swung into action. She heaved Al into a fireman's lift and with a quiet, 'See you in the morning,' strode off down the hall to the bedrooms complete with her burden.

George lay for a while in his bed. The light was still burning and he had one eye open. It was his own patented method of avoiding the room spinning when he'd had a drink or two. It only delayed the inevitable though. His open eye would tire and as soon as it drooped the bed would feel like it had turned over, suspending George underneath it. At such times the only cure was projectile vomiting. George hastily and wearily headed for the bathroom.

9

An insistent buzzing filled the inside of George's head. He shook it from side to side but the buzz wouldn't go away. Warily he opened one eye. 'Jeez, where the hell am I?' he thought. He was sitting on the bathroom floor with both arms around the toilet and the insistent buzz was still with him. Wearily he struggled, first to his knees and then to his feet. The room started to spin and he sat down again, quickly.

A short while later and the buzz was getting louder. He started to get to his feet again and this time staggered as far as the wash basin. He turned on the tap and gratefully sluiced water over his head. So far, so good. There was no towel hanging on the rail so he rubbed his arm over his face and peered around him. His mouth tasted foul and he would have liked to sit down again but he resolutely headed out of the bathroom towards his bed.

'*Salaam wa aleikum,*' said a cheerful voice and George looked round. The servant was happily pushing a vacuum cleaner up and down the hall. That solved the problem of the buzz.

George tried to remember the Farsi for 'What's the time?' but it didn't come to him. He tapped his wrist and then shrugged and to his amazement the servant pushed up his sleeve to display a gold Rolex watch.

'*Sahat hasht,*' said the man, grinning from ear to ear.

'Bloody hell,' muttered George. 'That's eight o'clock.'

'*Baleh. Sahat bloody hasht*,' the man said again, grinning even more widely.

George puzzled for a minute. 'What was it he had to do, and why was the bloody fool man grinning like an ape?'

He looked down and solved the question of the grin. He was completely naked. He ran for the bedroom door and as he did so he solved the second riddle. He had one hour to get himself and his baggage on to the plane. Safely inside the bedroom George tried to focus his bleary eyes. 'Suitcases,' he thought, and bent over to drag them from under the bed. His head spun so he dropped to his knees. He found he could get the cases and stay reasonably steady as long as he kept his head upright. He fumbled in the top of his case and came up with a clean pair of underpants. He lifted one leg to put them on and fell in a heap on the floor again. 'Holy shit!' he muttered, and sat upright. He carefully pulled up the underpants and then stood up. His pants were on back to front, so he sat down again.

He repeated the epithet and then the process, this time getting it right and then he repeated it with the trousers that he found lying on the bed. He also found the shirt without the gin stains and pulled it on too. Socks and shoes followed and he then struggled to his feet again. There was a mirror on the dressing table and he peered into it. Apart from looking rather green around the gills and red around the eyeballs he thought he would pass muster. He made sure the cases were shut and headed for the living room.

There he found Al, already dressed and looking as if he didn't have a care in the world. Al looked up. 'Jesus, George, what have you done to your eyes? You'd better shut them before you bleed to death.'

'You should see them from my side,' replied George in a voice near to a whisper. He had found that any more vocal volume threatened to burst his head.

'Better have a hair of the dog,' said Al and headed for the remains of the bar.

George felt his stomach churn and ran back for the bathroom. 'Keep going like that and you'll bring up your toenails,' came Vi's soothing voice behind him. George couldn't get out a suitable reply. He was busy.

Feeling slightly better George swayed his way back to find Al. 'How do I get to the airport?' he asked.

'Slowly and carefully, by the looks of you,' said Al.

Vi came into the room. 'Ignore him, George,' she said sympathetically. 'The bus is on its way.'

George waved a hand in thanks and sank gratefully into a chair.

Luckily for George both Al and Vi came to the airport with him. It was even luckier that they carried his cases and showed him where to book in.

'How heavy are you, Captain?' asked a scruffy, unshaven clerk.

George looked blank and Al took him by the arm and lead him to a large set of scales and pushed him on to them.

'One-forty-four!' shouted the clerk, 'Now what about the bags?'

Al swung them onto the scales. 'Eighty-eight,' screamed the clerk and entered some figures on a dirty, dog-eared form.

All this activity washed over George, who was by now wondering if he would live through the day. 'Never again,' kept popping into his mind, but he knew it wasn't the last time. Somehow he would have to get through life until he could go back to bed and sleep it off.

He peered out of the airport waiting room wondering where the plane was. There was nothing on the runway. He also wondered where all the other passengers were, as there were only four or five stragglers hanging around.

There was a hum of engines and it slowly grew louder. George's head throbbed and into view came the smallest plane he had ever seen. 'You're on the Dove,' said Vi. 'Nice planes. Only take an hour back to civilisation.' The plane stopped and shut off the engines, much to George's relief, and a gaggle of passengers tumbled down the steps on to the tarmac apron.

'Passengers for the mainland,' screamed the clerk in George's ear and George took his leave of Al and Vi.

'See you around, old son,' said Al, shaking his hand. 'Get a transfer back down here soon. We'll miss you.'

George turned to Vi and she kissed him on the cheek. 'Take care, George,' she smiled, 'And get something for your head when you get to the mainland.'

'If I live that long,' said George, a rueful grin spreading over his ashen face. 'Reckon it must have been a good party.'

He struggled up the steps and ducked into the plane. Only four seats on either side, so he took one near the back. The cockpit door was open and George could see a hatchet faced old pilot sitting with his feet up on the dashboard. The pilot turned, and in an American accent called, 'Last one in close the oven door.' The door thudded shut and the oppressive heat in the cabin made George feel queasy again. He looked around and found that at least there was a small toilet compartment at the back of the plane. Hopefully he wouldn't need it. He tightened his seat belt and sat back with his eyes closed. Maybe he would be able to sleep.

The Dove's engines snarled into life making the cabin vibrate. George opened his eyes, and noticed that the pilot was taking his feet down. He turned and thrust his chiselled features into the cabin. 'Hold on to your hats,' he called, and the plane leapt forward and thundered onto the runway.

'Hold on to my groceries,' thought George, willing the plane into the air and the engines to quieten to a dull roar.

The plane swooped into the air and immediately one wing dipped violently towards the ground. George's stomach churned as the plane turned, then levelled out and settled into a steady climb. Cold air suddenly spurted from the vents above the passengers' heads and George adjusted a nearby vent so that it blew on his face. He started to feel better. Maybe he would live to see his wife and children after all. He dozed as the plane droned on.

Twice during the journey he opened his eyes and peered around. The other passengers were reading or sleeping and it looked to George as if the pilot was doing the same. He was sitting sideways in his cockpit seat and had a book in his hand. 'Hope it's not a flying manual,' thought George and closed his eyes again. If they were going to crash, he didn't want to know.

The nose of the plane dipped and George's stomach churned. A glance at his watch told him they must be getting near and he tightened his seatbelt another notch. 'I've made it this far,' he thought. 'I can't throw up now.'

He was right. Although his head swam alarmingly and his stomach jumped through hoops, he managed. The plane swooped low over Abadan airport perimeter fence and touched down lightly before coming to a halt outside the domestic airport hangars. George staggered down the steps and swayed across the tarmac to the small terminal building. There didn't seem to be anyone waiting for him so he slumped in a chair until his suitcases were delivered to the door on a rickety wooden cart. He lifted them down and stood in the burning morning sun feeling like something the cat had dragged in. Wondering what to do next he sat on his cases and took stock of his situation. Stuck in the middle of nowhere, in a foreign country, and with no idea of how to get in to town and the only thing in his head an insistent ache. Dying was starting to seem an attractive option when along the road bumped Captain Robinson's dilapidated Hillman.

'My God, you look like shit, Penroy,' came the cheerful greeting. 'The jungle drums tell me it was a good party. Suppose you'll want the rest of the day off?' he continued.

George mumbled a greeting and dumped his cases in the boot of the car. It sank on its back springs alarmingly but they piled into the seats and roared off towards the town. 'You're staying with Pat tonight,' said the Super, 'Then tomorrow he'll take you to the housing office to sign for your bungalow and get the keys. You start on shift with Pat the next day as Brian goes on leave tonight.'

George tried manfully to take it all in and to answer sensibly but he could only mumble monosyllabic replies. Once again he was getting concerned for the state of his stomach. Would his job survive if he throw up in the super's car?

They rumbled on into the town, past the large modern cinema and into a maze of bungalows. George lost count of the twists and turns but they eventually came to a stop outside a green and cream painted house. 'This is it,' said Captain Robinson with a grin. You'd better get some sleep this afternoon and try to sober up a little. Don't ask the houseboy for water. Pat has him trained to serve only vodka.' He drove off in a cloud of dust leaving George to wonder how he knew about Pat's drinking habits.

George pushed open the iron gate and walked up to the front door. He rang the doorbell and waited. After what seemed an age the door slowly opened and George was greeted by a houseboy. The man smiled, revealing a set of teeth like a moonlit graveyard, and ushered George inside. He went in and followed the servant along a hallway and into Pat's living room. There sat Pat, empty glass and a plate of congealing bacon and eggs at his side on a small table.

'Hello, lad,' said Pat. 'Want some breakfast?'

'No thanks,' said George. Before Pat could ask he continued, 'Don't think I need a drink for about a week, either.'

Pat grinned. 'Gave you a good send off, I suppose?'

Pat called for his houseboy and told him to go and get George's bags. 'Better not leave them out there for long or some of the local lads might have them away.'

'You'd better go and get some sleep,' said Pat. 'When you wake up tell Hassan if you want anything to eat. Whatever you do don't ask for scrambled eggs. I reckon he boils the damn things and then squeezes them between his toes to get the right consistency. He's not bad on toast though.'

Sleep sounded rather a good idea to George and he followed Hassan and his bags towards the bedroom. The shutters were closed over the windows and the air conditioning unit in the wall purred quietly. George threw off his shoes and crawled under a cover. He was asleep in two minutes.

BOOK 2

THE HUSBAND

10

George and Pat got up early the next morning. George had slept solidly part from two hours during the evening before. Eighteen hours of rest had seen off the alcohol in his system and George was a new man.

'Fine company you were last night,' said Pat. 'I ended up going to the club by myself.'

'Sorry about that, Pat,' apologised George, who really wasn't sorry at all. He knew he couldn't have taken any more high life.

Hassan served them breakfast. Bacon and eggs, toast and marmalade, washed down with hot tea for George. A glass of Pat's water was ceremoniously displayed on a separate tray.

'Hope he doesn't tip any of that water into the house plants,' thought George to himself. 'It would be certain death for the spider plants and cacti.'

They chatted for a while about mice and men and what April was getting up to in Kharg. Pat loved to hear all the gossip and would feed it to others at a regulated rate whenever he thought it might have best effect. He thought the story of Robbie and Olwyn was priceless and Pat made George go over the details twice in case he'd missed anything out.

Pat eventually stirred in his chair. 'Well, George,' he said, 'If you want to get a house for you and your family we'd better go and see the Oil Company Housing Department."

George thought that was an excellent idea and he and Pat went to get dressed. Like many tug men Pat didn't drive himself around town. George had wondered if it was because of the alcohol level in Pat's system, but evidently only a few expatriates bothered to buy cars. The taxi system in town was highly developed and the cost minimal. For ten rials per person you could go anywhere in town as long as you didn't mind other people being picked up and dropped off as well. For fifty rials you could have the taxi to yourself. You could also phone the nearby taxi rank and then the likelihood was that you would get One-Eyed Ibrahim, who made his living by driving the ferangis who always paid him well over the odds.

The nickname was accurate if not particularly inspired. Ibrahim had one walleye that wandered alarmingly from side to side. The way he drove suggested that his other eye might not be that good either but he didn't have too many accidents and was fairly fluent in colourful English. He would also transport anything in his car boot from contraband to cart wheels so was fairly useful as a general carrier.

They called the taxi rank once they were ready and within five minutes the taxi sounded its horn at the front of the house. Sure enough the beaming face and portly figure of Ibrahim was behind the wheel. 'Where you go, Mr. Pat,' he asked.

'Housing office, Ibrahim,' replied Pat and they sped off.

Half as mile down the road they swerved into an open yard and skidded to a halt in front of a group of offices. 'Wait for us,' ordered Pat and Ibrahim switched off the engine and lay across the front bench seat with his eyes firmly closed before they had time to get out.

'We'll have to wake him when we come back,' said Pat. He explained that Ibrahim worked twenty-four hours a day, sleeping and eating whenever he could and saving his money so that he could retire, with his family, to his home village near Bushire. He was known to drive quite erratically if he hadn't slept for a while.

They pushed their way into the offices and joined a queue in one of them. It seemed more like a rugby scrum than a queue to George, but they shouldered their way towards the front and eventually reached the desk. A flashy looking Iranian slumped behind it and when he saw the two expatriates shouted at the others in the queue until they moved back.

'What can I do for you gentlemen,' he asked with an oily smile.

'House for Captain Penroy,' said Pat.

'Ah, yes,' said the official and shuffled through a huge pile of filing on his desk. He pulled out a sheaf of papers from near the bottom of the pile causing a landslide with all the others, which he deftly caught before they spilled onto the floor.

'One five seven four,' he intoned. 'All cleaned and painted, and ready for moving in. Sign here.'

He pushed a paper towards George and jabbed a finger at the bottom. George glanced at the paper. One the left was English script and on the right Farsi.

'Don't read it,' said Pat. 'Just sign or we'll be here all bloody week.'

George signed and a large bunch of keys was handed to him. The official said something in Farsi and before George or Pat could move the throng pushed back towards the desk. Over the hubbub George gathered that their business was finished, so he shoved his way clear of the melee and found Pat had done the same.

'Let's go,' said Pat. 'We'll go and have a look at the place to see everything is OK.'

They woke Ibrahim with a shout, and Pat gave him the house number. 'One-five-seven-four,' he said, and Ibrahim set off without further ado.

'It's only just down the road from me,' said Pat. 'Within walking distance.'

He was right and in a few minutes they arrived at the house and stopped in the drive. House number one-five-seven-four was at the end of a line of bungalows and stood in its own garden surrounded by an overgrown privet hedge.

They pushed open the wrought iron gate and found themselves in a wilderness of couch grass and spindly trees.

'Looks like you'll need a gardener,' commented Pat as they walked up the path to the front door.

'Certainly will,' said George. 'I know sod all about gardening at home and about half of that about gardening here.'

George selected a likely looking Yale key and opened the front door at the first try. It led into a long hall with cream painted doors leading off it. The floor was tiled with green tiles that reminded George of a urinal but at least it was clean. They began investigating and found that each room had the basics for living. Two bedrooms, each with a pair of iron single bedsteads, a dining room with chairs and table and a living room that resembled a barn in size. A door lead from the dining room into the kitchen, which seemed to contain all the necessary utensils. A gas stove, some work surfaces and a stone sink with old-fashioned hot and cold brass taps suspended by pipes above it. George tried the stove and a hiss of gas escaped. He had no matches with him so he turned it off again and tried each tap in turn. A rusty piddle of water dribbled into the sink but gradually the flow increased and the water cleared.

'Seems OK, Pat,' he said.

'I'd advise you never to drink it,' said Pat.

I won't but maybe the wife and kids will,' grinned George. 'I'll have to get some bedding before I move in,' he continued. 'I'll need mattresses, sheets and blankets for a start.'

'That's no problem,' said Pat. 'We'll send Ibrahim down to the bazaar in his taxi and he'll deliver some foam mattresses in no time. Give him five thousand rials and he'll bring you the change.'

'Right,' said George and went out to make the arrangements. He came back to find Pat in the kitchen, investigating a large sized Kelvinator fridge.

'Makes a bit of a racket,' he said but it seems to be working OK. 'We'll head for the store later and stock up with beer and soft drinks. The food can wait till later. We'll eat at my place for a few days.'

Pat was evidently looking after the necessities of life so George asked what he should do next.

'We're on duty tomorrow,' said Pat, 'So we'll get some sheets and blankets off the tug when we come ashore. If anyone asks they are going to the laundry. The company can afford a bit of bedding. Don't suppose you'll mind having 'Property of the Oil Service Company' stamped over them, will you?'

George didn't suppose he would and it would save some of his hard-earned cash. It was going to take a quite a while to get everything set up and probably a great deal of the folding green stuff. He wondered what his wife would think of it all.

The doorbell rang and George went down the hall to see who was calling. He opened the door and was greeted by a snaggle-toothed apparition wearing filthy working clothes and a greasy felt skullcap.

'*Salaam*,' said the apparition. 'You want gardener?'

'Pat. Come and have a look at this,' called George and Pat came to the door.

'Hello Ali,' said Pat, 'Didn't take long for you to get here.'

Pat turned to George. 'This is Ali,' he explained. 'He works for most of the expats. Cost you two thousand rials a month and he'll fix up your garden. That's about ten quid in real money.'

'Is he any good,' asked George.

'Probably as good as you'll get,' replied Pat. 'Why don't you give him a try.'

'OK,' said George and the bargain was sealed. George had employed his first servant.

They settled down to wait for One Eyed Ibrahim to return and before long George was the proud possessor of one

93

double and two single mattresses to put on the four single beds in the bedrooms. They headed back to Pat's house, satisfied with the progress and after lunch and a short siesta made for the club for the evening. They met up with the usual group of off duty tug men and their wives and after a few drinks went to the Taj Cinema which was showing a moderately up to date film. George sat through the film, which wasn't very interesting and wondered about the next day. It would be his first as a genuine shipmaster. It might only be a little old-fashioned tugboat but it would be his to command. 'I've arrived at last,' he thought. 'This is what I've worked towards for the last twelve years.'

The next day dawned as bright and clear as usual. George was out of his bed at Pat's house and drinking a cup of tea when Pat surfaced. 'We won't have breakfast here,' said Pat, 'We'll have it on the tug when we get there.'

That was agreeable to George and he went to the bathroom for a shower. He dressed in shirt and slacks and packed a pair of shorts and his sandals in a small grip. He also packed the novel that he'd been reading. He was ready for the fray.

Pat carried a similar bag with him and they went outside to wait for the minibus to arrive. For the first time George found it noticeably cooler and remarked on it to Pat.

'Aye, lad,' agreed Pat, 'The summer's coming to an end. We'll be OK now until next April.'

The minibus screeched around the corner and swayed to a stop. They climbed aboard and were still shutting the door when they took the next corner on their way to the jetties. George produced his dog-eared paper pass to the guard on the gate while Pat flashed his official identity badge and they were into the jetty area. The bus shuddered to a stop again at the tug jetty and they tumbled out. The departing men were already half way down the gangway and they passed each other on the jetty. They were evidently glad to be heading home.

'Reckon the next ship will be about mid-day,' they called, and the minibus pulled away in the customary cloud of dust.

Pat and George climbed aboard and were met by the butler. 'Breakfast, *sahib*?' he asked and they nodded their agreement. 'Might as well start with a full stomach,' thought George, and went to change into his shorts. He paused outside the cabin door, looking at the brass plate above it with some satisfaction. 'Certified for Master' it read and a shiver of pride ran down George's spine.

Captain Penroy headed for the saloon, breakfast and whatever else the day might bring.

11

It was three weeks later and Captain Penroy was getting excited again. Telegrams had been sent and answers received and George was waiting for a date for his wife to arrive. It was now November and by the middle of the month he hoped his wife and children would be in the care of British Overseas Airways and on their way to Iran. George thought back to his own first flight and wondered how his wife would get on, travelling by air for the first time with two small children. He was apprehensive about the anecdote of the expatriate wives that the acronym BOAC should be translated as 'Better On A Camel', especially when applied to children's travel.

George was now settling in to his job on the river and starting to enjoy it. His first few trips on his own had been a bit nerve wracking but he was now getting into practice at berthing and unberthing the ships in the river. He had also moved into his own house and had employed a servant, who had proved to be very good so far. He had employed a local woman in her mid thirties who was evidently divorced. This was not an uncommon situation in the Muslim world, where men could divorce wives at the drop of a hat, often leaving them in disastrously poor circumstances. She was to be Nanny to the children and also a general servant, a position she seemed to suit very well. She had cleaned and polished the house until the green tiled floors were like an ice rink.

George had also unravelled the mysteries of the Commissary, or as it was more generally known, the staff store. He had discovered, much to his surprise, that the basic foods were easily available and not unreasonably priced. The Oil Company imported large quantities of food, drinks and other supplies and distributed them through the staff stores. The goods came from Britain, America and other European countries, and the selection was extremely good. There was even a daily supply of bottled milk which you had to collect but George had found that Ali the gardener doubled as milkman for most of the expatriates. You just handed him your milk ration card and he would appear at the back door each day with a toothy grin and a fresh bottle of milk.

The back door was the Nanny's preserve. She had moved into the rooms at the rear of the compound and was slowly furnishing them in typical Middle Eastern style. George was a bit apprehensive about this, as he had no idea if his wife would approve. However, he knew from the others that servants could be changed as often as dirty socks if necessary, so was just crossing his fingers and hoping all would be well, at least for a start.

Now that George was on a regular shift he had plenty of time to himself. One day on duty, one day on stand-by and two days off left plenty of time for setting up house and for socialising. He had been to the Theatre Club one evening with Pat and met up with several other tug men. Dave, the first skipper he'd met, and Bob, the swearing engineer, plus several wives were all there and also many of the refinery staff. They were all in old clothes and all extremely busy.

The club building was in a long avenue, lined by palm trees, and looked, from the outside, like a large house. On investigation George found that it was two semi detached houses knocked into one and used as a theatre by the Amateur Dramatic Society. The members were busy in building a new stage, some new dressing rooms, and a stepped auditorium. It had been under construction for some time and was now in urgent need of completion before the annual Christmas show. This was right up George's street. He had long been adept with hammer and saw and was quite handy at making things. He supposed he'd inherited the skills from his father, who had been a shipwright and he was quite willing to pitch in and help out. He was soon working, sleeves rolled up and sweating profusely, on the wooden framework of the new bar area. There was a regular input of Shams and the men bought rounds in turn. The women were also busy as there were costumes to sort, props to make and make up to apply to the few arty types who were rehearsing in one corner. In all, it was a busy place.

'Volunteer required,' came a call from the depths and George made his first mistake of the evening.

Will I do?' he asked.

The call had come from what George was already thinking of as the arty-farty group and an effeminate looking man of around forty looked him up and down before saying, 'You'll do, sailor. We want somebody to read a part. We're one actor missing.'

He handed George a sheaf of papers and within a few minutes George was well into a Christmas sketch. He'd soon got into the character of the part and was enjoying acting it up. There were two other men and two women in the short play and before long they were reacting to each other's cues and getting into the feel of things. Time sped by and after they had run through their lines twice George was surprised to find that it was eleven o'clock. Not only that, but most of the construction crew had long gone home.

'We'll just go through once more,' said the effeminate one, who was evidently the producer, 'Then we'll go round to my place for a night cap.'

The others all agreed, so George didn't like to drop out. They went through the play again.

'How did you like that, George?' enquired the effeminate one who was called John.

'Seemed to go OK,' replied George, non-committally.

'Well,' continued John, 'Will you do the part?'

This was something George hadn't considered and wasn't too comfortable with. He back peddled, fast. 'Don't know if I can get the free time,' he spluttered.

'Don't worry about that,' said John. 'Captain Robinson is a member. He'll arrange it for you. He'll probably be in the show himself. He likes to do a bit of singing.'

George's first reaction to the situation was to think, 'Oh shit!' but after a short walk to John's house with the other actors, and a night cap or three, he started to get used to the idea. At three o'clock in the morning he wended his weary way back home, driven by One-Eyed Ibrahim, and that was his second mistake of the night. It cost him two hundred rials instead of ten. Luckily he had enough in his pocket to stump up the extortionate fare.

He didn't wake up very early the next morning but it didn't really matter very much. It was his second day off. After ploughing his way through a mound of corn flakes he wandered around his house trying to see what he could do to improve it. It was exceedingly bare and it still echoed hollowly. He would have to explore the world of Persian carpets but would need some advice before he bought anything. He would also wait for his wife to arrive. George had little idea of colour coordination, whilst his wife, like many females he knew, had a built in sense of colour.

Half way through the morning George plucked up courage and phoned for a taxi. He was going to make his first foray into the bazaar by himself. He had always gone in the company of others before and had got a rough idea of the layout. The hooting of a taxi horn announced the arrival of none other than One-Eyed Ibrahim, who did not seem any the worse the wear for sleeping in his taxi.

George climbed in the front seat. '*Salaam, Ibrahim*,' he said. 'Take me to the bazaar.'

'OK, Captain,' smiled Ibrahim and they pulled out into the road, narrowly missing a blind beggar and the small boy with him.

George was getting used to beggars and had been given the low-down on most of the well-known ones. They were professionals and made a reasonable living, especially those with some bodily defect or other. Their approach was similar, whatever the defect. They would clutch the sleeve of any passing *ferangi* whilst moaning pitifully and crying, '*Baksheesh*'. George had met the blind beggar before and was eager to find out how the man could distinguish *ferangis* from locals, as the boy didn't utter a single word. He had his suspicions but as the man's eyeballs were pure white he couldn't confirm them.

They soon arrived in the central square of the bazaar and Ibrahim skidded the taxi to a halt. 'You want I wait, Captain?' he asked.

'No thanks,' replied George and noted with satisfaction the look of disappointment on Ibrahim's cash register face. George resolutely put his hand over his wallet in his trouser pocket. He'd heard that there were pickpockets around the bazaar.

His first call was at a barber shop. It had been nearly two months since George had had his hair cut in Kharg Island and it was falling around his collar. The top was still thin though and George had considered changing the style to try to cover it up but he'd finally decided against it. All the men in both his parents' families were bald and George was slowly resigning himself to looking like a mobile billiard ball one day.

George sat in the queue of Iranians listening to the music playing over the radio. He doubted if his ears would ever attune themselves to the wail of Asian music. He could watch people passing the shop though and was interested in the contents of the barrows pulled by donkeys and in the immense bundles carried on the heads of the porters. That such skinny men and beasts should carry such burdens was a source of continual amazement.

Several times beggars came into the shop and with unerring ease selected George for their attention. The barber would head them off, shouting and waving a cut-throat razor and then apologising to George in a stream of Farsi. George could only guess at what he said but smiled and nodded his thanks.

It was soon his turn in the chair and George pointed to a picture on the wall to show what he wanted. The barber first piled all his implements into a steel dish. Scissors, steel combs, razor all went in and then he added what looked like methylated spirits. George watched with undisguised interest as the barber then set light to the dish with a flaming taper. It suddenly occurred to George what was going on. He was sterilising the tools to get rid of lice. George started to itch.

Once the instruments had cooled the haircut proceeded and George watched apprehensively in the fly blown mirror. Strangely enough it turned out to be a good cut and was followed by a scalp massage, which left George's head tingling. The cover was whipped from his shoulders with a theatrical gesture and the barber smiled, waiting for approval.

'Very good,' said George, not wanting to try out his elementary Farsi. 'How much?'

'*Pange toman*,' came the reply, which fooled George completely. He had expected to be told a number of rials.

He took a hundred rial note from his wallet and hopefully handed it to the barber. The barber thanked him and gave him back fifty rials in change. 'Excellent,' thought George, and handed the fifty back to the barber as a tip. He couldn't have paid the man a better compliment. He was brushed down, his hand was shaken vigorously and he was given a round packet covered in gold foil. It reminded George of the chocolate coins that were hung on the tree at Christmas and he put it into his pocket hoping it wouldn't melt. He was ushered out into the street by the barber, and he walked away happy. First job accomplished.

He wandered through the narrow covered alleyways looking into the open stalls to see what was on offer. There was evidently a plentiful supply of fruit and vegetables, although he wasn't sure how clean they would be. They looked good to him though, and he bought a kilo of bananas, which would come in handy as a snack. There were many fruits and vegetables that George didn't know, including bundles of a green substance that looked suspiciously like grass. The locals were buying it in large quantities and George wondered if perhaps they kept rabbits. He came out from an alleyway to find himself in a row of more modern looking lock-up shops, and it was here that he found the second thing he was looking for. Crockery and eating utensils. Those in his house were on loan from the Oil Company until he bought his own and he knew that his wife would soon want to buy some.

He poked around in the shop, badgered by a swarthy assistant and then left without buying anything. He made a mental note of how to get to the shop though for future reference. He had seen what he thought might be acceptable wares.

He was starting to feel sweaty and itchy. Tiny pieces of hair had got inside his shirt and he felt uncomfortable. It was time to go back to the house and get a shower. He found his way back to the main square and waited for a taxi. He didn't have to wait long before a battered Fiat in the ubiquitous black and white colours drew up. George got in.

'One five seven four,' he said to the driver who replied with a stream of Farsi. It took a few moments for George to realise that he had found a driver who had no English at all.

'Bawarda,' he said with a flash of inspiration, and the taxi headed off in the right direction. It took nearly half an hour for George to find the right way, pointing left, right and straight ahead to the driver as they came to intersections. They finally pulled up to the house, and George indicated the notice that gave the house number in both English and Farsi script.

'One five seven four,' said George clearly.

'*Punsda haftoda chahar*,' replied the driver, nodding his head.

George gave the driver a fifty rial note and walked into the house muttering, '*Punsda haftoda chahar*,' to himself, over and over again.

The phone rang, making him jump. It was the first time that it had rung since George had taken over the bungalow. He wondered who it could be as he picked up the receiver. 'Penroy,' came a disembodied voice down the receiver.

'Yes. Who's calling,' he enquired.

'Captain Robinson', came the reply. 'Your wife and children will be arriving on flight BA 143 from Heathrow on the twenty-second.'

'Thanks very much,' said George, searching for a pen and paper so that he could write the information down. He repeated the details to make sure they were right and then went in search of his work roster. Great! He was day off so wouldn't have any problems getting to the airport. 'Bet there's a flap on at home,' he thought. 'They'll be packing things up and trying to get everything sorted out in the next few days.' He had left it for his wife to arrange the letting of their house through an agent whilst the family were abroad and hoped that it was all in order. It would really be some-thing to have some other silly bugger virtually paying the mortgage for him. The Penroy Clan might even be able to save some money at long last.

Over the weeks he'd been away George had written many letters home. Gradually, as he found out what went on, he had sent more and more instructions and requests for things to be brought out to Iran. His wife and children would have air freight when they arrived, and then any large items would be sent by sea freight and would arrive later. George hoped he had covered everything, as their freight would have to see them through a further twelve months before they had any leave back in England.

He showered and then had a light lunch of bread and cheese. He then sat over a cup of coffee making out a list of things to do before twenty-second. The servant hovered until he'd finished his coffee and then snatched away the cup for washing up. George was starting to appreciate this business of not having to clean up after himself. 'Think I must have been born to it,' he thought. 'Reckon the missus might appreciate it too,' he grinned.

12

The following Friday George tried out another club. He was already learning his lines for his part in the Christmas show and he thought perhaps it would be a good idea to check out something that the children could take part in. At three in the afternoon the tug staff minibus arrived at his door, bursting at the seams with children and their parents. George squeezed in through the door and perched on the corner of the seat whilst Swearing Bob pulled the sliding door shut, narrowly missing the seat of George's trousers. The bus groaned into gear and slowly built up speed.

There was a general hubbub of noise in the bus and children squealed and shouted as they swerved around the corners. They were evidently used to this performance and the older ones egged the youngsters on. After about a quarter of an hour they headed out into the desert and five minutes later they pulled in to what George could only describe as an urban oasis. A garden of palm trees and bushes surrounded a huddle of single story buildings and they pulled into a nearby sandy car park.

They were met by the sound of tuned engines, which was not what George expected of an oasis but was definitely in keeping with the purpose of the club. The Khuzistan Karting Club was holding its weekly race meeting. The track was laid with asphalt and it wound round in a complicated pair of connected circuits on the far side of the club building. High steel railings surrounded the whole club and outside the fencing a huddle of ragged, bazaar urchins cheered the go-karts on.

The children piled out of the bus, followed by the adults. 'Get your arse in gear, George,' said Bob. 'I could die of thirst waiting for you to buy a round.' They trooped into the clubhouse and into the air-conditioned bar to be met by many familiar faces. The arty-farty group from the theatre club was also in residence and they were crowding around the bar along with several people in boiler suits. These were the karters and they looked rather like pandas as their driving goggles had left white eye patches on their otherwise dirt grimed faces. George recognised Dave, the tug Captain, who waved a greeting with an oily hand.

It was plain to see that there were no rules in the club about drinking and driving. Every half an hour the bar would empty and a race would be held. Ten minutes later drivers and spectators alike were back in the bar. The children played happily and accepted Coke and Seven Up from anyone at the bar who was foolish enough to offer. Uncle George was getting to be a favourite, as he couldn't resist the kid's requests.

At five o'clock the children suddenly deserted the bar and the parents followed. George went to see what was going on. Suddenly, from the garage area, a miniature steam train appeared driven by one of the older children. A model vintage car also followed and a crowd of children rushed up to the gate in the track fence. The train and car came to a stop by the gate and one of the adults opened it and stood back. The children surged towards the train and car and climbed aboard and the vehicles moved slowly off, bells ringing and horns hooting, to the delight of the youngsters.

'How's it going, George?' said a voice at his elbow. George looked round to see Dave.

'Pretty good,' replied George. 'Looks as if this is where I'll be bringing the kids on Fridays.'

'Reckon that'll be right' said Dave, coughing convulsively as he lit another cigarette from the stub of the last one. 'Ever tried karting, George?' he wheezed.

'No, but I'll have a go one day.'

'You sure will,' agreed Dave. 'How about today. You can have a few runs round the circuit in my kart if you like.'

George was swiftly kitted out with a spare boiler suit and a helmet, neither of which really fitted and he waited impatiently for the children to finish their rides. It was getting dark by the time the train and vintage car went back to the garage.

George lowered himself into the bucket seat of the kart, and looked at the controls. Only two pedals were on the machine. 'Accelerator on the right and brake on the left,' said Dave. 'Put your foot down a bit and we'll give you a push to start.'

Two other volunteers joined in and they started to push George's kart around the track. Suddenly the engine coughed into life and George was away. He'd forgotten to pull down his goggles and his face felt like it was getting sand blasted but the ride was exhilarating. He quickly got the feel of the steering and started to enjoy powering into the corners, braking and then accelerating out again. He was just approaching one of the bends when a roaring sound rattled his eardrums and another kart screamed past him only inches away. George could see the driver grinning and he pushed the accelerator hard down to catch up.

Nose to tail the two karts roared around the track with George trying frantically to overtake. His opponent was wily though and cut off George's attempts with apparent ease. All to soon a figure leapt out into the track waving a red flag in front of the karts. They skidded to a halt. A grinning Dave walked up to George and helped him out of the kart.

'Enjoy that, George?' he asked.

'Do you need to ask?' said George. 'It was great. Who was the other driver.'

'Meet Khalaf,' said Dave. 'Best smuggler and worst driver in town.

A swarthy Iranian shook hands. 'You come race with me next week,' He said.

'Maybe,' answered George. 'That's if I can borrow a kart.'

'We've hooked another one,' called Dave to the crowd of other drivers who had been watching. 'He must like having his bum near to scraping the ground at fifty miles an hour.'

They headed for the bar. It was too dark for any more racing but not too late for thirst quenching. George had a mouth full of Iranian desert and his ears and nose were in a similar condition. The next Shams wouldn't touch the sides.

About an hour later all the families gathered up their children and belongings and loaded them into the tug services bus again. They were much quieter on the return journey and one or two of the smaller children nodded off on their mother's laps. One by one they were dropped off outside their bungalows and they trailed into their houses for a late supper. The older children would be back to school the next morning. George went into his house and straight into the bathroom for a shower. When he undressed he found that oil had seeped through the boiler suit he had worn and stained one of his good shirts. He threw it into the laundry basket. The Nanny would find it in the morning and would get it clean. He suspected that she flogged his washing against a big smooth stone but at least it came back clean. Wouldn't be long till some of his gear would need replacing though as some of the seams were already getting a bit frail.

George passed the evening reading a book. He had given up writing home, as his letters just wouldn't get there before his wife left to join him. It was a change to have spare time and not to have to write. For the past twelve years writing had always filled much of his spare time. Mail was the link to home and real life for any seaman. In his early days at sea George had written to his parents and sisters from each port and later to a succession of girl friends. Once courting became a major part of his life he had always had an ongoing letter to hand. He would add to it daily until reaching port, by which time his letters were twenty or thirty pages long, depending on the voyage.

Mail was the lifeline to home for all the sailors and could be the source of great joy or the utmost despair. Long range relationships were never easy and it was a regular occurrence for some poor sod to get a 'Dear John' letter. This was the accepted term for a letter that ended any relationship and any-one who got one was instantly recognisable. The miserable look and the constant re-reading of the letter were a source of great hilarity for the rest of the crew.

There was a standard sailor's revenge for a 'Dear John' letter that many a hard hearted girl must have received. The sailors would collect up any old photographs of girls that they had and give them to the sufferer. He would then put them in an envelope and reply to the girl saying, 'Thank you for your letter. Please select your photo from these and return the others as I can't remember which one you are.'

George was on duty the next day. He was getting used to working with Pat who looked after him well. He would spend a lot of time on the bridge giving George advice es-pecially when they were doing something new or different. George was preoccupied with counting the days now. Only four more duties before his family arrived. He had checked and re-checked his house and thought that he had all the household basics now. His larder was stocked with food and the family would be able to eat for at least the first few days. By that time George knew that his wife would have the intricacies of the staff store worked out and he would be able to end his shopping forays.

He had now arranged for two club subscriptions to be deducted from his pay. The Oil Company Club, where you could get a meal in town and the Theatre Club where he would be taking part in the Christmas Show. Now he would probably join the Karting Club so that his children would have entertainment at the weekends along with all the other families. He might also enquire how much a second hand go-kart would cost him. Driving had been fun.

The day passed and others followed slowly. Time was dragging now and it seemed that the awaited day would never come. Eventually it dawned like all the others, bright and clear. George was excited. Somehow he got through the day and by sunset he was showered and ready to go. He had ordered the tug minibus for seven in the evening and he was ready and waiting for it for it by six. The plane wasn't due in until nine thirty.

He checked the house once more. Beds were made up for the children. The built in wardrobes were clean and ready for clothes even if the doors had so many coats of paint that they wouldn't close. Food was in the larder and a vigilant servant and the occasional dose of DDT powder kept the cockroaches at bay. There was a supply of tea, coffee and soft drinks and a fresh bottle of milk was in the fridge.

He wandered around the house wondering what he had forgotten, and jumped out of his wits when the telephone rang as he passed it. It was Pat.

'How are you, lad?' he asked. 'Got everything ready?'

'Sure,' said George, and then realised, too late, that it was the wrong thing to say.

'Right,' said Pat. 'Pick us up in the bus at seven. We're all going to the Theatre Club for a few drinks.'

'Bloody hell,' George muttered to himself after putting down the receiver. 'I'll have to watch they don't Shanghai me and make me miss meeting the plane. That would really put me on top of the shit list.' He went through his check list once more to make sure everything else was ready.

He primed the servant with the time he expected to be home with his wife and children and then phoned for the tug minibus again. In no time there was the sound of a horn outside the door and after a last glance around George went out. He was greeted by the driver, Ali, who was idly gunning the much-abused engine of the aged minibus. '*Memsahib* coming today?' asked Ali.

'Yes,' replied George and added a stern warning. 'We're going to the theatre club first but I must be at the airport by nine o'clock.'

'*Sahat no*,' confirmed Ali, pointing to the correct time on his watch and nodding seriously.

They made the rounds of the bungalows, picking up the other off duty men and the wives and headed for the other end of town and the theatre club. Twenty minutes later, after no more than three near brushes with death on the road, they arrived, and pushed their way in through the doors of the clubhouse. The place was alive with music and chatter and just about everyone that George knew was there. They were celebrating the completion of the changes to the building that now looked like a small theatre instead of the storeroom of an ironmonger's shop.

The arty-farty group were installed in one corner of the bar and called George to join them. 'I'll just have a shandy,' said George in reply to the usual question.

'You'll have a real beer, like the rest of us,' came the shout, and a foaming Shams arrived in front of him. Before he could finish the first one there were two more lined up in front of him and he casually slipped away to the toilet. Once inside he glanced at his watch. Eight o'clock and all was not well. He ran his hand through his ruffled, thinning hair and headed back for the bar. 'Back in a minute,' he called to the actors and made for a group of tug men.

'Hello, George,' said Scotts Bob. 'How's yer bum off fer wrinkles?'

A time honoured query in Merchant Navy circles to which George gave the required response, 'Not so bad, mate. How's yours off for spots?'

Bob grinned and pushed another Shams towards him. George sipped at it slowly, determined it would be his last. He could already feel the effect of the first ones. He drifted from group to group, holding his bottle by the neck and tilting it to his mouth occasionally. He wasn't going to let it get less than half full or some kind misguided soul would get him another.

At half past eight he slipped quietly out of the door and looked for Ali. He was nowhere to be seen and neither was the minibus. George went back inside wondering what to do. He waited for five minutes then went out again. There was still no sign of the bus so he went back in and found Bob. 'Seen the tug bus?' he asked.

'Sure,' replied Bob, 'Pat's sent it off to get some food supplies. We thought the party could do with some.'

'Bloody hell,' said George, 'When will it be back?'

'Ali's getting kebabs,' said Bob, 'They'll take about an hour to be ready and then he'll have to drive back from the bazaar.'

'Bloody fat lot of help, that is,' said an anguished George. 'If I'm not at the airport by nine-thirty I'll be strung up by the short and curlies. The wife's arriving tonight.'

'Don't get your knickers in a knot,' laughed Bob. 'There's always plenty of taxis around. Telephone for one.'

George grabbed the phone from its rest and dialled the taxi rank number. Nothing happened. He tried twice again before he realised that there was no dialling tone.

'Don't waste your time, George,' called one of the arty-farties. 'It hasn't been reconnected since the alterations.'

A moment of panic passed and George hurried out into the street. He would hail a passing taxi and still make it in time. Despite the cooler autumn weather he was dripping with sweat from head to toe. He knew where the airport was, so walked in that direction, glancing over his shoulder from time to time when he heard a car approaching. Not a single black and white taxi came along and he glanced at his watch with increasing frequency. He couldn't believe how fast the minutes were passing.

Despair wasn't far away when at last a taxi came in sight. It stopped when he waved and George found it was already occupied by three locals and a live chicken. He squeezed into the back and thanked his lucky stars that he had learned the Farsi word for airport.

'*Forootga*,' said George and felt his shoe slide in something on the floor. The taxi pulled away and plunged into the back streets. At intervals it let off the three other occupants and the last one dragged the protesting chicken after him on a long piece of string. George guessed they weren't too far from the airport then, as he heard the scream of engines in reverse thrust quite clearly. He looked at his watch again and saw that it was nine-thirty. He cursed BOAC silently for being on time and urged the driver on with explicit English instructions that the man clearly didn't understand.

The taxi careered around a roundabout and suddenly was on the approach road to the air terminal. George could see the lights of the building at last and behind it the long low profile of a VC10. There was no mistaking it and the Union Jack on the tail plane confirmed George's worst fears. He was late.

He paid of the taxi and ran into the ramshackle terminal building. There was the usual crush of figures and he could hear a voice he recognised. It was April from Kharg Island and she was saying loudly, 'I expect the bastard is on the piss somewhere.' George cringed and wondered what poor soul was the object of April's wrath when the crowd parted and April came into view. His face dropped when he saw that April was addressing her tirade to his wife and bewildered looking children.

He pushed through the crowd and called to his wife. She looked round and saw him and so did April. 'Where the bloody hell have you been hiding, George?' boomed April, 'And what the devil is that bloody evil smell?' George smelled it at the same time and glanced down. His shoe was covered in chicken dung.

He put his arms round his wife, carefully keeping his dirty shoe well back, 'Hi, Kay,' he said and kissed her. 'How was the trip?'

Before she could answer a small voice piped up. 'Dad, I was sick,' said his four year old daughter, Louise, 'All over Mum,' she added.

'She's not joking,' said Kay. 'Just got cleaned up from the first time and it happened again. Had to look after John as well, as he looked like he was going to follow suit.'

John was looking out from behind Kay. At two years old he was not very sure of all this activity around him. Big, tired, blue eyes peeped out from under a thatch of white blonde hair. He wasn't going to say anything until he was confident that he wasn't going to lose his Mother. He held tightly to her skirt.

'Well, don't just bleedin' stand there,' said April, 'Take the poor girl home. She looks tired out.'

'I'll just get the cases,' said George, 'And then we'll get a taxi. Shouldn't take us long to get back to the house.'

He struggled outside with the first of the cases and to his relief found One-Eyed Ibrahim sitting in his taxi. Ibrahim grinned and put the first case into the boot. 'Cost extra for cases, captain.'

'Two hundred rials,' said George firmly, 'And don't drive too fast or the kids will probably puke.'

'Not understanding this puke,' muttered Ibrahim happily to himself as he stowed a second case on top of the first and mentally added another small fortune to his day's takings.

George plunged back into the airport and picked up the remaining hand luggage. 'Thanks for looking after them,' he said to April, 'What are you doing here, anyway?'

'Got fed up with life on the happy isle and decided to go home for some therapeutic shopping,' she replied.

What does Mike think about that?' he asked.

'How should I know,' said April with a grin. 'He doesn't bloody know yet.'

George led his family outside to where Ibrahim was waiting. They climbed into the back seat of the taxi and set of for their new home. George held Kay's hand as the children settled between them.

'Hope your hands are cleaner than your shoes,' she said, smiling for the first time. 'Where were you tonight?'

'Don't ask,' said George, 'You wouldn't believe it.'

By the time the taxi reached the bungalow John was asleep and Louise was getting very quiet. They both roused when the car stopped, and Ibrahim helped them out with their baggage. The front door opened and the servant appeared. She bowed to Kay and took the two children by the hands. They immediately pulled back and hid behind their mother, so George and the servant carried the baggage inside the door and they all went inside. Slowly the children came out from behind their mother and George said to them 'Come and see the house,' and held out his hands. Louise took his hand and John followed suit after checking that his sister was going with George. They trailed off around the bungalow.

'Where's the carpets?' asked Louise.

'Haven't got any yet,' said George, and that seemed to satisfy her. It wouldn't be long before she was back to her inquisitive best though.

There was a ring at the doorbell and George went off to see who it was. Ibrahim stood at the door with his hand out. George had forgotten to pay him. He quickly settled the bill, and they all headed back into the living room.

'Ought to get the kids to bed pretty soon,' said Kay. 'They've had a long day. Let's find them some pyjamas and give them a drink and they'll soon drop off.

She opened up an overnight bag and produced pyjamas for the children and a washbag containing toothbrushes. 'What have you got for the kids to drink?' she asked.

'All sorts,' replied George, 'But they'll probably be best of with orange juice.'

They went out to the fridge in the kitchen and found the nanny waiting to do whatever was required. She quickly produced two orange drinks, adding an ice block to each, which fascinated the children.

'What's that?' asked John of his mother. The first words he had spoken since arriving.

'Ice, to make the drink nice and cold,' she replied, and that seemed to satisfy his curiosity for the time. The drinks were swiftly finished and they herded the children into the bathroom for a quick wash down. George helped and in a very short time the children had cleaned their teeth and were in their beds. They were used to sleeping in the same room and happily lay down as soon as they got into bed.

'We'll leave the hall light on,' said George but two sets of eyelids were already drooping. They had had a long and exciting day and they probably wouldn't stir before morning.

'What time is it,' Kay asked, as they went back to the sitting room.

'Eleven o'clock,' said George. 'But it's only seven in the evening in UK.'

'Feels as if I haven't slept in a week,' she replied. 'It's been pretty hectic getting everything packed up and ready. Let's head for bed.'

George thought that was a rather good idea but before he could reply the doorbell rang.

'Who the hell can that be?' he wondered as he went to the door.

He opened the front door to find Pat, Dave and several others laughing and joking on the front step. 'Hello, lad,' said Pat, 'We just thought we'd check to see if you got back OK.'

'Lying sods,' said George, 'You just thought you'd check to see if I had any booze in the fridge. You've got no chance tonight but if you want to come round sometime in the morning I'll see what I can do. I might as well let the wife know what sort of company she's got herself in to as soon as possible.'

'Right,' said Pat, turning to the others. 'The pub's got no beer. Lets all go round to Dave's place.' They trudged off

116

still shouting to each other merrily and George went back into the house.

'A narrow escape,' he thought. 'If I'd let them through the door they'd be here for hours.'

He went back down the hall and found Kay in the kitchen. She had already established a working language with the nanny, who was nowhere to be seen. 'She'll be back in harness early in the morning,' said Kay. 'I've got a few things for her to do.'

George marvelled at the ease with which Kay was taking over the household.

'Let's get a few things out of the cases and head for bed,' she suggested. 'When do you have to go to work?'

'Not till the day after tomorrow,' he replied. 'We'll have time to look around and meet a few people before then.'

They went into their bedroom, where George had pushed the two single beds together and covered them with the foam double mattress. 'It's the best we can do at the moment,' he explained. 'We'll get ourselves a proper double bed once we settle in.'

They undressed quickly and after a quick visit to the bathroom they got into bed. It was over three months since they had seen each other and they lay in each other's arms and talked for a while. Before long passion took over and they could no longer hold back. Two bodies joined together and they quickly reached a peak of excitement. Their climax was accompanied by a squeal of steel castors on the tiled floor as the two single beds parted company and they were deposited gently on to the floor between them.

'You're not supposed to laugh at a time like this,' said Kay, and burst into a fit of giggles herself. 'We'd better stay on our own side of the bed until we find a way of getting it together.'

'Oh well,' sighed George, 'At least this is better than not getting it together at all.'

13

A peaceful night followed. The children slept the sleep of the just and George and Kay followed suit. Kay woke slowly, wondering at first where she was. Memory flooded back when she saw the fan in the centre of the ceiling and she sat up in bed. George stirred even more slowly. He never woke quickly if he hadn't set an alarm.

There was a patter of feet along the hallway and Louise and John came into the bedroom. 'Breakfast,' demanded a monosyllabic John.

'Dad, can I have this chocolate money?' asked Louise.

'Whatever have you got there?' asked George.

She showed him a gold foil covered disc and George remembered the bazaar barber giving it to him.

'OK,' he said, 'But don't open it now. You can have it later in the morning.'

They climbed out of bed and went through to the dining room to find the servant ready and waiting.

'Corn flakes,' decided George and four plates magically appeared on the table along with fresh milk and sugar. They ate slowly and the children chattered. At least, Louise did. Her brother just smiled and nodded most of the time and if anyone asked him a question Louise would reply for him. He was in a little world all of his own and he had his own personal interpreter to speak for him.

'What's her name,' asked Louise, pointing at the servant.

'Don't point,' said Kay, automatically, 'It's rude.'

'But what's her name,' she asked again.

'Ask her yourself,' said George, so she did.

'Minouche' said the nanny, glad to be involved. '*Esme mal-e-man, Minouche. Esme shoma?*'

Louise looked puzzled.

'She says her name is Minouche and she's asking you what your name is,' said George.

'I'm Louise,' said the mystified girl, 'And he's John,' she continued, pointing once again, this time at her brother. 'Why does she talk like that?'

George explained how different countries had different languages and it seemed to satisfy her. She lost interest in the nanny and idly started to peel the gold foil from the disc she had found earlier. The nanny shrieked and grabbed the coin from the child.

'Whatever's wrong?' asked Kay and the servant went into a torrent of Farsi. She held out the coin to Kay, who continued unwrapping it. She suddenly put it in the pocket of her dressing gown and, with her face rapidly going red, asked George, 'Where did it come from?'

'From the barber in the bazaar,' replied George. 'Why?'

'I'll tell you later,' she replied. 'Off and clean your teeth,' she told the children. They scuttled away.

She pulled the gold disc out of her pocket and handed it to George. He peeled the foil from it to find it contained a condom. 'Just as well the Nanny knew what it was,' he muttered. 'Saved a few awkward questions. I'll get rid of it.'

An hour later they were dressed and ready to go out. 'We'll try the bazaar,' said George and phoned for a taxi. They went out into the garden to wait for it to arrive. The family had come from winter at home to bright sunshine and warmth and the children revelled in it. Ibrahim's battered black and white Opel roared to a stop outside and he tooted the horn. They went into the street and piled into the back seat. 'Bazaar please, Ibrahim,' said George and off they sped.

The children enjoyed the ride, unaware of the lethal speed they were travelling at or the near misses. There were things to see and they were full of questions. Louise asked hers and translated John's and they were especially interested in the animals. Donkey carts, chickens in cages, goats on rope leads; they were all of interest. They went into the heart of the bazaar and Ibrahim grinned when he got paid a tip. 'See you later, Captain,' he shouted and drove off.

Kay and George took a hand each and led the children around the stalls. The children weren't too sure when the beggars approached asking for money, but took heart when George chased them away. 'If you want to give them something do it just before you get into the taxi to go home,' he told Kay, 'Otherwise word will go round and they'll all come to ask for something.'

They looked at all the unfamiliar fruit and vegetables, and hurried past the butchers shop where they were dismembering something unfortunate on a wooden block. They turned a corner and Kay exclaimed, 'This is more like it.' They had arrived at the material shops where bolts of gaily coloured cloth were ranged across what passed for a pavement. She went into the first shop and looked at the materials closely. 'Cotton?' she said to the proprietor who was hovering nearby.

'Cotton,' he confirmed, unrolling material from the bolt. 'Cotton,' he repeated, again and again, pulling more bolts off shelves and displaying them.

'How much?' asked Kay, pointing to one of the materials.

'Hundred rials a metre,' came the reply. George was about to calculate the equivalent in Sterling but before he had a chance Kay was back in action.

'Three metres,' she said, holding up three fingers to the man. 'Three hundred rials, George,' she demanded, holding out the other hand.

George meekly doled out the dog-eared, tattered notes and the cloth was cut and parcelled up in brown paper. They left the shop and went into three more before Kay was satisfied. 'The cloth I bought will make me a dress,' she explained 'And there'll be enough left for one for Louise. My sewing machine will be coming in the sea freight. Now, where do we find crockery?' she continued.

George led the way and before long Kay was into discussion with three stall holders who had crockery for sale. She went from one to the other, comparing prices and looking for bargains, and getting cheaper offers all the time as they competed for her custom. George was impressed. Even after years at sea and visiting the Middle East regularly he had never really picked up the art of haggling over the price.

They eventually left without buying anything and George asked if she hadn't seen anything that she really liked. 'Oh yes,' she replied, cheerfully. 'I liked one set of crockery a lot, but they were asking too much. I'll go back in a few days and have another try. They'll come down in price, slowly.'

The children were tiring by this time and weren't interested in more shopping. 'John's hungry,' announced Louise.

'We'll go and get them a cold drink' said George. 'Have they ever tried Coke?'

'Don't think so,' said Kay, and they went in search of a shop selling cold drinks. When they found one it happened to be next to a bakery. 'Come and see this,' said George to the family and they crowded into the baker's cluttered shop.

Inside were two huge clay ovens with roaring fires in the bottom. Electric fans which blew over the coals assisted heating, and a large round stone was set in the centre of each fire. The stones were shimmering and glowing red with heat. Two sweating bakers were making the flat round bread of the middle east, tossing the dough until it formed a large circle and then flipping it on to the hot stone for a few seconds. It turned a rich brown colour and formed bubbles on the surface and was scooped out of the oven and placed on top of a pile, waiting to be sold. The children were fascinated and when George bought half a dozen *chupattis*, freshly baked, they quickly learned how to tear off pieces to eat. There was soon nothing left but crumbs.

They went next door and bought Coca-Cola. Both children quickly decided it was good to drink, and satisfied with their morning outing they all went in search of a taxi. They were plentiful and soon they were getting in to another battered car. '*Punsda haftoda char*,' said George, and spent the rest of the journey teaching the children and Kay the number of their new house.

'I can see I'll have to get Farsi lessons,' said Kay.

'Good idea,' said George, who was too lazy to try anything requiring much thought. 'I'll stick to teaching the kids how to swim once the hot weather really comes again,' he said.

The children were satisfied with their morning out and were content to play around the house afterwards. They hadn't many toys with them as twenty kilos of airline luggage per person didn't allow for too many of their bigger toys to be brought. However, Louise's imagination was quite enough for her. She talked continuously to dolls, imaginary people and her brother but he consistently never bothered to reply. As long as he had a couple of toy cars to push around the floor he could play happily.

They hadn't been at home long when the telephone rang. It was Dave's wife, Margaret, who invited them round that afternoon for coffee and to meet Kay and the children. Her own two daughters would be there but Dave was on duty. They accepted and told the children they would be going out that afternoon. They were happy when they knew that two similarly aged children would be there. George thought he would be like a spare end in that company but agreed to go so that Kay could meet some new people and get all the local inside information from another woman.

An hour after lunch they set out on foot for Dave's house. It wasn't far away and the children scampered back and forth along the pavement in front of George and Kay. They turned into the drive at Dave's to be met by ferocious barking from a black labrador. The children decided it was prudent to stand behind their parents for a while and George tentatively opened the gate. 'Down!' he growled to the dog, which immediately rolled over on its back, wagging its tail so furiously that its whole body moved. The front door opened and Margaret came out, smiling a welcome.

'Don't worry about Cindy, she's all bark as long as you're European.' She turned to Kay.

'You must be Kay,' she said, 'Come on in and have a coffee. It takes a lot of time getting used to this place. You must be quite bewildered with it all.'

Margaret's two children, along with Louise, John and the dog had stayed in the garden. There was a swing and a small slide that had taken their interest. It didn't take long for them to settle down and they were soon playing happily. There were at least two satisfied customers.

Margaret's house was well furnished. She had already been in Iran for three years and knew her way around. She showed Kay around the house and soon George was drinking coffee whilst the ladies talked about houses and furnishing, food and cooking, where to go and what to do and anything else in general. George finished his coffee and slipped out into the garden. He knew when he wasn't needed and this was one of those times. They would soon be on to children and child bearing and that just wasn't his scene.

He joined the children in the garden and for the next half hour shouts and squeals of enjoyment rang out as they played 'What's the time Mr Wolf?' Of course, George had to be Mr Wolf and each child had to be caught in turn but they all enjoyed it thoroughly. By the time they went into the house they were hot and thirsty and Cindy, the dog, was panting furiously. Margaret gave the children their first taste of 7-Up and calmed them down, whilst George sank gratefully into a chair. 'Hope it's a quiet day at work tomorrow,' he commented to no one in particular.

'Typical man,' said Margaret to Kay. 'Half a day with the kids is about as much as they can take and they're supposed to be the stronger sex. Better have a beer, George,' she added. 'You've got a pile of books and magazines to carry home.'

George accepted gratefully whilst Kay looked at him in surprise. Drinking in the afternoon wasn't something she expected. 'Don't worry about it,' said George. 'They all do it here.'

'No need for you to join in though,' said Kay but she realised it might be a battle she couldn't win. Luckily she knew that George would soon settle back to normal, with a little prompting from her from time to time.

On the way home Louise and John weren't quite so full of energy. 'Looks as if it will be an early night for them,' said Kay. She was wrong though. Whilst she cooked a meal the children decided to investigate the compound and the servants rooms. Minouche was glad to see them and soon they were sitting down, cross-legged on the floor, and watching cartoons on her television. It didn't seem to matter that the cartoons were in a foreign language. They were also given a small cucumber each and quite happily munched their way through it. They didn't realise it but they were already on their way to becoming multi-cultural.

After their meal the children played for a while before being packed off to bed. They were already settling to their new life and accepted things readily as long as George and Kay were nearby. It would take George and Kay a lot longer. Kay immersed herself in the magazines that Margaret had given her but George prowled around not knowing what to do. There was no TV for him to watch and Kay showed no sign of wanting to go out. He tried his radio for a while but couldn't find the BBC Overseas service and gave up. He then read his book for a while but he could read on the tug between ship movements. He packed his bag ready for the morning and then hovered around the living room.

'For goodness sake settle down, George,' said Kay. 'Find something to do. You're putting me off from reading.'

'What are you going to do tomorrow?' said George pleased to have got some response.

'I'm going to the commissary with Margaret,' she said. 'She's offered to show me round. I'll ask her round for coffee afterwards so the kids can play. Now, how about first you give me some money for tomorrow and then you let me read in peace?'

George handed over a fist full of Rials and then got out pen and paper and started to write a letter. He wrote a couple of pages to his father and then three more to one of his sisters. It seemed strange not to be writing to Kay but he settled down to it and quite enjoyed putting pen to paper. It might also bring some mail in return one day.

He finished his letters and wandered out into the kitchen, idly opening and closing drawers to see what they contained. All his borrowed crockery had been stowed neatly away by the nanny before he had even seen some of it. In one drawer he came across a ball of string and he pulled it out from under a pile of knives and forks. He went through to the bedroom and threw the clothes from the bed. He then set about lashing the two single beds together with seaman's knots and before long had them trussed up securely. 'Great.' He thought as he tested the knots and then put the mattress and covers back on to the bed. 'Now for the bitter bit.'

'Kay,' he called.

When she came through to find what he wanted he made her an offer that she could hardly refuse and the string stood the test.

14

Days passed and Kay was getting used to the new routine. She had met several of the other expatriate wives and their husbands and was getting to know her way around. She had yet to venture out in a taxi without George but was getting to know the Commissary and the small shops in the immediate area. She had come across a small local store just a block away and had found that it had many interesting items for sale.

The store was called '*Anbar* Adib' or Adib's Store in English and was run by the owner. Mr Adib was pleased to see any expatriates, as they were an additional source of income that he couldn't normally rely on and he would come out from behind his counter and personally see that Kay got good service. Kay soon learned that he spoke good English and was pleased when he would repeat in Farsi anything that she asked for. She quickly caught on to the basics of 'Good day', 'How are you?' and 'Goodbye' and soon added a variety of 'I would likes'. This was backed up by talking with Minouche in the house and they were quickly both picking up enough of each other's language to have a good basis for communication. George was left far behind with Farsi as his day to day working languages were English at home and Hindustani on the tugs.

Kay was finding out where there were children for Louise and John to play with and had started on the wives' coffee morning routine. They would visit anyone whose husband was on duty on the tugs and pass an hour away with coffee and conversation whilst the children played around the garden. There would often be several wives visiting so the garden would usually be alive with the piping voices of pre-school children. Kay had also invited many of the others to their house and found that an endless supply of coffee was required, much as George had found that an endless supply of Shams beer was required for the men.

The children were settling down. John was his usual quiet self, happy to let his sister do all the talking and Louise was finding that she had many new friends to share her days. They had now quite taken to Minouche and Kay and George were fast approaching the day when they would go out in the evening and leave the children to her care. Several times George had gone to rehearsals for the Christmas Show and Kay had stayed at home but soon they were going to take the plunge. They would have to make it before long as the show was getting nearer and the rehearsals longer.

On the days when George was at work they often tried to meet up in the evening. The Seaman's Club was open to the wives and families of the tug crews and if there were no ships to move the duty Captains and Engineers would also go there for the evening movies. The club had an indoor and an outdoor screen so it was possible to sit outside in the cool of the evening and watch a film. The men would buy drinks from the bar for the families and they would all watch whatever movie was showing.

The start of each performance was always preceded by the playing of the National Anthem of Iran, accompanied by a picture of the Shah in full dress uniform. There was always a problem with some members of the ships crews who did not understand that they were required to stand for this performance, but the wives and children soon learned that this is what happened. The expatriates generally tried to count the monarch's medals before the end of the anthem, usually failing by the time the song ended and they had reached the upper fifties. Muffled laughter would often accompany the ever-present gecko walking across the screen in search of flies, especially if it was strategically positioned as if to crawl up a royal nostril.

The movie would start at seven and was usually over by about eight thirty. This gave the wives time to get tired children back home to bed whilst the men sat on for a while chatting and drinking. The evening would break up around ten when most people would head for home and the duty men would go back to the tug.

George was also finding that his sex life had been given a boost. For the first time in his life he could look forward to days, weeks and months when he would see his wife most days. For the first few nights life was a whirl of love making, then slowly George was becoming grateful for his nights on the tug. Could the old saying be true? 'Once a king, always a king but once a night is more than enough.' He was starting to wonder.

On the first Friday that George was off duty the whole family joined the throng heading for the Karting Club. Louise and John were instantly overjoyed to see all the other children and to find that there were swings, slides and a sandpit for them was a bonus. By the time they had ridden on the miniature train their day was complete.

Half way through the afternoon a novices race was announced. Any members or visitors who were not accredited drivers could take part and a kart would be loaned to them. George borrowed Dave's kart and this time put on a boiler suit that fitted. He climbed into the driving seat and waited for the other competitors to take their places. Slowly more volunteers donned boiler suits, crash helmets and goggles whilst George plotted on how he would drive and win.

At a given signal all the karts were push started and they went slowly round the track in formation. When they completed a lap the green flag was waved and the race started in serious. George got away to a good start and soon found himself in second place, ahead of the pack. Ahead of him was a small figure, completely swathed in helmet, goggles and a scarf, taking the corners in style and keeping his distance in front. George floored the accelerator pedal. Serious speed was required if he was going to catch the flying front runner.

Slowly George caught up with the leader but, try as he would, he could not pass. He would have to get a faster kart and some serious practice if he were going to be good at this. He was still about five feet behind when the chequered flag waved and he continued round the track slowly until he came to the pits. He pulled into the side of the track, stopped and heaved himself out of the kart.

'Better show good grace and congratulate the winner,' he thought. He looked round to find the winner climbing gracefully out of his kart.

'Flash sod,' he thought as the winner unwound his scarf. The goggles came off, followed by the helmet and blond hair spilled out from under it. He had been beaten by Kay.

'Where did you get to, George?' she laughed.

'Wait till next time,' said George, 'That was only beginners luck. Anyway, winner buys the drinks.' Arm in arm they went back into the bar.

Later that evening George and Kay were sitting at home. The children had long been in bed, tired after their afternoon at the Karting Club. George was starting to think of heading for bed when the phone rang. He quickly went into the hall and answered it, hoping that it wouldn't wake the children. It was Dave and he'd evidently had a few drinks.

'George,' Dave shouted, making the phone rattle George's eardrums, 'Are you coming to the night club with us?'

'Who's us and where's the night club?'

'Us is me and the wife, Bob and Moira, and old Pat, and the bloody night club is in Khorramshahr, a few miles up the road. All seven of us can get in a large taxi.'

'Let me check if we've got a baby sitter,' said George, hoping that Minouche hadn't gone out. 'I'll give you a ring back in five minutes.'

'Don't take too bloody long,' advised Dave. 'We don't want to miss the show.'

George went in to tell Kay what was going on. He thought it would be best to join in with the gang and was pleased that they had been invited.

'What am I going to wear?' asked Kay.

'The little black dress, I should think,' said George, checking on the contents of his wallet. He supposed it would set him back a couple of thousand rials but it should be worth it.

Minouche was at home and immediately brought her bedroll into the house.

'I stay inside with children,' she announced, much to Kay's relief. At least the children would see a familiar face if they woke up. Not that it was likely. Louise was a good sleeper and John wouldn't bother to get out of bed as long as Louise was nearby.

George returned Dave's call.

'Pick you up in five minutes,' yelled Dave, so George got his skates on and threw on a clean shirt and tie.

'No need for a jacket in this weather,' he thought.

Kay was soon ready, so after leaving final instructions for Minouche they went out into the street to wait for the others. They didn't have long to wait.

Ibrahim's battered black and white Opel hove into sight and lurched to a halt at the house. The back door opened and a voice said, 'You get in first, George and Kay can sit on your knee. George peered inside the taxi to find four people already piled onto the back seat and Pat who was lording it in the front. They climbed in and with great difficulty closed the door.

'Hotel *Khalij*, Ibrahim,' directed Pat, and they set off, slowly gathering speed.

'For Christ's sake don't hit anything, Ibrahim,' said Bob. 'This thing must weigh in like a small tank.'

'No problem,' smiled Ibrahim, who was busy working out how much he could expect from this little jaunt. 'A few more rials towards retirement,' he thought.

They piled out of the taxi twenty minutes later, outside a nondescript two-story building. A flickering neon tube announced it to be the Hotel Khalij and they paid Ibrahim his small ransom. 'I take you home?' he asked, hopefully.

'Bugger off,' replied Bob in his usual forthright fashion. 'We'll find a taxi here.'

They all went in through a darkened doorway, past a stocky doorman, and headed for the dim lights and low music. They were met by an Iranian *maitre d'* who showed them to a table near to the dance floor and asked what they would like to drink.

'We'll have a kitty,' decided Dave. 'Five hundred rials apiece to start with and we'll have beer for the men. What about the women?' he wondered.

Kay asked for a shandy whilst the other ladies had a gin each and they all settled down to see what was happening. On the dance floor several couples were slowly circling to music from a five-piece band which was on the nearby stage. George didn't recognise the tune and by the sounds of it neither did the band. The only recognisable sound was an insistent waltz beat from the drummer and this seemed to satisfy the needs of the dancers.

'The show starts in ten minutes,' said Bob. 'Better get another round in now, before the bar closes down for a while.'

'Good idea,' said Dave and went off in search of a waiter.

Just as the drinks arrived all the lights dimmed. The band scuttled off the stage and a single spotlight picked out the *maitre d'* who announced, 'Ladies and Gentlemen, the Hotel Khalij international floor show.'

Distorted pop music leapt from the speakers at the side of the stage and eight scantily clad girls cavorted around, vaguely in time with each other. The music rose to a crescendo and a single male dancer in tights and a leather waistcoat pranced to the fore.

'Walks like he has the hairs of his bum tied together,' said Bob in a stage whisper and three of the dancing girls collapsed with laughter. They slowly got their act together again and continued the show.

They were followed on stage by a lady in a bikini riding a unicycle and then by a troupe of Czechoslovakian jugglers, neither of whom excited much applause. The dancers then returned, this time topless, which caused some excitement amongst the hard core of Middle Eastern gentlemen who sat at the bar. They were evidently evaluating the possibilities for later that night.

More beers arrived at the table and the kitty diminished accordingly. 'Don't think much of the show,' said Kay in George's ear.

'Good for a laugh,' replied George, ' But not exactly the '*Folies Bergere*' is it?'

The dancers left the stage and were replaced by a motley crew of Iranians, each holding a chair and some sort of musical instrument. They proceeded to seat themselves and on the count of three from their leader they launched into the wailing tones of Arab music. 'What the hell is that instrument that sounds like a strangled cat?' asked George.

'It's a bandolerium,' replied Bob in a serious voice. 'It was developed from a Jew's foreskin, stretched tightly over a five barred gate and strummed gently with a navvy's shovel.'

'Bob! That's dreadful,' said Moira

'Sure is. Let's have another drink and hope the bugger goes home soon.'

The show came to a close and recorded music replaced the band. Vaguely recognisable dance music now came from the speakers and the dance floor once again filled with people. The entire group except Pat joined in and the time passed pleasantly until with a sudden commotion April burst on to the floor with a stumbling male companion.

'What in God's name are you lot doing here?' she squealed, as she whirled the unfortunate looking man past their table. 'It's long past your bloody bed time.'

George turned to Kay and she whispered in his ear, 'George, have you seen the time?'

He backed off slightly and glanced at his watch. It was past two in the morning. 'Checking up on me, are you, George?' called April across the floor. 'You can tell Mike that this one is pretty useless,' she continued. 'No stamina at all. I'll be lucky if he lasts out for this dance.' She pushed the hapless dancing partner ever faster.

'Lets round up the others and take off before she comes and joins us,' whispered George. 'I don't have to go to work in the morning. Dave does though and if April gets into her stride we'll never get away. Wonder how she got away from the Island without Mike?'

It was half an hour later that they slipped out from the Hotel, only to find that there wasn't a taxi in sight. It was cold in the night air and by the time a taxi turned up they were all glad to pile into the back and huddle together for warmth. They sped back to Abadan and dropped each couple off in turn, leaving Pat with the remainder of the cash from the kitty and the job of paying the driver.

George and Kay quietly went in the front door and crept into their bedroom. It was half past three. 'Let's hope the kids don't wake us at six,' said George as they undressed and he wondered where April would be staying that night.

George and Kay's first visit to the nightclub was the start they needed. Once they had successfully left the children with Minouche for the first time they found themselves going out in the evening more and more. They had never had so much freedom before and they made the most of it.

When George attended the Theatre Club to rehearse for the Christmas show Kay went along too and it wasn't long before she signed up to do makeup for the actors. They now had an interest in common which regularly took them out of the house. The show was taking shape and it was soon close to the dress rehearsal, which would be held during an afternoon at the weekend. All the children were invited as an audience and they would be given free fizzy drinks in the interval.

'Just like taking them to a pantomime at home,' commented Kay.

Whilst the children didn't understand some of the more risqué jokes they made up for it by recognising the actors and actresses and cheered them on when there was any audience participation required.

The dress rehearsal went without too many hitches and all was then ready for the show. It would be held on three consecutive nights with the last night being on Wednesday so that a party could be held afterwards. Those lucky people with every weekend off could then take the advantage of a two-day recovery period. Tug personnel like George were not quite so fortunate. He would have to arrange a relief so that he could attend each show and then pay back the time later. Still, as he told himself, 'It beats the hell out of going to sea.'

The show played to a packed house every night and just about every expatriate attended. It went down very well and George and Kay found their circle of friends widening quite quickly. They had several invitations to go out to dinner that Kay was very happy to accept. However, as she told George, 'We'll have to invite people back, soon.' The prospect didn't sit too well with George even though he knew it was true.

Work on the tugs was becoming a routine for George. He was now familiar enough with the job and enjoyed being in command. There were changes being talked about though and George found them unsettling. The river port was restricted by the depth of the water and the size of the tankers that came was relatively small. Improvements in shipbuilding techniques during recent years had meant that new ships were much bigger than the older ones and required much more depth of water. The site of the refineries was changing too. Where once they were close to the oil wells it was now more usual for them to be in the developed western world. Large crude oil tankers would export the raw product and the refining would be done near to the clean, refined oil markets of Europe, America and Japan.

It was rumoured that the port of Abadan would soon be closed and any clean oil exports would go from the deeper port of Bandar Mashur. All crude oil exports would be from Kharg Island where there was enough water for the very largest super-tankers. George worried about the prospect of the port being closed and wondered if he would have to go back to sea on tankers when it happened. He kept his thoughts to himself though. Kay was enjoying the freedom and life of an expatriate.

15

Christmas had passed and Easter followed and the rumours of change still abounded around the expatriate community. Many families were unsettled but life went on. It was spring again and the weather was getting warmer. Soon everyone would start up the air conditioning in the houses and the searing heat of summer would return.

The end of the Easter period brought a big change in the family's life. Although Louise would not be five years old until September she was considered old enough to start at the Abadan Oil Company School. George had registered her on arrival in Abadan and along with several of her friends she started in the reception class of the kindergarten.

George would have liked to see her start her first day but he was on duty, so Kay went with her on the first morning. Two of her friends were starting at the same time; one of Dave's children and one of Bob's brood of fanatical Scots. All three mothers got together and hired Ibrahim to take them. The children soon settled in and their mothers went home, leaving them to the tender care of Camille, an elderly Canadian lady who loved to teach small children. By the end of the morning the children came home reciting the first part of the alphabet in a North American twang. 'A is for apple, b is for ball, and c is a cookie with a bite out of it.'

When George got home the next day Louise had already left for her second day at school. This time she had been picked up by the school bus along with all the other expatriate children. She would return home for lunch and then go back for her first afternoon session. George met her from the bus and she told him excitedly of all that had happened. Teacher was evidently the best thing since Adam was a cowboy and a supreme being who could neither do nor say anything wrong.

Louise chatted all through lunch and was ready to go back to school immediately it was over. Meanwhile John was at a loss for something to do. For the first time in his life he didn't have his sister to do the talking for him and he had to make up his own mind what to do next. It was going to take him some time to adjust.

A few days later George was on duty and was lounging in a deckchair on the tug's fore deck reading a novel when he heard the sound of a car approaching. He glanced up and recognised the battered red Hillman belonging to Captain Robinson, the Superintendent. 'Wonder what he wants,' thought George, putting his book to one side. He slid down the ladder to the after deck and was waiting at the gangplank when Captain Robinson arrived.

'Morning, George.'

'Morning Captain,' he replied. 'What brings you out on a fine morning like this?'

'First things first,' puffed the Super, 'How about a coffee and I'll have one of those smuggled cigarettes of yours. I've run out.'

They went into the saloon and were soon followed by George's engineer, Harry. Harry was a gentle, grey haired Geordie in his late fifties and had been on the tugs for years. George got on very well with him and they always enjoyed their days on duty.

'Right,' said the Super, once he had his coffee in front of him and had lit up one of George's cigarettes. 'I want you to get hold of everyone, masters and engineers, to tell them that there will be a meeting in my office tomorrow morning at ten. Phone round from the jetty today and make sure that they all know. I'll expect everyone to be there.'

'OK,' said George. 'What's it all about.'

'It's about the new working arrangements starting in a few weeks time. Don't ask me any more. You'll all get to know tomorrow.'

With that he pocketed George's cigarette packet, swilled down the rest of his coffee and stood up to leave.

'Give you something to do other than read that novel,' he said as he went out the door.

'Wonder what that's all about,' said Harry.

'Search me,' replied George, 'But he's not as daft as he looks,' and he went out onto the jetty to start telephoning the others.

They all wanted more information than George could give them, especially Brian. He was the senior master and thought he should know what was going on. Captain Robinson enjoyed keeping Brian in the dark though and George wasn't going to enlighten him or to second-guess what was happening.

A fleet of taxis arrived outside the office next morning and the complete complement of the Abadan tug service piled into the anteroom. The engineer superintendent stuck his distinguished, snowy white head out of his door and directed them all to the liferaft shed that stood out on the jetty. It was large enough for everyone to crowd into and Captain Robinson followed them in and took the only chair.

'Well,' he started, 'The port of Abadan is closing down. All shipping operations will be centred on Bandar Mashur and Kharg Island and the majority of tug staff will be accommodated in Abadan. Some will be left on Kharg Island for emergency purposes, but most will live here and be transported to work at one or other of the ports.'

There was dead silence for a few seconds before everyone started asking questions at once. Captain Robinson restored order by roaring for quiet and he then explained what arrangements there would be for travelling to work.

Those who were to work in Bandar Mashur would be taken by taxi across the desert early in the morning and would work for twenty-four hours. They would then be relieved the next morning and would return by taxi to Abadan. It was expected that the one hundred kilometer journey would take about two hours and the car would be air-conditioned. It would take two masters and two engineers each day.

Those who were required to work in Kharg Island would be collected in the morning by the tug bus and would be taken to the domestic airport. There they would board a company plane to Kharg and would work for twenty-four hours. They would be relieved the next morning and would fly back to Abadan.

'Any questions.'

'Yes,' shouted Bob, 'Are you sure we get a taxi and not an arse bustin' bus?'

Above the hoots of laughter Captain Robinson was heard to quietly reply, 'I have never stooped to arranging travel by an arse bustin' bus, whatever that is.'

They soon got down to who was to work where and George found he was assigned to work at Bandar Mashur. He would have preferred Kharg Island as he knew the port already but at least he wasn't surplus to requirements. There would be more work for everyone. One day on duty and two days off would be the standard. 'Still better than going to sea,' thought George.

The meeting broke up shortly after and they all headed for Brian's house. The senior tug master wanted to discuss matters further. George went along even though he knew Kay would be anxiously waiting his return. 'Better not upset the senior man. Easier to placate the wife.'

The beer in Brian's fridge was soon exhausted and Ibrahim delivered a further crate to the door in his taxi. He was making another sizeable contribution to his retirement fund again. Little was settled other than a duty rota for those who were to work in Mashur and George, being the junior man, was to be on duty on the first day in the new port. 'Sod's Law,' he thought, wryly. 'Wonder what it will be like.'

As soon as he could get away George went home. 'Good news and bad news,' he told Kay, who met him at the door.

'Good news is that we are still in a job. Bad news is that I have to work in Mashur and will get one less day at home during each duty cycle.'

'Could be worse,' she said, 'Anyway, at least we're together.'

'So we are,' he agreed. 'What are we going to do this afternoon?'

'Thought we'd give the swimming pool a try. It opened yesterday for the summer and the kids are itching to go.'

They certainly were. As soon as Louise got home from school they got out their swimming costumes and were jumping up and down in anticipation. George changed and they went on the short walk to the pool. The water turned out to be cool but at least it was refreshing and it woke George up. He played with the children in the paddling pool. He eventually persuaded them to come into the big pool and both he and Kay had their hands full as it was too deep for either of the children, even in the shallow end.

They managed to get Louise to put her head under the water and John automatically followed suit. They both thought this was great fun. 'They won't take long to learn to swim if we come every day,' said Kay.

Several of the other wives appeared with children and it was then possible to leave the children to play in the shallow pool. The kids all had an affinity for each other and for water so they were happy. George found that the pool café served ice cream, soft drinks and beer, so he left them to it for a while and bought drinks for everyone. He was happy too.

The pool became a regular venue for the family and George attended whenever he was off duty. It wasn't long before Louise was able to dog paddle across the width of the big pool and John was showing signs of wanting to follow suit. He wasn't strong enough to keep his head up though so he eventually accomplished a width by taking one enormous gulp of air and swimming under water. At the half way stage he surfaced and took another monstrous gulp of air to see him the rest of the way. He had to be watched like a hawk though, as he sometimes became disorientated and swam off in the wrong direction.

George enjoyed the diving boards at the deep end of the pool. He found he could make an acceptable dive without making too much of a splash and would entertain the children when they got tired. Both Louise and John wanted to learn how to do it so George started them off by letting them jump into the deep end. There would be great whoops of glee as they competed to make the biggest splash. Their faces were a picture and Kay brought the camera into play to record the event for the family back home.

Gradually both children became bolder and it wasn't long before they were both diving from the springboard and jumping from the higher boards. Tales of their prowess soon got round and the number of expatriate children at the pool each afternoon increased. George had found himself a spare time job. One by one all the children learnt how to swim and then how to dive and George was in constant demand to watch one or the other as they accomplished something new.

By May there was an influx of new children. Slowly, families were being moved from Kharg Island and Bandar Mashur and were being re-housed in Abadan. George's expertise was much in demand and he and Kay were soon like the Pied Piper each afternoon. A procession of children would knock at the door soon after school and they would all follow George and Kay to the pool. Their parents would come along later for a drink at the bar and to take the children home. This suited George even though he didn't often get time for a beer. He was starting to get very fit with the continual exercise.

The trip across the desert to Bandar Mashur had started and the tugs at Abadan were lying idle. George was getting used to the drive but he didn't like the new port as it wasn't surrounded by palm trees and buildings like Abadan. It was a tidal sea water inlet in a flat wind blown area of scrub and desert with only a few oil tanks to relieve the monotonous sandy horizon. On one side of the inlet were seven jetties and on the other was a wreck. Some years before a tanker called the Louisa had caught fire and exploded, sinking in the middle of the harbour. A salvage company had cut up the wreck to clear the port and the pieces were dragged to the southern shore and left to rot. There had been talk that a scrap iron company would come and take the pieces of the Louisa away but rumour had it that the authorities wanted the company to pay an exorbitant price for an export license and that had put an end to the project. The stark reminder of the dangers of oil remained.

There were three tugs based in the port and George was finding out their characteristics. Ships were always referred to as 'she' and he knew very well why. They were all very different and all had a will of their own. Two of the tugs were Empire class and chugged along powered by their steam engines. The third tug was much more modern and was driven by a diesel motor. It rushed along at nearly twelve knots and had all the power needed to handle the bigger sized ships. It was older than the Farahdast, George's favourite tug at Kharg and the engines weren't bridge controlled but nevertheless George enjoyed working her. He still had the cheerful Harry as his engineer, so despite the dismal outlook of the port he enjoyed his days at work.

There were new people to work with as well. He knew of the men from Bandar Mashur by reputation and was slowly getting to know them personally. One or two were of similar age to George and he found that he enjoyed their company. Their wives were also of a similar age to Kay and she was finding firm friends amongst them. All in all George was feeling very satisfied with life.

Evenings were also taking on a different aspect. George and Kay got together most evenings with one or two of the younger set and were finding that they had much in common. They had discovered a badminton court that they could use and once a week they would all go to play. Mixed doubles became the order of the day and after a couple of hours of rushing around the court they would repair to the local milk bar for an evening meal of burgers or steaks and chips. This pastime was much derided by the older set whose prevailing sport was Shams beer but George hadn't been so fit since he'd left school. The long years of forced sporting inactivity aboard ship were slowly being reversed.

He had nearly served a year in Abadan and would be due for home leave soon. He wasn't too worried about having time off but was concerned that he would end up in England during the winter. He would have to see the Super and find out when he could have some time back at home. He talked it over with Kay who put another slant on the matter.

'The children are fast running out of clothes,' she said. 'There's nothing in the bazaar here for them and they've both grown out of their shoes. John is in danger of having to wear Louise's cast off underwear and we'll have to find something new for her somewhere.'

'Hadn't thought of it that way. I suppose I'd better go and see Robinson and make the arrangements. I'll do it tomorrow morning.'

The next morning George called for the ever-willing Ibrahim and went to the office. He knocked on the Super's door and went in. 'Morning, Captain Robinson.'

'Whatever it is that you want, the answer is no. I've already had a procession of your lot in this morning for one thing or another.'

'I just want to know about my leave,' said George. 'Is anything scheduled yet.'

'Okay, I think we can manage to fit you in somewhere.'

The Super pulled a sheet of foolscap out of a drawer and spread it out on the table. 'I've had to combine the Abadan and Bandar Mashur leave schedules,' he said. 'I've put you down for October and you'll have forty five days due then.'

'Can't it be a bit earlier than that?' asked George. 'My kids have just about run out of clothes.

'Sorry, George,' said the Super, 'They'll have to look like urchins for a little while longer yet. Besides, you are an actor and I need your services in September. The Theatre Club is putting on the first ever production in Iran of Gilbert and Sullivan. We need both you and Kay.'

'I can sing,' replied George, 'But Kay couldn't hold a tune in a basket.'

'So what?' said Captain Robinson imperiously. 'It's HMS Pinafore and we have to mock up a ship on stage. You've just volunteered. In case you're interested I'm playing the Admiral, so you're outranked as usual. Kay can do my makeup.'

'I'll let her know,' said George. 'She's only just got used to sleeping with a captain and now she's got to touch up an admiral.'

'Don't be coarse, George. Now bugger off and leave me in peace. I've got to learn my lines.' He took a book from his desk, found his place and started to mutter to himself as he read.

Okay, Admiral,' smiled George and hastily left the office. He found Ibrahim dozing in his cab, woke him and went back home to tell Kay the news.

'Bet he won't be wearing his sister's vests when he's an admiral,' she snorted. ' I'll just have to see what I can do on the sewing machine again.'

16

Throughout the heat of the summer the expatriates in Abadan worked, sweated and played. The refinery belched steam on a twenty-four hour basis and the storage tanks filled with oil products. Tankers no longer called at the jetties along the river. The products flowed out through the huge pipelines that snaked across the desert to Bandar Mashur to be exported to the ever hungry countries that had no oil of their own. The tugs that had graced the Shatt al Arab had been sold to local owners and had moved up river to Khorramshahr on the River Karun. Cargo ships occasionally called at Abadan to bring food, spares and parts for the Oil Company but most ships sailed on past to Khorramshahr or on to Basra in Iraq. The once popular Seaman's Club had been taken over by the Oil Company and was being turned into a club for their employees. The nightly seaman's cinema show was closed and the expatriates now had to go the Oil Company Cinema instead. The old outdoor screen had been demolished and the geckos had found new homes elsewhere.

The old Anglo-Iranian Oil Company had started building the modern Taj Cinema in 1938 but, before the imposing auditorium had been completed, the Second World War brought an end to building supplies. The ship bringing the new cinema seating was torpedoed and sunk as she ran the gauntlet of U-boats through the Mediterranean, so although the exterior of the building and the projection room had been finished the auditorium remained a stark, bare cavern. The oil workers of the day had declined to suffer any loss of entertainment due to Mister Hitler's megalomaniac ambitions and throughout the war had taken their deckchairs, kitchen chairs, camp stools and even their armchairs with them when they went to the movies. Such are the contributions to morale that help to win wars. It was not until well after the end of hostilities that the cinema was finally fitted with seats.

George's off duty days were filled from early morning till late at night. Preparations for the forthcoming Gilbert and Sullivan show took considerable time and most of the tug men were kept busy. A sailing ship was being built on the stage at the theatre under the direction of Captain Robinson and all the skills of seamanship went into the building and rigging. A lot of ingenuity went into building the set as room had to be left for a rather large cast of singers and an even larger chorus. Many a morning was spent splicing ropes and making cardboard yardarms that looked real.

The afternoons were then spent at the swimming pool where the children were really progressing with their swimming lessons. John still spent much of his time under water but Louise was improving daily. More and more children were being entrusted to George and Kay and it was getting difficult to manage them all, especially the latest arrivals in town. The Irish had arrived!

George had known Paddy O'Connor during his sea going days. Paddy hailed from a small island on the West Coast of Eire where his family owned the local hotel. He boasted of what he called a mixed marriage, as he was nominally a Protestant and his wife was very definitely Catholic. They had three children. All were girls, and all had inherited their father's 'What will be, will be,' attitude. Each one had a charming and complete disregard for normality. They had lived in Bandar Mashur with Paddy for the last five years and the stories of their laid back way of life were legend. Paddy worked as master on the tugs, when he could be found and many a time had gone walkabout for days whilst others covered his work for him. It was easy for someone to cover for him whilst they all lived in Mashur but now all the staff lived in Abadan and had to travel for two hours to get to work. Life for Paddy had become a little more difficult.

His children would turn up at the swimming pool each afternoon and attach themselves to the Penroy clan. This was no worry, but when no one turned up to take them home things became a little more difficult. One afternoon, when George and Kay wanted to go home the O'Connor girls were still happily swimming. The oldest was only nine, and the youngest five, so in desperation George phoned Paddy's house. After what seemed an age Mary O'Connor answered the phone.

'Is Paddy there?' asked George.

'I think himself has gone out,' she replied. 'Wait though. I hear someone shaving in the bathroom, I'll go and see if it's him.'

She came back after a few minutes.

'It wasn't him,' she reported, leaving George to wonder who the devil it was if it wasn't Paddy.

'Your children are at the pool by themselves, Mary. I don't want to leave them without an adult. Do you want to come and collect them?'

'Oh sure and I'll be right down,' came the calm reply and over an hour later she arrived, looking as if she had just been out on a photo shoot for Vogue. 'Sure, you shouldn't have worried, George,' she said, gaily. 'They would have been just fine on their own.'

George wasn't so sure and could imagine what would be said if something untoward happened because he had left the girls alone. He was glad Mary had finally arrived to take them off his hands.

The summer wore on in a seemingly endless blaze of shimmering sunshine. George's family slowly turned brown and the contrast of tanned skin with the children's bleached white blonde hair was quite startling. They were grateful that the children's hair remained white. With some types of blonde hair there was a reaction to the chlorine in the swimming pool and the result was blonde hair with a definite tinge of green colour to it. Many an Iranian stopped the children in the streets and pinched their cheeks in admiration. The children hated this common Iranian form of appreciation and would hide behind their parents if they thought a cheek pincher was on the loose. This usually encouraged the prospective pincher to greater efforts, much to the children's disgust. George and Kay would be torn between protecting the children and not offending against an accepted local custom.

The whole family was now used to seeing beggars in the bazaar and also with those who came knocking at the door asking for *baksheesh*. According to Muslim custom the giving of alms was encouraged and George and Kay would give a small amount to most deserving causes. However, once it became known that this *ferangi* was an easy touch there was a continuous stream of supplicants awaiting their share. There was only one tried and trusted way of keeping the hordes from the door of the family home and George and Kay took it.

On a bright Thursday morning they piled into Ibrahim's taxi and went up town. They had heard of an event in an expatriate household and wanted to take advantage of it. They arrived outside their destination, went up the garden path and knocked the door. The door opened and a smiling man, two small children and five dogs greeted them. It was the dogs they had come to see.

The brood of five consisted of a bitch and four puppies. The mother was a beagle and her relatively short legs were only equalled by her long undercarriage caused by having puppies. 'If her legs were any shorter she'd be in real trouble,' thought George, imagining the poor hound unable to put a foot on the ground.

'Please,' said the owner, 'Please, please take a puppy. My children want to keep them all but we just can't manage that many.'

Louise and John were only too happy to oblige and they spent the next quarter of an hour trying to decide which one they would have. Eventually they settled for the biggest one on the grounds that it would survive best without it's mother and without more ado they jumped back in the taxi, complete with a dog and went home.

By the time they reached home the dog had been christened Tommy and he was happily climbing all over the children. They thoroughly enjoyed it and as soon as they reached home let the dog loose in the garden. Tommy would have to grow a little before he would be an effective beggar deterrent but in the meantime he was going to be great company for the children.

Louise's first term at school was already over and the long summer holiday had started. John knew all about it as his sister now wanted to play at schools all the time and she always had to be the teacher. His respite always came in the afternoons at the swimming pool when Louise went off with all the other school aged children and he could then play with his new sparring partner, Peter, a boy of his own age. His new friend was even worse off than John. He had two older sisters.

Peter's parents had come from Bandar Mashur and had moved into a nearby house. George and Kay got on extremely well with them and they were fast becoming firm friends. They had similar interests and were very close in age. They were also doers and for the first time George and Kay had assistance at the swimming pool in the afternoons.

Peter's father was also Peter, which could have caused a problem of identification. However, the family came from Scotland and they solved any uncertainty by referring to lad as Wee Peter. It seemed a complicated system to Kay who would never have called a son of hers George but nevertheless it worked. The elder Peter now worked at Kharg Island but fortunately his work schedule was the same as George's so they had the same days off. His wife, Liz, was an attractive blonde girl who had once been a schoolteacher. Her quiet

East Coast accent hid a wicked sense of humour and she often made George laugh.

The summer wore on passed and the rehearsals for HMS Pinafore came thick and fast. The only accompaniment for the singing would be a single upright piano and it was certainly taking some heavy punishment. The lead singers often practised at home but most evenings would see the chorus belting out a song, accompanied by the rhythmic sound of saws and hammers as the scene builders plied their trade. Most of the builders were now so familiar with the production that they were able to saw and hammer in time with the music.

George had not signed up for a singing part in the production and was content to work with the back stage gang. Kay was well into makeup though and was regularly practising her art on anyone who would sit still for a few moments. They were both looking forward to seeing the finished show and thought that the children would enjoy the dress rehearsal too. Louise's schoolteacher was in the chorus so she would no doubt be enthralled as her teacher still stood head and shoulders above all comers.

When the dress rehearsal finally arrived it was, as usual, attended by all the children. In one or two places the singing was decidedly shaky but the children didn't notice. They also didn't seem to notice when a song was repeated for practice and they followed the simple plot with apparent ease. Captain Robinson, who had grown a magnificent set of mutton chop whiskers, was a great success as the admiral and the children cheered whenever he came on stage. Four and five year olds took in the lyrics and melodies of Gilbert and Sullivan with apparent ease and went home singing happily. George had watched from the wings and was impressed with the standard of the production. He was resolved to take a part in a play before too long.

The performances came and went during the first week in August and the last night party went with much Shams rocket fuel being consumed. Thirsty singers and the hottest summer temperatures required large quantities of liquid, whatever the quality. Dave and his wife Margaret were at the party and were also celebrating the end of another year in the Middle East. They were flying out on their six weeks annual leave the next day. When they returned it would be time for the Penroys to head for home and a cooler climate for a while. The last twelve months had been great fun and George was no longer sure that he was ready for time back in England. New friends, a great job, a settled family life and so much entertainment were a lot to give up. For once George agreed with Harold Macmillan, a recent British Prime Minister who had caused much caustic comment by saying, 'You've never had it so good.'

Several days after the show had finished George was summoned to the office.

'What have you been up to now?' asked Kay.

'Search me. Far as I know I've done nothing wrong. I expect Captain Robinson has another show in mind. Hope he hasn't forgotten we are due on leave.'

Ibrahim was phoned at the taxi rank and George went off to the office. The superintendent wasn't in so George hung around waiting for him. He went round to the liferaft shed and found a bunch of engineers surrounding Mr. Morris, the engineering super.

'Come to join with the intelligentsia, George?'

'Not me,' George replied. 'Anyone seen the admiral?'

He'll be back in a while,' replied Mo Morris. 'When are you going to join a real club, George?'

George knew that he meant the Golf Club and suspected that half of the engineers worked harder at the Golf Club than they did on board the tugs. He would have quite liked to play but knew that Mo was the kingpin at the club and he didn't want to be under the thumb of any engineer.

'Daft game,' said George. 'The better you are the less hits you get,' and he wandered back to the offices to await Captain Robinson's return.

He was just starting to get really hot and sweaty when the rusty Hillman chugged into view, trailing a foul cloud of evil smelling smoke.

'Morning, George. You don't look too happy. Come on into the air conditioning and we'll see if we can put a smile on your face.'

They went inside and the super delved into his desk drawer. He came up with a sheaf of papers that he slowly shuffled, finally selecting one that he laid on the desk.

'Read that.' He commanded, and George turned it towards him and quickly read.

'In consideration of.........the salvage of....... you are awarded.......' He turned the page. 'The sum of seven hundred pounds!'

'Jesus H,' said George, 'When do I get the money?'

'Now,' came the reply and a cheque was handed to him.

George couldn't wait to get home. He hurriedly left the office and searched for a taxi in the street. It didn't take long to find one and he was soon opening the front door and calling for Kay.

'Come and see what I've got,' he called. 'Play your cards right and you might get more than just a lollipop.'

Kay came out to see what the noise was all about and deftly took the papers out of George's sweaty palm.

'What is it?' she asked, glancing at the papers.

'Salvage money for that ship that went on fire last year. What are we going to do with it?'

She turned the paper over and carefully read the amount.

'Good Lord,' she gasped, sitting down on the nearest chair. ' I don't know yet but I'll think of something. It means that we'll be solvent throughout our leave, whatever happens.'

Plans for the forthcoming leave were progressing. They would be paid during their home leave anyway but the extra money would certainly come in handy. Prior to coming abroad they had just been keeping their heads above water economically and keeping one step ahead of the bailiffs. Now the higher pay rates for service abroad meant that they had a relatively healthy balance in the bank for the first time in their married life. Money coming in from the renting of their house in England covered their mortgage payments and the Penroys were definitely on the way up.

'You know, George,' said Kay, slowly, 'I think we'd better open a deposit account at the bank when we get home. It's time we had some money behind us.'

'Good idea. We'll have a joint account in the names of Captain and Mrs. Penroy. That'll make that snooty bank manager sit up and take notice.'

'Perhaps it will,' smiled Kay.

The days flew past and the friendship with Peter and Liz Longford blossomed. Louise would meet up at school with Carol and Julia, the Longford daughters and John and Wee Peter were becoming inseparable. Slowly the two families were becoming known as the in crowd and others were becoming attracted to the group. Dave and Margaret who were on leave were part of the crowd and their great friends Martin and Greta from Ulster completed the set. Most evenings the telephones between the households would run hot and they would end up congregating at one of the clubs or one of their houses. If one of the men were on duty his wife would be invited out for the evening with the others. She would be entertained throughout the evening and then escorted back home by one or other of the men.

On the evening of Dave and Margaret's return from home leave the rest of the in crowd all went to the airport to welcome them back. Later no one remembered whose idea it had been but they all agreed it had been a good one. The plane was actually on time and right on cue Dave, Margaret and their two daughters came down the steps from the aircraft and walked across the tarmac into the arrivals lounge. They were quickly through customs and then everyone piled into the tug bus so that it groaned under the weight of ten people and several suitcases.

Dave looked very pleased with himself and announced to everyone, 'I've brought a bottle of booze back with me. Who's coming to my place to help me drink it? There was a general murmur of assent and shouts of encouragement to Ali, the driver, not to spare the horses. Ali couldn't have understood the idiom but he certainly knew the tone. His foot went to the floorboards and the old bus struggled to do a few more miles per hour.

They all tumbled out of the bus when it arrived at Dave's and Margaret handed her children over to her Nanny who was more than ready to resume her duties. Dave plunged into a large bag and produced the bottle with the air of a conjurer producing a rabbit. The bottle was far bigger than any rabbit though. It was a gallon bottle of J and B whisky.

'Customs allow one bottle of booze per person to be brought into the country,' Dave explained, 'But they didn't say how big the bottle could be. Do you reckon we can do this one justice?'

They certainly tried and next morning when George was on duty he still had a decidedly heady feeling. It lasted throughout the taxi journey to Bandar Mashur. Luckily there were no ships to move until late in the evening and George spent the time horizontal in his bunk. His engineer, Harry, was most concerned until George explained the problem and then all sympathy vanished.

'Self inflicted injuries, George. Just sleep it off before we have any work to do.'

George was only too happy to do just that. It was his last day on duty and he and the family would be flying home to

England the next day. He would have time to get changed and finish packing before going to the airport and he would need all of his faculties. The children were already over excited with the prospect and it would be one long, long day.

He arrived home the next morning to find his garden full of children. The in crowd and their families had all turned up to see the Penroys safely on their way. Louise and John were dressed to kill and Minouche hovered nearby trying to keep them clean. Kay was looking rather stressed.

'Get a shower and get changed, George. Let's get on the way before the children drive me potty. They've been running wild since you left yesterday and I haven't been able to get them to calm down.'

George did as he was asked and then started to get the suitcases ready at the door. Ali, the bus driver arrived and took over. He took the cases and piled them safely in the bus. George went back for Kay and the children.

They said their farewells and climbed into the bus and Ali started the engine with a roar. They had just started to move when Dave hammered furiously on the side of the bus. They screeched to a halt and George opened the door. Dave stuck his head inside and with a grin said, 'Hurry back, George. It's your turn to bring back a gallon bottle this time.'

They started off again, craning their heads round to see the others who were waving goodbye.

'Well,' said Kay, 'We're on our way.'

'We certainly are,' replied George. 'And for the first time ever I didn't want to go on leave.'

'I know what you mean,' said Kay. 'We've got two homes now and I'll be quite happy whichever one we are in.'

BOOK 3
THE TUG MASTER

17

The VC10 flight droned over Europe and onwards, deep into Asia. George Penroy sat beside his small son, John, who was curled up and asleep. In the seats in front of them sat Kay Penroy and their daughter, Louise, who stubbornly remained awake even though she had risen very early that morning. The family was on their way back to Iran after six weeks of home leave and George was deep in thought remembering his holiday.

They had arrived in England in October and the chill wind of autumn had struck home immediately their plane landed in Heathrow. It was late in the afternoon and the last rays of sunlight still vainly struggled with approaching dusk. Customs had not unduly bothered them and they had been met by the bored representative of their car hire firm who had delivered a stately Morris Oxford Estate car to the airport. Soon the documents had been completed and the family had shivered their way through the airport tunnel and on to the road for the South Coast.

Half an hour later they drew in to a service station and parked on the forecourt. George had to study the controls and find out how to switch on the lights and how to switch on the heating inside the car. He hadn't dared to stop before as his eyes were glued to the unfamiliar road and to the traffic that seemed to be driving on the wrong side of the road. The heat soon warmed the car interior and they headed south again. The children soon got drowsy once the car was warm and Kay and George chatted for the rest of the journey.

It was completely dark when they arrived home but lights were on in their house. George's father had been busy that day, stocking up the larder and generally preparing for the wanderers' return. Dad was a widower and needed to do things so that he forgot that he was lonely. The front door opened and the children woke up. They rushed into the house and Louise instantly remembered her grandfather. John was too young to remember sixteen months back but greeted the stranger because his sister evidently knew him. The children rushed from room to room, exploring, whilst George struggled inside with their battered suitcases.

The first priority for Kay was to get new clothes for the children and to stock up for another year in Iran. How much would they grow in another twelve months? They went into town on the first day home to start the process. It was dull and rainy and the children had to have new shoes immediately.

It was market day in town and they parked a little way from the shops. John was extremely slow as they made their way through the crowds and he kept staring up in the sky.

'Come along, John,' said Kay, who was getting wet and cold.

'What's that?' he asked still staring upwards

George, Kay and Louise all looked up but couldn't see anything unusual.

'What's what?' asked George.

'Those black things,' said John, pointing upwards.

They all looked.

'They're clouds, son.'

John had been so young when he left for Iran that he had forgotten what thick, black rain clouds looked like. They hurried along to the nearest shoe shop wondering what else he had forgotten.

They fitted both children out with new shoes and then, to the surprise and consternation of the assistant, bought the next three bigger sized shoes too. The process was repeated for underclothes, dresses and trousers too, by which time the children had had enough and wanted to go home. George thought it a good idea too as his bank balance was decreasing in inverse proportion to the time they spent shopping.

The short, wintry days had passed quickly. They had friends to see and family to visit and a year or more of home news to catch up on. Previously, when George was away at sea, Kay would keep him up to date with everything that had happened. Now they were all in the same boat. The children missed the warm weather of Iran and did not like having to wear sweaters and coats whenever they went out. They did enjoy the toyshops and sweet shops though and they especially liked the places that were already starting to have Christmas gifts in their windows.

Kay was planning for Christmas and was often out and about whilst George looked after the children. They would be sending freight back to Iran as well as using their weight allowances for baggage on the plane. Hidden away from the children were all sorts of new toys and games that would eventually be brought out for Christmas and birthdays. Kay hadn't had so much retail therapy in a long time and was enjoying the sensation.

All too soon the time had passed and very early that morning the family had climbed into the Morris Oxford for the last time. They handed it back at the airport before breakfast time and then all had bacon and eggs in the airport restaurant before boarding the plane. Their well-worn suitcases were bulging at the seams and it had taken all of George's charm to get the smartly dressed girl at the check in desk not to charge for excess baggage. Beneath the seat lay a further package purchased in the duty free shop at Heathrow and George hoped that the Iranian customs would take no notice of it. Despite a loud and lengthy protest from Kay about the cost, another gallon bottle was preparing to meet its fate.

The day passed slowly and the time dragged. They had trailed around Cairo airport for an hour whilst the aeroplane refuelled but since they had boarded again the children had been restless. They were served an evening meal but the children did not like the tasteless meat and nameless nauseous sauce that covered it. They brightened a little when offered Coca-Cola by a passing stewardess but the pleasure was short lived. They wanted to be free to roam around and not to be tied to an adult seat where their feet couldn't reach the ground.

Eventually the aircraft wing dipped towards the desert and they commenced their descent, across the river and in to Abadan. John awoke and protested loudly at having to fasten his seat belt and only quietened when offered a boiled sweat to suck. Louise was starting to turn green around the gills and Kay was busy trying to divert her attention whilst all the time standing by with a paper sick bag. They touched down without any problems and when the plane doors opened the children were ready to scramble out. They left George and Kay to carry all the trappings of travel despite being told to wait and were first in the queue to leave the plane. They had had enough of aeroplanes for one day. By the time George and Kay reached the tarmac the children had already passed through the arrivals lounge. They had casually walked straight past the immigration desk and customs men and were happily chatting to the 'in crowd' who were forming a welcoming committee.

George and Kay stood in the arrivals hall and waited for their baggage to be delivered. It was the first day of December but the weather felt pleasantly warm compared to the English chill of that morning. George took off his jacket and threw it on top of his baggage when it arrived. To George's relief the customs men waved them past without bothering to open their cases and they went out to find the children. There were handshakes and kisses all round and much excitement from the children.

'Hello, Ali,' they said to the driver of the bus that was waiting for them. 'Everyone is coming to our house.'

'Okay, *sahib*,' said Ali.

'*Punsda haftoda chahar, Ali*,' said Louise, remembering her Farsi. '*Zoot bash.*'

Ali grinned and climbed into the driving seat.

'*Zoot bash*,' he agreed and put his foot to the floor in his own inimitable, Middle Eastern style.

Young John was sitting on Liz Longford's knee and watching out of the window as they roared past familiar scenes. The brightly lit refinery that belched steam, the company hospital, the bazaar where you could buy *naan* and Coca-Cola and then the Taj Cinema. John was happy to be home.

'Auntie Liz,' he asked, 'Where's Wee Peter?'

'He's in his bed, John, but you can come and see him tomorrow.'

Liz guessed that John had missed his young friend's company and also knew that Peter would be glad to see him back. A man could only play schools for a limited time before he wanted football, fighting and Action Man.

'Penroy Mansions, everybody out,' someone shouted and they all climbed from the bus and found Minouche waiting to greet them. With many cries of '*Salaam*,' she fell on the children and whisked them inside. They rushed happily around her and were soon outside in her rooms and watching a cartoon on local television.

'Before you crack open the bottle give me a couple of minutes to phone Brian,' George insisted. 'I'd better report in.'

Two minutes later he wished he hadn't bothered.

'Blasted man tells me I'm on duty first thing tomorrow morning,' he moaned. 'We'd better postpone the welcoming ceremonies for a couple of nights.'

'What did you say to him, George?' asked Dave.

'Told him that when they were giving out heart he must have stood in the arsehole queue.'

'Nice one, George,' said Kay. 'That's really how to make friends and influence people.'

'No one has to work first day back. I'm sure he could have found someone else.' muttered George and the others nodded their agreement.

'Never mind, sunshine,' said Dave. 'We'll leave you in peace and come round to drink your booze another day.'

They all left for home and George and Kay went to find the children. 'Time for bed,' they told them and amidst a chorus of complaint packed them off in the direction of the bathroom to clean their teeth.

'Nice to be home?' Kay asked them as they jumped into their beds.

'Nice,' they agreed and in a few moments were fast asleep.

'Think we might as well follow suit. I've got to be up early for work,' said George so they unpacked a few necessary items from their cases before retiring to their string lashed bed.

18

At half past six the next morning the taxi called for George to go to work. He threw his workbag into the boot and climbed into the middle seat at the back. He knew the others would tell him it was his turn in the middle. It was the seat that everyone hated, as there was nothing to lean on. What else could he expect on his first day back? The four tug men would take it in strict rotation to sit in each seat so that once in four journeys you got to sit in the front where there was more space and the air conditioning was at its best. The front seat man always had the extra job of seeing that the driver stayed awake for the monotonous journey across the desert.

They quickly left the town and crossed the rickety iron bridge which spanned the muddy brown Bahmanshir River. As usual the religious beggar was at his post near the bridge. The bridge only took a single lane of traffic that was controlled by a traffic light and the beggar was invariably sitting cross-legged nearby. He was always stripped to the waist, whatever the weather and would strike himself with his fists repeatedly, first on the left shoulder, then on the right. His shoulders and upper chest were blue with bruising but he didn't seem to feel any pain and would continue a cheerful sing song chant asking for money to be put in his begging bowl.

The tug men usually tossed him a few coins as they passed. It was a ritual with all of the men except Scots Bob. Bob steadfastly refused to pay but regularly leaned out of the window with a different offer.

'I'll give you a hundred rials if I can take a poke at you,' he would shout in his broad Scots accent, grinning broadly.

It was hard for the tug men to follow Bob's accent sometimes, let alone an Iranian religious fanatic. The man seemed to understand though and so far Bob's offer had always been politely declined with a shake of his head.

Once across the bridge the desert road stretched out to the horizon. Ninety kilometres away the first bend lay in wait for all those drivers who weren't paying much attention. A tow truck was regularly to be seen pulling dented and crushed cars back onto the road. George slept for much of the way and only started to wake up as they took the bend and his head slipped sideways onto the shoulder of Harry, his engineer. They passed the desperately impoverished village of Sarabanda where the villagers queued patiently at a single water tap and in the distance the silvery storage tanks of Bandar Mashur shimmered in the morning desert sun. They were nearly there and would soon get the chance to stretch cramped limbs.

They passed through the gates of the installation and made for the jetties. Hopefully the tugs would be waiting for them at one of the empty berths, saving a ride in a small, dirty and oil stained boat. They had no such luck and to make matters worse they were met by the Chief Fire Officer who informed them that there would be a fire practice in half an hour.

'No peace for the wicked,' said Harry as their boat bobbed alongside the tugs. 'I'd better go and check the fire pumps before the siren goes. Bloody man always picks our shift for his fire practice.'

George went into the Captain's cabin and called for the steward. 'Coffee, please, and tell the *Serang* I need to see him.'

The *Serang* arrived and George spent five minutes explaining the jobs he wanted done that day. He also quietly gave the *Serang* the news that there would be a fire drill and explained what he wanted the crew to do. The old Indian showed his few remaining teeth in a grin and left the cabin to go and make arrangements.

On the dot of nine-thirty the wail of the fire sirens interrupted the peace of the desert morning. George went up to the bridge and the crew cast off the lines from the mooring buoy. Harry already had the fire pumps going and, as the tug approached the empty jetty where the fire exercise was supposed to be, he opened up the valve for the fire monitors. Water gushed from the nozzles as the tug neared the jetty. The Chief Fire Officer watched with satisfaction as the tugs approached. 'Very good,' came his voice over the radio, 'You can stand down now.' Normally the crew would turn the monitors away from the jetty but today they casually turned the monitors towards it instead. The Fire Chief took the full cascade of water on his chest and slipped off his feet, thrashing around in a vain attempt to avoid further soaking. His peaked cap washed gently over the side of the jetty and into the murky water below. The water from the monitors abruptly stopped as Harry shut down the pumps and the Fire Chief climbed damply to his feet and sorrowfully watched as his soggy hat sank beneath the surface.

'Sorry about that,' called George over the radio, trying to make it sound like an abject apology whilst he was still shaking with laughter. 'Bit of a misunderstanding by my crew.'

They sailed the tug back to the mooring buoy and the crew tidied everything up. A few minutes later they all reported outside George's cabin.

'Sign for your monthly overtime,' said George, smiling broadly. They put their mark, an inky thumb print, as a signature and all happily received two hours more pay than they had worked for. There would be blank looks from the crew if anyone ever asked how the Fire Chief came to be hosed down. No one would even remember such an accident. George felt much happier.

'Don't think we'll have any more fire drills for a while,' he said to Harry over lunch.

'Don't think we will,' Harry agreed and then headed for his afternoon nap. George followed suit.

Later that day two tankers arrived in the port and George was kept busy. He took the tug down river to meet each ship and as it approached he took the tug alongside the bow and made fast. The ship was then turned around and pushed and pulled into its appointed berth facing downstream. It was quite a simple manoeuvre and didn't require too much thought or effort on George's part. He was beginning to wish he could transfer and work at Kharg Island where there were lots of different manoeuvres and many more ships to move each day. He had approached Captain Robinson more than once but so far there was no chance of a change of work. He would have to stay where he was for a while yet.

'Perhaps I'll ask again after Christmas,' he thought to himself as he daydreamed through the taxi ride home the next day. 'There will be plenty to keep me occupied till then.'

For the second year running George was appearing in the Christmas show at the Theatre Club. He was in two small skits and was also busy as usual helping to build all the sets. Kay would be helping with makeup again and had also volunteered for front of house work. It sounded important but would probably mean serving in the bar that was at the back of the auditorium. In the intervals it would be packed with thirsty theatregoers and a small fortune would be made to go towards the costs of the next production.

There was only one problem with Christmas this year. George was on duty on Christmas Day. He would have time to see the children wake up and open their presents but then he would have to go to Bandar Mashur for twenty-four hours. When he had seen the work schedule he had finally realised why he had been asked to work on his first morning back from leave. It fitted him neatly into the roster so that he had Christmas day on duty. Someone had been pretty crafty and he suspected it was Brian.

'That's the last time I get caught like that,' he had vowed 'Next time I shall know better. The phone will be off the hook the night I get back from leave.'

Some weeks later George had a new engineer to work with. The new man was a bachelor and had arrived in town whilst George had been on leave. He would eventually be part of a small squad of engineers who would form a maintenance crew but meanwhile he was relieving Harry who was going on leave. John Henson was a big, bluff Yorkshireman who had been at sea on tankers for several years and he was one of the rare exotic breed known as a 'Professional Third'. They were men who had served an engineering apprenticeship before going to sea but who had no interest in gaining deep-sea qualifications. Accordingly they could rarely progress further through the ranks than Third Engineer.

John was a similar age to George and they immediately worked well together. John had worked mostly on motor ships but was gradually getting used to the steam engine and boiler on the tug. When John wasn't busy in the engine room they spent their time playing cards and had settled on canasta as their preferred game. They were also teaching it to their opposite numbers on the other duty tug and the four of them would play whenever possible. If a call to a ship came during the playing of a hand it was most unpopular and considered a worse infraction of protocol than an interrupted meal.

The four duty men were deep into a hand of canasta one evening when one casually said, 'Did you hear that Dave and his engineer, Bob, are being sent down the Gulf on a job?'

George pricked up his ears. 'No,' he replied.

'As far as I know one of our company tankers had a serious engine breakdown and fire a week ago and has been anchored ever since, waiting for a tow.'

'Where will they tow it?'

'The rumour is it will go to Bahrain and then one of Schmidt's tug will come from Suez, take over and tow it to Europe.'

'I wouldn't mind having a go at that,' said George, thoughtfully. 'Make a change from parking ships around Mashur.'

The next morning, on their way home, they stopped at the office to put in a requisition for stores. Captain Robinson was shuffling papers at his desk as George passed his door.

'Any news about the tow job?'

'None that's good,' replied the Super. 'One of Dave's children is sick and he doesn't want to go. I'll have to find someone else.'

'What about me?' said George.

'You haven't got enough experience yet.'

'How much do I need?' grinned George.

'Sod off,' said the Super. 'Some poor village must have lost its idiot when you came here.'

George left and thought no more about it till he got home.

'Robinson thinks I don't have much experience,' he told Kay later.

'Don't go volunteering to go back to sea, George. We've only just got used to living together,' said Kay. 'Think of what you'd be missing.'

'Just thought it might be fun,' said George.

Two days later George was called to the office.

'So, how would you do this tow job, Penroy?' asked the Super.

'Easily,' replied George.

'For God's sake be your bloody age and give me a sensible reply,' said Captain Robinson in his best Gilbert and Sullivan Admiral's voice.

'Okay,' said George. 'I'd need a crew that I know and one of the new motor tugs. Then I'd need someone to share the watches whilst towing, so would the engineer, so I'd get the second mate and third engineer off the ship. And maybe an Apprentice as well, if there's one on board. He could be a gofer. A set of Admiralty Charts for the

Gulf is a must and if possible one of those portable Decca Navigators so that we would know exactly where we were. That's just for a start.'

'So far, so good,' grunted Captain Robinson. 'Do you know how far it is to Bahrain?'

'No, but I can soon find out.'

'It's 330 miles, and if you could make three or four knots it would take between eighty and a hundred and ten hours. Do you think it could be done?'

'Well, four days is a long time, but with the right time off to prepare and more time to recover I reckon it's quite possible. Of course, if there were more accommodation on the tug and another officer to share the duties it would be better. Could we find enough cabin space on board for a couple more?'

'We'll think about that. What about towing gear?'

'All the books say tow with the ship's anchor cable, so we'd have to go with that. Shackle our heaviest towing gear on to the cable and then slack away the cable until we've got a really long tow.'

'Do you think one of our tugs could control a fifteen thousand ton deadweight ship in ballast?'

George thought for a while.

'As long as we don't have to go into any restricted areas I can't see too many problems. We pick the tow up in the open sea and we take it to within striking distance of Bahrain but not into the buoyed channel. We leave it at anchor outside until the deep-sea tug comes to get it, while we go in to port for some rest and recreation before coming back. I hear Bahrain is a nice place for shore leave.'

Captain Robinson sat quietly for a while, evidently thinking about the possibilities. Eventually he sighed deeply and said, 'Right, George, I'll get on the phone to the Company in London and see what they have to say about it. It will save them thousands if we can move the ship to Bahrain. The less time that they have to hire a deep-sea tug the happier they will be but if we cock this up and lose a tanker we're going to be up to our necks in deep brown stuff without a paddle. Which engineer would you want?'

'Might as well stick with the devil I know,' said George. 'What about John Henson? He's a bachelor and would probably enjoy a bit of salvage. Which reminds me. What do we get paid for this little jaunt?'

'Don't push your luck, George. I expect the company would be grateful and that's as much as I'll say. I'll give you a call if there are any developments.'

George went home, excited at the prospect of something new. He told Kay all about it and was quite surprised when she suggested he had better leave it to one of the others.

'Why,' he asked.

'It won't make you very popular with the others if it's a great success,' she explained, 'And you won't be satisfied to go back to pushing ships around Bandar Mashur afterwards.'

It wasn't much later that the telephone rang. It was Brian, wanting to speak to George.

'I hear you've volunteered for the towing job,' he said.

'Doesn't take long for the jungle drums to get the message around.'

'Just to let you know that I've now volunteered as well,' said Brian. 'Can't have Robinson thinking you're the only one with the nerve to do it.'

'Please yourself,' replied George, 'Do you really want the job? I'm happy to come with you if you want an assistant.' He thought that it would serve Brian right to have him as assistant.

Not twenty minutes later the phone rang again. It was Captain Robinson. 'Thought I'd tell you that the job is off, George. The company is going to let Schmidts handle the whole thing after all. Thanks for volunteering though. I'll keep you in mind if anything else comes up.'

'How about a transfer to working in Kharg instead?' he asked. 'The work in Mashur is pretty mundane.'

'I'll see what I can do and you'll be top of the list,' came the reply, 'But don't hold your breath. Most people prefer the work in Kharg so it's difficult to find a place for you.'

George thought no more about things until the weekend when he met up with Brian at the Karting Club.

'You shouldn't have volunteered without talking to me,' said Brian, testily. 'Makes us all look bad.'

'Tough shit,' said George, losing his temper and raising his voice. 'Even if the rest of you were scared out of your wits, I wasn't. You should have been first in line, instead of skulking at the back of the queue.'

'Is that what you think?'

'If the cap bloody well fits then wear it,' said George and he stomped off into the bar to find a cool beer.

Kay found him there, deep in thought, half an hour later.

'Penny for them,' she said, taking his arm.

'I always have to pick the most senior man around to argue with, don't I?' he said, morosely.

'That's probably because you've always wanted to be the boss yourself. Don't worry. You'll get there one day.'

19

Spring was in the air and the days were getting warmer. The Iranians would soon be celebrating *Now Ruz*, the Iranian New Year, which falls on the twenty-first of March each year. The official religion in the country was Muslim but, being an independent minded nation of ancient origins, the Muslim lunar calendar was not used. The Iranian solar calendar gave the country the unique date of thirteen forty-four. However there would soon be a big change. The *Shahanshah* had directed by Royal Decree that the following year would be re-numbered and the new basis of counting would start from the beginning of the reign of Cyrus the Great, the first King of Persia. It meant that the date would be two thousand five hundred and thirty five and it was causing great amusement to the *ferangis*. A few years previously there had been a pop song in the hit parade which started with the words, 'In the year twenty five thirty five, If we're still alive,'.

Now Ruz was the excuse for thirteen days of celebrations, starting with the ceremony of *Haft Sine* and culminating with a picnic day on *Sisdah Nowruz* when the spirit of *Haji Firooz* was known to be out and about. Presents were exchanged, visits were made to relatives and much food was eaten, especially the sickly sweet *halva* which the Iranians so loved. Pistachio nuts would be gorged by the kilo and there would be lavish dinners and dancing at the clubs. The less religious of the adult men would drink vast quantities of *Makhsous* vodka and a general air of gaiety would prevail. Most holidays in the Muslim calendar were grave and solemn but Now Ruz was just the opposite.

Abadan would be full to bursting during the holiday. In the North of Persia there are mountainous areas and in the winter they get extremely cold. Teheran would regularly grind to a halt under enough snow to seriously disconcert a brass monkey. It was therefore the practice of anyone who had relatives living in Abadan to visit them for the holiday. The spring weather was just what the Northerners needed after a long hard winter. The *Teheranis* were a liberated lot, especially the young girls. Under their voluminous *chadur* the hair and make up would be the very latest in fashion, whilst on a lower level their mini skirts were shorter than the average pelmet. The girls were a wily bunch who knew how to keep one step ahead of their chaperones.

When George and Kay were at the company club for a dinner and dance the previous year they had watched some of the visitor's tricks. The young female visitors had all attended the dance along with the youthful males of Abadan who, unlike the girls, had relatively few restrictions put on their behaviour. The chaperones sat at the edge of the dance floor like roosting black crows, watching their female charges who were the model of prim decorum whilst dancing in their line of sight. However, a tight outer ring of well-behaved dancers concealed the inner circle from the chaperone's view, and within that inner arena there were no holds barred. 'I think it must be a dance called The Freestyle Grope,' said George as he danced sedately round in the outer fringe with Kay.

A few days before *Now Ruz* George was again called into the office by the Super.

'Got a job for you, George,' said the Super. 'You're always looking for something new.'

'What is it?'

'Firstly, it will be to bring the Narimand through to Abadan for annual dry-docking. The floating dock will be ready in about two day's time. Once the docking is over there is a barge to be towed down the Gulf so you can do the job with the Narimand.'

'Where is the barge going?' asked George.

'Dubai,' replied Captain Robinson. 'It will be loaded with drums of a special lubricating oil that they want down there for their new oil wells. You'll discharge the drums at Dubai Creek and then you can bring the barge back to Abadan.'

'Great,' said George, 'Who's coming with me?'

'You can take your friend, Henson, as engineer if you like. Otherwise it is just the Indian crew to back you up.'

'Sounds okay to me,' said George happily. 'When do we start.'

'I'll send a taxi for you and John Henson tomorrow morning and you can go over to Mashur. Take over the tug and as soon as you have customs clearance you can bring her round to number eight jetty at Abadan. She has enough fuel to get her here and you can top up again after docking.'

George went home in high humour to tell Kay what was happening. 'I should get a chance to have a look round Dubai whilst the barge is discharging. They tell me there's stacks of duty free stuff worth buying and I can bring it back on the tug without any bother.'

'How long will you be away?' Kay asked.

'Reckon we can make about six or seven knots,' said George, 'So it shouldn't be more than three and a half days to get there. Two days in Dubai then back at eight or nine knots. Should get back here in around nine days.'

'Do you think you can last that long without home comforts, George?'

'Don't think they would let me take you with me, so I suppose I'll have to, unless some dusky, dark-eyed maiden takes pity on me in Dubai.'

'Don't even think about it, sailor,' said Kay with a glint in her eye. 'Harm could definitely come to a young lad when he got back, so wind your neck in, or anything else you've got out.'

'Please don't beat me again, Master,' said George, cowering back in mock horror.

He went out into the garden and turned on the hose. He found that he could think clearly whilst he sprayed water over his blossoming, well-kept garden, so he planned out the coming trip round from Mashur. It was no more than a hundred and fifty miles by sea but he would count it as his first deep-sea command.

He was up bright and early the next day, waiting for the taxi. It would make a change to have just two of them in the car instead of four. Room to spread out. It arrived at the appointed time and he threw his workbag in the back and climbed in. In a few minutes he had picked up John Henson from his bachelor flat and they were on their way, discussing the prospect of the trip to Dubai as they sped across the dusty desert highway.

They arrived safely at Bandar Mashur and went in to the agent's offices. The office of Gray Mackenzie and Co was a dingy room with bars on the dusty windows and piles of shipping documents strewn all around it. George recognised the company's representative and asked him to arrange for customs clearance for the tug later that morning.

'I'll bring the official documents along in about half an hour,' said George.

'Okay,' said the rep, who was more concerned with the contents of his nostrils than doing any real work. 'I fix.'

George went out into the bright morning sunlight and joined John on the jetty. There was no sign of a boat to take them out to the tug, which lay at the mooring buoy. After five minutes they gave up and went into the shipping office where there was a VHF radio. They greeted the shipping clerk, who happily let them use the radio and they called up Dave on the duty tug.

'Dave, will you come alongside and collect us? The boat has gone walkabout.'

Dave's reply dwelt mainly on how much he would charge for the service but a few minutes later they could see a puff of smoke from the duty tug's funnel as she got under way and headed for shore. George and John walked down to the empty jetty.

Dave's tug landed gently alongside the jetty and his voice floated down from the bridge.

'Get a bloody move on. I haven't got all day to waste on you two prima donnas.'

They threw their bags aboard and jumped down onto the deck. The bags were whisked away by the crew and they went up to the bridge.

'Hello sailor,' said George.

'Don't know how you'll find your way to Abadan,' said Dave, gruffly. 'Can't even find your way on board your tug without my help.'

'You love us really,' said George, blowing him a kiss, 'Where's the coffee then? Damn poorly run tug this is.'

'Sod off to your own tug,' muttered Dave with a grin. 'Use your own stores, not mine.'

In a few minutes they arrived alongside the Narimand and they jumped across. Their bags were tossed after them, and George called for the *Serang* as he went up to the Master's cabin.

'All ready to go, *Serang*,' he asked.

'*Atcha, sahib*. All ready.'

'Good,' lets get under way. 'We'll go alongside the jetty first.'

The *Serang* left, calling for the crew to go to their stations, whilst George changed into his working gear. Feeling more comfortable in a shirt and shorts he went up to the bridge. His first move was to put the pilot chair within easy reach of the bridge telegraph and he climbed into the seat and made himself comfortable.

'Penroy's first rule of navigation,' he said to the quartermaster. 'Plant bum in comfortable position before sailing. Seafaring's good for the soul but hell on the piles.'

The quartermaster didn't understand what George had said but he grinned happily. The crewmen were all eagerly looking forward to doing business ashore in Dubai. They had heard about the gold souk and were intent on acquiring some of it to take home to India. It would fetch a good profit in Bombay.

'Second rule.' Continued the recumbent Captain, 'Always make sure that the Captain has coffee. Where's the steward?'

The quartermaster understood this time. He leaned out of the bridge window and shouted down to the men on deck. They took up the shout in turn and within a few minutes the steward appeared on the bridge complete with silver tray and a steaming mug of white coffee.

'Thanks,' said George, and the steward turned to leave.

'Wait up, sunshine,' said George and the man turned back. 'Any beer on board?'

'Only half case, *sahib*,' said the steward.

'That's OK for today,' said George and he fished in his pocket for his wallet. He extracted five hundred rials and handed it over. 'Get plenty in Abadan,' he said, 'And take your taxi fare out of that too.'

The steward smiled happily. He would walk to the beer shop and carry the cases back on his shoulder, keeping the taxi fare for himself.

George hurried to the agent's office as soon as they came alongside. The clerk was still idly picking his nose but stopped when George arrived. He casually wiped his fingers on his trousers and handed George his sailing permit.

'Pilot ready for you at Bandar Shapur, Captain George,' he said and turned away to resume his interrupted occupation.

'His flaming head will cave in one day,' thought George as he walked back to the tug.

'Let go everything,' called George as he jumped down on to the main deck and he went up to the bridge. The tide had already pushed the tug away from the jetty as George climbed into the pilot chair and he kicked the telegraph handle to full ahead with his foot.

'Steady as she goes,' he ordered and the tug surged ahead, building up a bow wave under the for'ard fender.

'First stop Bandar Shapur,' said George as John's head appeared at the top of the ladder. 'We'll pick up the *Khor Musa* pilot and then arrange some lunch. What do you fancy?'

They sailed down stream and a short time later a pilot boat came alongside and a surly unshaven pilot climbed aboard. He wasn't happy as he knew he wouldn't see anyone or get any help on the way out to the sea. On a tanker there would be an officer on watch, plus a helmsman and a lookout, and access to food and drink. On the tug he would usually be left with the Indian quartermaster and a bottle of cold water. He brightened when George offered him lunch and asked if he wanted a drink. He settled for curry and a beer.

Having seen to the pilots needs George told the quarter-master to call him when the pilot was ready to leave and then went down to his cabin. He could get in a couple of hands of canasta with John before a drink and lunch. Better limit himself to one beer though. Once the pilot went he would have to stay on the bridge until they reached the next pilot station off the mouth of the Shatt al Arab.

George could feel that they were leaving the *Khor Musa* when the tug started to pitch gently. They were approaching the open sea. He went up to the bridge to find the pilot all alone and steering the tug.

'Where's the quartermaster?' he asked.

'Just gone to get me a few stores,' replied the pilot.

The quartermaster scuttled back up the ladder and handed the pilot a bottle of Scotch Whisky and a carton of Camel cigarettes. In return the pilot handed him a thick wad of rial notes. They were approaching the pilot cutter and it was time for the pilot to leave. He said his goodbyes and went down to the maindeck, stuffing his shopping into a paper carrier bag.

'Good business?' George asked the quartermaster.

'Good business, Captain *sahib*,' he replied. 'Pilot he pay double price.'

'You sure you weren't a bandit in India?'

The quartermaster smiled and felt the wad of notes in his pocket. He would be a rich man in his village when he went home for his annual leave.

The pilot cutter pulled away from the side of the tug and once again they went back to full speed. George checked his chart and called out a course to be steered. He marked the position and time on the chart and then stepped off the distance to go to the next pilot station. There would be nothing to see except sea and they would run on dead reckoning. It should be over four hours before they picked up the first buoy in the Shatt al Arab channel. George put on the echo sounder. It was the only navigational aid, apart from the standard compass and at least it would tell them if they were getting into shallow water. He settled down in his chair with his feet up on the ledge beneath the bridge window and lit his tenth cigarette of the day.

'Smoke if you want,' he said to the quartermaster and they both added their toxic contribution to the silvery plume that lazily streamed aft from the tug's single funnel.

Four hours later they were still steaming towards the setting sun. George would be glad when it set and meanwhile he was wearing his sunglasses to counteract the glare on the horizon. Once it was dusk he would be able to see better and the lights on the buoys would start to flash. George knew he wasn't far from where he wanted to be as on the port bow he could see a cargo ship heading Northwards. It could only be heading for the pilot station and was probably bound for Khorramshahr. He adjusted the course so that the ship was dead ahead. He would follow behind it once it had safely crossed his bow although according to the seaman's Rule of the Road he could have stood on. No point in racing with him thought George. He's a lot bigger than we are and the pilots will go to him first anyway.

The sun dipped below the horizon and almost immediately the flashing lights of buoys appeared in the distance. George checked the time between the flashes to identify each buoy and was pleased to find that they were right on course. Soon he would be able to go below and get his dinner. It had been a long afternoon.

The cargo ship picked up his pilot and slowly headed north. George took the tug in close to the pilot cutter and called on the radio for a pilot.

'No pilot available for you,' came the reply. 'Anchor and wait.'

'How long?'

'Maybe four hours,' the disembodied voice replied.

'Can I follow the cargo ship in without a pilot? asked George.

'Affirmative.'

George swore to himself and pushed the telegraph to full once more. He took over the wheel and sent the quartermaster below to find John. He steadied the tug on the stern light of the cargo ship muttering to himself.

'Four more bloody hours. Soddin' lazy Iraqi pilots should be rogered to death with the rough end of a pineapple.'

In a little while the quartermaster returned and took over the wheel and John followed close behind him.

'Cancel the evening canasta,' said George. 'It's DIY day on the lovely Shatt al Arab.'

'Can't win 'em all.'

'Can't even bloody draw, today,' moaned George, watching the lights of the cargo ship disappear as it turned a bend in the river. He crossed his fingers, hoping that they would see the lights of the ship again before the cargo boat disappeared behind the palm trees around the next bend.

'See if you can rustle up a few buckets more steam, John. Damn ship has got the legs of us and we're struggling to keep up. If we lose him we'll have to anchor till daylight and I want to get home tonight.'

'Hold on to your hat,' said John as he slid down the ladder towards the engine room.

George breathed a sigh of relief as the tug rounded the bend in the river and the cargo ship was in sight once more. John must have opened up everything as the waves under the bow fender hissed and bubbled as the tug picked up speed. They started to close on the ship ahead.

John didn't reappear so George guessed he had stayed below and it wasn't until they were in sight of the Abadan refinery that John came back onto the bridge. He was in his boiler suit and was sweating profusely.

'You know you asked for more speed? Well we've got problems. The manoeuvring valve is jammed and now we can't bloody stop.'

'What the hell can we do?' asked George. 'We can't go up and down this god forsaken river until we're out of fuel. It would take days.'

'There's only one thing to do and that's shut the steam valve off on the top of the boiler. If we do that the engine will stop. You'll just have to give me a shout when we get near the jetty. I'll shut off the steam and with any luck we will stop near enough to put a man ashore with a rope.'

'Good thinking, Batman,' said George. 'I'll just cross a few fingers and toes so that you shut the valve in time to stop us steaming right through the damn jetty and out the other side and onto the refinery road.'

They neared the berth and George heard a dull clang behind him. John had lifted a grating just forward of the funnel and was crouched down over a valve with a wheel spanner in his hand.

'Just going to make sure the valve works,' he called and

George muttered a short prayer to any God that might be listening.

'It's free,' shouted John.

'So are my bloody bowels,' replied George, estimating roughly how far they had to go.

He steadied the tug on a course for the jetty, taking into account the tide in the river and watched carefully until they were within about twenty yards of the berth.

'Now,' he bawled and John furiously turned the valve. Magically the tug slowed but it wasn't enough.

'Get a man ashore,' he called to the crew. 'Hard a' port.'

The bow swung away from the berth and the tug clouted the jetty fenders broadside on. Before it bounced off again a crewman leaped ashore and a heaving line snaked after him. By the time they had a mooring line on a shore bollard the tug was twenty feet back out in the river and still going ahead

'Is that poxy valve shut?' called George to John.

'It is now,' grunted John, giving the spanner one final pull and the tug came to a halt.

'Hard a' starboard,' ordered George and the quartermaster spun the wheel over the other way. Slowly the bow turned towards the jetty again and the crew took up the slack on the mooring rope. They bumped gently alongside this time and more lines were soon ashore and fast.

'Finished with engines,' sighed George. 'Just as well this old bucket is going into dock. In this state she couldn't pull a soldier off your sister.'

'Let's go and have a beer before we go home,' said John. 'I could really do justice to one right now. And, by the way, I haven't got a sister.'

'That's a bit sad for the army. I reckon we deserve the beer though. We'll have to be back tomorrow morning at slack water for taking the old tub onto the dock. At least the tide isn't until eleven, so we won't have to be up at the crack of sparrow fart.'

20

The following morning the Narimand was dry docked without further problem. She was pulled and pushed by several small launches out into the middle of the river where the floating dock was submerged and then nudged inside and made fast. She was held securely in position by her mooring ropes whilst the ballast was pumped out of the dock and gradually the tug was raised clear of the water. The tug filled the space in the dock and when fully lifted it looked as if it were perched on top of the water like some enormous, garishly coloured sea bird. The crew on the dock set to work scraping and washing the barnacles and weed from the hull whilst it was still wet. The Indian crew remained on board and hastily locked all cabin doors against the marauding hordes that flocked all over the tug. Anything not nailed down was likely to disappear.

George had stayed aboard during the docking and had cleared all the equipment from the bridge. When they eventually sailed he would need charts, binoculars and azimuth mirrors for the trip and didn't want to have to find them from where they had been sold, in the back streets of the bazaar. He took the boat ashore once everything was complete, leaving instructions with the *Serang* to call him if necessary. He hoped for several days of peace and quiet before the tug was refloated.

Once ashore he went to find the barge which he would have to tow to Dubai. After much searching he finally located it in Braim Creek, an evil smelling backwater about a mile upstream from the port. George was horrified to find that it was a flat topped, dented and rusty hulk that looked as if it was a relic of the Second World War Normandy landings. He stepped gingerly aboard and picked his way amongst the filthy debris of wires, ropes and empty cans that littered the deck. He peered into the hatches that were open and was surprised to find the interior of the barge dry. The hatch covers lay nearby but there was no sign of their securing bolts. He went despondently back to the super's office.

'Have you seen the state of the barge?' he asked. 'I've seen cleaner Bovril boats on the Thames.' He was referring to the ships that took the sewage sludge from London for disposal in the North Sea. 'I reckon Noah could have been the last Master and the crew didn't clean up after the animals.'

'Keep your hair on, George. Let's see what we can do whilst the tug is docked. We can use the tug crew and pay them overtime. Save them from getting sores on their bums.'

George sat down and they planned what was needed to bring the barge back to a seaworthy state. If they took the crew to the creek each day in the tug service bus, along with whatever paint and equipment was needed, there was a chance the barge might be in a reasonable state for sailing in a few days.

'Take the *Serang* up to the creek today, George. Let him have a look at the barge and he can then get together all the stores he needs.'

That afternoon George took the *Serang* to show him the problem. The *Serang* smiled broadly when he heard that the crew would be on overtime.

'I bring engine crew too, *sahib*?' he asked.

'Sure.'

The *Serang* smiled even more. He would probably be taking a cut of each man's overtime.

'What do you think of the barge?'

'Same like Bombay bum boat, *sahib*. No problem. I fix.'

'Three days enough, *Serang*?'

'Maybe five day,' he replied, calculating how many hours overtime that would be.

'You want me here?' said George crossing his fingers behind his back.

'No, *sahib*. You take rest with *memsahib*,' replied the wily old *Serang*. Without George around he would be able to sell off some of the stores and make a little extra profit.

George left things to the crew for four days before going to see the barge again. The transformation was stunning. On the shore was a pile of rusting junk, empty paint cans and general rubbish, whilst in the greasy brown water of the creek floated a shining, freshly painted barge. The hatches were all secured with stainless steel bolts, stanchions were welded around the edge of the deck and a safety chain was strung between the stanchions. Old car tires hung neatly along the sides for use as fenders and new mooring ropes were coiled neatly in wire cages. The topsides of the barge were painted black, the decks were dark red and the edges of the hatches were white, so that they showed up clearly. The tug crew had rigged an awning and were sitting underneath it, brewing tea over a portable stove.

'*Chai, sahib?*'

'Yes please,' said George, squatting down amongst them. 'I think maybe five days overtime pay.'

'*Atcha, sahib*,' came the universal reply as they happily sipped their strong, black tea. They were well pleased.

George reported back to the super's office feeling much happier.

'The dry dock boss reckons three more days before he finishes all the repairs,' said Captain Robinson. 'They've even fixed the boiler, so the old girl should be in top condition. What's your programme once she comes off the dock?'

'Well,' replied George, 'I reckon to give her an hours run up and down the river on trials before we go up to Braim Creek to collect the barge. Then we'll bring the barge here to number eight jetty until the Oil Company is ready to load the cargo. Our crew will then check that the load is secured properly before we sail for Dubai. We'll have the barge alongside the tug for manoeuvring in the river but when we get clear of the Shatt al Arab we'll tow over the stern.'

'Sounds as if you've got it all planned out. I've just got one thing more for you to do.'

'What now,' asked George.

'When you're in Dubai pick up my new deep freeze for me. It will be crated up, so just put it on the barge and bring it back. If you bring it straight to this jetty I'll get it ashore before the customs come on board.'

'Crafty old sod,' thought George. 'A freezer will be about half the price in Dubai and I get to take the risk of bringing it in through customs. If he can get away with it, so can I. Wonder what I'll bring back?'

Captain Robinson's estimate of three days to finish repairs to the tug turned out to be rather optimistic. The repairs stretched to four and then five days and then it was Now Ruz and an extended weekend with no work. It suited George fine. The tug crew continued their work on the barge, welding new steel plates over the deepest dents in the sides. They put a second coat of paint on everything too, so the barge was in better condition than it had been for years. The crew also made up a new towing rope especially for the trip to Dubai, so everything was ready. George, Kay and the children took advantage of the time that he spent in Abadan, and George was much happier than when working in Mashur. They were out and about during the *Now Ruz* holiday and went to the bazaar and to the clubs. George even arranged for the family to visit the dry dock to see the tug. The children had a great time and were royally entertained by the crew, whilst Kay and George sat drinking the obligatory *cha* with the *Serang*.

On the tenth day the Iranians returned to work and preparations were made for undocking the tug. They had to wait for the high tide so that the dock could submerge but late in the afternoon all was ready. Both George and John Henson were on board although the boilers hadn't been started up and the tug would be towed back to the jetty.

Inch by inch the dock slowly submerged until the tug floated off the stout wooden blocks that supported her. The motor launches hovered around the dock as the mooring ropes on the tug were slacked. The newly ebbing tide eased the tug astern and out of the dock and the launches made fast to her sides. The last rope was cast off and the tug was floating free once more. Cautiously the launches nudged the tug towards the Iranian shore and number eight jetty. Ten minutes later the tug was made fast at the jetty and the last of the launches cast off.

'We'll flash up the boilers,' said John, 'And she'll be ready for a trial run tomorrow morning. What time shall we get on board?'

'Ten o'clock would be a nice time,' said George. 'Give us time for a run and to go and collect the barge before we have the afternoon to sort out any last minute problems.'

'Okay, George. See you in the morning.'

John disappeared into the bowels of the engine room and George went home. Hopefully the Oil Company would load the barge with drums the next day and then they would have a good nights sleep before their trip.

When George got home their was a lorry outside his house. He hurried inside and found Kay directing several Iranian workers.

'Hi, George,' she said, gaily. 'They are taking our beds away down to the bazaar.'

'What for?' asked a puzzled George.

'We're finally going to get rid of the string that ties them together. They are going to cut springs apart and re-weld everything together to make a six foot wide double bed.'

'How did you arrange that?'

'I got talking to the Armenian family across the road and they said they knew a good welder in the bazaar who could do the job. We'll find out tomorrow if that's true, when they bring it back'.

The men pushed and heaved the beds outside and on to the lorry and it went off up the road in a cloud of hazy blue exhaust.

'I'm not sure where they are taking it,' admitted Kay. 'I hope they don't just sell the single beds.'

'I hope so too,' muttered George. 'Where are we sleeping tonight.'

'On the floor.'

'Charming,' said George. 'Let's hope that won't become a permanent arrangement.'

George thought the same thing the next morning. He awoke bright and early and tried to get out of the covers that were scattered across the bedroom floor.

'What's all the noise for?' asked a sleepy Kay.

'I'm as stiff as a skinhead's boot,' groaned George. 'Reckon it will take me all day to get mobile again.'

'Rubbish,' said Kay. 'You'll get on board that tug with Henson, lubricate yourself with a couple of Shams beers and you won't feel a thing.'

'Sounds a good plan,' said George. 'What's the damned noise outside?'

'Try looking,' said Kay.

George shrugged into a dressing gown that had seen better days, rubbed his eyes and went to the front door.

He opened it and peered out to find four shrill voiced Iranians trying to get a six-foot wide bed through the gate. He hurried back into the house.

'Better get out of your pit before you have company,' he said. 'The bed is back.'

Kay jumped up, pulling on a housecoat and George hastily pulled on a pair of trousers and a shirt before returning to the open front door.

The struggling men had reached the front door and pushed their way into the hall.

'In here,' directed George, pointing to the bedroom, and the sweating group turned in through the door. The bed just made it, clearing the lintel by a fraction but scraping a layer of paint off the door. The workers lay the bedspring on the floor and went back for the head and foot. Surprisingly it all fitted together and the foreman of the group presented George with the bill.

'One thousand rials,' said George. 'Not a bad price.'

He added a further two hundred rials to the amount and paid it to the foreman who shook his hand and bowed. Kay spoke to the foreman in Farsi and he bowed even deeper. 'Wonder what she said,' thought George, but he didn't ask. She was far better than George at the language but he hated to admit it.

George ushered the men out and came back to the bed-room.

'Looks okay to me,' he said, bouncing on the springs. 'Let's try it out?'

'On your bike, sailor. Get some breakfast for yourself and the children and then go to work. I'll get a new six foot square mattress in the bazaar today, and I'll sew together some sheets and a blanket later. Maybe it will be ready for tonight if you don't get in the way.'

George went and did as he was told. Once Kay started organising he knew it was time to get out of the way or he would be given a job that he wouldn't want to do. He hurried the children through their breakfast and then phoned for transport. He showered and dressed whilst waiting for the tug bus whilst Kay busied herself in the bedroom.

George arrived at the tug early and found the crew bustling around, cleaning up the accumulated refuse of many days on the dock. They were in a cheerful mood and glad to be getting back to normal duties again. A thin column of white smoke curled from the tug's woodbine funnel. Things were evidently warming up in the engine room.

'Chief Engineer aboard? He asked.

'Yes, *sahib*,' replied the quartermaster.

'Tell him I want to see him, please.'

The quartermaster scuttled away and a short while later John appeared at the cabin door. He was already in his boiler suit and was looking pleased with himself.

'All systems go, George,' he reported. 'The boilers bubbling fit to bust a gut, so we might as well give her a run and try everything out.'

'Okay,' said George and made for the bridge. He rang stand by on the telegraph and it clanked an immediate reply. The crew poured out on to the deck and at a wave from George they threw off the mooring ropes.

'Hard a' port.'

The tug turned slowly away from the jetty and the engines answered the telegraph's call for slow ahead. Slowly and sedately they cruised into the middle of the river and headed down stream. A few minutes later they cleared the last of the oil jetties and were heading into Bawarda Reach, a wide expanse of river with plenty of room for manoeuvres. John climbed the bridge ladder and George lifted one eyebrow quizzically.

'Can we give her a good work out now?' George asked.

'Do your worst.'

George pushed the telegraph to full ahead and the tug surged through the water. They were just reaching full speed when he pulled the telegraph back to full astern. The old hull shook and the funnel and mast stays rattled and shook as the propeller bit into the murky water. The bow swung to starboard in a classic display of transverse thrust and George put the telegraph back to full ahead. The tug shook herself again and the binoculars danced along the chart table. John caught them before they fell to the deck and put them in their box.

'You might need them,George.'

'Reckon I will, too. If she doesn't shake herself apart we could soon be on our way to Dubai.'

They put the tug through her paces for another half an hour without any defects appearing so George then pointed her in the direction of Braim Creek. 'Might as well collect the barge,' he said to nobody in particular.

At the entrance to the creek he slowed the tug to a crawl. The creek had not been surveyed for years and it was anyone's guess what unseen hazards lurked beneath the stagnant waters.

They nudged carefully alongside the barge without a problem and two crewmen jumped aboard. 'Make fast alongside,' George called, and ropes were passed onto the barge and the eyes were dropped over the bollards.

'Make sure they're tight.'

The windlass motor purred to life and the ropes were hauled bar taught before they were stoppered off and made fast to the bollards.

'Put out a stern line too.'

Another rope snaked over from the after end of main deck and was soon heaved tight with the capstan.

All was ready and George rang for dead slow astern. The water churned and gurgled under the stern but nothing happened.

'Shit,' thought George, realising that he hadn't let go the ropes holding the barge to the shore. He hoped no-one would have noticed and called to the crew, 'Let go the barge from the shore.'

The sailors threw off the moorings and leapt back aboard the barge as it started to move back out of the creek. George stopped the engines and allowed it to drift. Short bursts astern and then ahead on the engine and putting the helm one way or the other kept them on a straight course and the tug and barge slowly backed out into the river. A sudden loud blast from nearby on a ship's whistle made George jump. He glanced up to find a sleek cargo ship bearing down on them as it headed down river from Khorramshahr.

'Hard a' starboard,' he called pushing the telegraph to full ahead. The barge turned quickly and the tug and tow gathered speed back towards the Iranian shore. The cargo ship swept close by them with several uniformed people glaring down from the bridge, waving their arms. The tug and barge bobbed furiously in the ship's wake and George gazed serenely back as if he hadn't a care in the world. Underneath his shirt his heart was thumping. He had learned several more important lessons that morning.

21

George rolled over and gazed at the ceiling. He was lying in the middle of his newly welded bed. The conversion was an unqualified success. Six square feet of cotton sheeted splendour in which to chase Kay around. He looked round to find that Kay had already risen. He stretched luxuriously. What would he do today? He looked at the alarm clock, that ticked contentedly on a nearby chest of drawers.

'Jesus H and General Jackson! Nine thirty already.'

He rolled out of bed and rushed into the bathroom. There was just time for a quick shower. The stream of hot water felt good but he didn't linger long. He dried himself and then wrapped the towel round his waist and hurried through to the dining room. Kay sat with the children, eating toast.

'Where's the fire?' she asked, grinning at George.

'I'm just late,' he said, grabbing a slice of toast from her plate. 'Why didn't you wake me? I wanted to be on board the tug by now.'

Kay laughed. 'You were flat out when I got up, George, so I put the clock forward an hour, just to see you get into a spin.'

'Thought I was supposed to be the comedian in the family,' George grumbled as he went away to get dressed at a more sedate pace.

He phoned for transport when he had finished his breakfast. It didn't take long before the toot of a horn announced that Ali had arrived with the tug bus and George went off to work.

The tug was alongside a loading jetty taking on fuel and the freshly painted barge had been moved to the cargo loading berth. Slowly the fifty-gallon drums of lubricating oil were loaded on board the barge. Each red painted drum was marked with a consecutive number and a description of the product it contained. A tally clerk checked each drum as it was lifted aboard, marking it off with a stubby pencil on a dog-eared sheet of paper. The drums were gently laid in position on the deck, on their sides, by the crane. Each drum was then jammed into position with wooden wedges before the next was lifted aboard. When all the drums were finally on board wire strops were tightened across the top of the stack to hold everything securely in place. They would not be able to move whatever rolling and pitching the weather might cause.

George and his *Serang* went along and inspected the loaded cargo carefully before deciding that everything was in order. They then recounted all the drums before George signed the cargo manifest. Now all that remained was to get customs clearance and a suitable weather forecast before sailing.

George went back to the tug bus and ,when he found the driver smoking in the shade of a thorn tree, told him to drive to the agent's offices. Mr Maroonian, the office manager, met George at the door of the office and then heaved his bulk into the bus for the short journey to the customs office.

'I'll fix everything for you, Captain George. Leave it to me.'

They went into the customs office, which was a hive of inactivity and approached the shabby, unshaven, uniformed customs officer at the desk. A ceiling fan lazily stirred the warm air in the room and dust motes danced in the stream of sunlight coming through a small, dirt streaked skylight. Maroonian let forth a stream of Farsi, waving his hands theatrically and thrusting the cargo manifest and tug's documents in front of the official.

'You wait,' replied the man in English with an insolent stare and he ambled slowly through a rear door, still clutching the papers.

They waited and then they waited some more. Twenty minutes passed.

'They're slower than the Second Coming,' hissed George through his teeth, hopping from one foot to the other.

'Not surprising,' said Maroonian. 'We didn't offer them any money.'

'Bloody hell,' exploded George. 'How much will it cost?'

'We'll try two hundred rials.' He held out a fat hand with nicotine stained fingers.

Reluctantly, George handed over two crumpled hundred rial notes from his pocket.

Maroonian lifted a flap in the counter and pushed his way through the narrow gap. He disappeared through the rear door of the office and George could hear muffled voices gradually increasing in volume. Maroonian came back through the door, still deep in argument with an unseen adversary but holding the necessary documents in his hand.

'Trouble?' asked George.

'None at all, Captain. Two hundred was quite enough to oil the wheels of commerce.'

George dropped Maroonian back at his office and went back to the tug to find that bunkering was completed.

'We'll sail on tomorrow mornings tide,' he told the crew and went up to the bridge to radio to the Iraqi pilot station at Al Wassiliya. He arranged for a pilot to board at ten thirty in the morning and went to find John to let him know the score.

'Suits me fine,' said John.

George left and headed for the Super's office.

'Morning, George.'

'Morning Captain Robinson,' he replied taking the seat that was offered. 'We're off tomorrow morning to the bright lights of Arabia.'

'Okay, George. I'll just offer some words of warning before you go. Don't take any short cuts. We don't want any rock dodging. Don't take any chances with the weather. And don't get into trouble in some house of ill repute in Dubai.'

'Chance would be a fine thing,' said George. 'Might find some decent beer there though.'

'Our agents in Dubai are Gray Mackenzie and they'll have a runner to meet you when you get into port. He'll give you all the help you need and he'll deliver my deep freeze to you as well. When you leave Dubai tell him to send me a telegram with your ETA and I'll be here to meet you when you berth.'

'Right you are, Captain. See you in about ten days, Allah and the weather permitting. You'll be able to freeze your assets when we get back.'

'You're a cheeky sod, George,' said the Super. 'Bon voyage, anyway.' George went home, whistling happily.

He spent the rest of the day with Kay and the children. Louise was still on holiday from school as Now Ruz coincided with Easter, giving the children an extended break. They went round to see the Longfords, which pleased the children and provided the adults with convivial company. The children played in the garden whilst their parents sat in deck chairs watching them. It was warm and pleasant in the afternoon sun and the time passed quickly.

'Are you going to the Taj tonight?' asked Liz Longford.

'What's on?'

'Don't you look at the weekly magazine?' she asked. 'It's Chitty-Chitty-Bang-Bang.'

'What the devil is that about?'

'It's a film about a magic car. Ideal for the kids.'

'Great, should suit me too,' said George. 'We'll come past just after seven and then we can all go together.'

It turned out to be a memorable evening for the children. They loved the film and were absolutely enthralled by it. When the wicked child catcher was caught up in his own net all the children broke into a ragged, spontaneous cheer. George hadn't realised how caught up in the story the children were. On the short walk home the boys ran ahead making noises like cars and chatting about the film. They would remember it for a long time to come.

'George,' said Kay, 'If you want to run on ahead and play cars as well, feel free.'

'Are you trying to tell me I'm not very mature?' he asked.

'Well, you like playing boats, so I thought you might like cars too.'

'Since we're talking about playing games, did you tell Liz and Peter about our new bed?'

'Behave yourself, George, or you'll find yourself on the settee tonight.'

They walked home arm in arm and put the children to bed. 'Can cars really fly, Dad?' asked young John.

'Maybe,' said George, smiling. 'I've never seen one but I'll keep an eye out and let you know if I do.' John was starting to have a mind of his own and no longer needed his sister to do the talking for him.

Kay and George lingered over a cup of coffee before going to bed. 'It will seem strange with you away,' said Kay. 'I've got used to us being together.'

'It won't be for long,' said George. 'What do you want me to bring back?'

'Just yourself but you could see what there is for the children.'

'I've been wondering about bicycles,' said George. 'Perhaps they'll have children's bikes the right size for them.'

'That would be fine,' Kay replied. 'Now. Hadn't we better see if our new bed can still take our weight without falling apart.'

'Best offer I've had today,' said George, draining his coffee cup. 'Let's go.'

George woke early the next morning. He wouldn't admit it but he was as excited as the children had been over last night's film. He got out of bed and went through to the kitchen where he put on the kettle to boil. He was still sitting at the table, day dreaming, when the kitchen filled with steam. There wasn't enough water left in the kettle for tea so he refilled it and started again. This time he remembered what he was doing and made a pot of tea. He carried two cups back into the bedroom and found Kay just waking up.

'Umm,' she said, 'Service in this hotel is improving.'

'Its not often I get up first,' said George getting back into bed with his cup of tea. 'I don't think it will become a habit.'

A few minutes later two blond heads poked around the door. All thoughts of another snooze were banished and they got up and got breakfast. George soon finished his and went off to get dressed. He wandered from room to room, whistling to himself, until Kay stopped him.

'Why don't you call the bus and get on down to the tug?' she asked. 'You're itching to get started.'

'Suppose I am. Is it that obvious? I'll give Ali a call.'

Within a few minutes the bus was at the door. George picked up his holdall with his spare clothes and toilet gear. The family all came to see him off.

'Take care,' said Kay.

'I will,' said George putting his arm round her waist and kissing her. 'Bye kids,' he called, but they were already more interested in playing with Tommy the dog. The hound was tearing around the garden chasing his own tail. Kay watched as George tossed his bag through the door and followed it into the bus. It pulled away with a clash of gears as he was closing the door. Kay waved as it reached the corner and she could see a hand thrust out of the window, waving back. She brushed her eyes with the back of her hand. 'Must be dusty this morning,' she said to herself and wiped away what definitely felt like a tear. George, meanwhile, was already deep in thought. How was he going to arrange watch keeping to the best advantage for everyone?

22

The tug bus stopped outside the bachelor flats and George went up the concrete steps to John's second floor flat taking two steps at a time. He jabbed his finger on the doorbell and heard it ringing inside the hall. Nothing happened so George rang the doorbell again, this time keeping his finger on the bell. There was still no answer. He rang for a third time and this time hammered his fist on the door too. A head appeared from the doorway next door.

'What's all the bloody row,' demanded the head, scowling furiously.

'Can't get any answer from John Henson.'

'Probably because he had one hell of a party last night. Half the bachelors in Khuzistan and every single female in the area were here. Leave the poor sod be, he'll have a head like Birkenhead this morning.'

'No chance,' said George, 'He should be at work. Does anyone have a spare key for his front door?

'I have' said the head and then disappeared inside the door like a tortoise going into its shell.

It reappeared a moment later, this time accompanied by an arm, a hand and a key.

'Thanks,' said George, grabbing the key.

'Put it back through my letter box,' said the head pulling itself inside the door once more. The door closed with a bang.

The key slipped into the Yale lock and smoothly opened John's front door. George went inside, turning on the hall light and wrinkling his nose at the smell of stale tobacco, stale booze and another sweeter smell that George didn't at first recognise.

'Wakey-wakey, rise and shine. Don't you know the morning's fine?' trilled George, loudly. 'Hands off cocks, put on socks.'

He walked carefully through the wreckage of the lounge, picking his way past overturned chairs and half-full glasses. There was still no reply from John so George went back to the hall and tried the door of the bedroom.

Inside all was in darkness, so George groped along the wall for the light switch. He smelt the sweet smell again and this time identified it as some sort of perfume. 'Smells like a tarts window box,' he muttered.

'Let there be light,' he bawled, throwing the switch and a scene of desolation met him. There were clothes thrown all over the room and in the middle was a bed with sheets and blankets strewn haphazardly over it.

A tousled head looked up from the bed.

'Oh shit,' said George. This head was definitely female.

'Where's John?' he asked, and in answer John's head appeared from beneath the bed covers.

'Time you were up,' said George, turning away from the apparitions in bed and he went back through to the kitchen and put on the kettle. He waited until it boiled and made two cups of strong black coffee. He found a tray in a cupboard so he put the coffee cups on it and went back to the bedroom where there were signs of life from both bodies.

George grinned as he recognised the lady as one of the schoolteachers from the expatriate school.

'Good morning,' he said, cheerfully. 'Do both of you gentlemen take sugar?'

He put the tray by the bed and hastily left the room, followed by two pillows that were aimed at his head.

Half an hour later they were on their way to the tug. John was still looking the worse for wear, as well as looking sheepish.

'Not a word of this around town, George, or you'll be right in it,' he said.

'Cost you a few beers,' said George.

They arrived at the jetty to find a van parked right by the tug nearly blocking the bottom of the gangway.

'What thoughtless prick left that there?' grumbled George.

'This thoughtless prick,' thundered Captain Robinson's voice from the deck of the tug. 'Thought you two were going to be on board well before this.'

'Unavoidable delay on the road,' said John.

'Didn't know they served beer on the road. Don't bloody breath near the van, you'll blister the paintwork. Get your backside aboard, George. We've installed a little something on the bridge for you.'

George went up the gangway and climbed the ladders to the bridge.

'*Voila!*' said the super waving his hand towards a large box of electronics that now stood behind the chart table. 'Don't say I never give you anything.'

George looked at the Decca logo on the box and at the display screen on the chart table.

'Decca Navigator,' he breathed. 'There must be a god somewhere after all.'

'Not God, George. Just me. There's a set of Decca charts in the drawer. That cargo of lubricating oil is worth a hell of a lot of hard cash and we can't afford to have it getting lost.'

'Well, we've got no excuses now. I suppose we'd better go and get the barge and be on our way.'

'Okay, George. Make sure Henson gets a bucket of coffee and don't let him try a hair of the dog. Best of luck and don't forget my deep freeze.' He casually waved a hand as he climbed into the van and left.

'As if I would,' said George and rang stand by on the telegraph.

He turned to the waiting quartermaster. 'I want to see the three quartermasters, the *Serang* and the *Tindal* in my cabin.'

'*Atcha, sahib.*'

George went down to his cabin, threw his hold-all into the bedroom and changed into his usual shirt and shorts. There was a knock at the door.

'Come in,' he called, and the five men crowded into the cabin.

'Salaam,' said George. '*Serang*, we're going to have three watches. I want you with one quartermaster and a sailor on one watch, the *Tindal*, the second quartermaster and one sailor as the second watch, and I will take the third watch with the third quartermaster and one sailor. The rest of the sailors will be on daywork as usual.'

'*Atcha, sahib*,' said the *Serang*, and translated the orders into Hindustani for the others.

'The *Tindal* will do the eight to twelve watch, you will do twelve to four, and I will take the four to eight. Understood?'

'Understood, *sahib*.'

'Okay. Stand by fore and aft. Lets go.'

The men went to their stations and George went back to the bridge.

'Let go everything,' he called and the Narimand started on its way upriver to collect the barge.

Within half an hour they were on their way down river again with the barge made fast alongside the tug. George called the pilot station on the radio to advise them that they would be ready for a pilot in five minutes and set course for the Iraqi side of the river and the small jetty at Al Wassiliya. He slowed the tug to a crawl and a small pilot boat peeled away from the jetty and headed towards them.

Two pilots climbed the ladder to the bridge. George knew one of them quite well from his time working in Abadan and the other was a much younger man.

'Trainee pilot, Captain George,' explained the elder man. 'He makes the work and I watch.'

'Great,' said George. 'Do you want me on the bridge?'

'Not necessary,' smiled the pilot. 'I call when we reach Rooka Buoy.'

It suited George well. He could check out the Decca Navigator to see that it was working properly before going below and taking it easy. He went behind the chart table and got out the northern Persian Gulf Decca chart. He unfolded it and put it on the chart table, putting chart weights on each end of it to hold it in place. He pressed the test button on the Decca Navigator and the dials all spun round. When he let the button go the dials all spun again and then re-settled in their places. He took the readings from the three dials, one red, one green and one purple, noting the figures down on a piece of scrap paper. He then transferred the readings to the chart, measuring exactly between the coloured markings before ruling in each position line. The three position lines crossed in a neat cocked hat, giving a position slap in the middle of the Shatt al Arab. George looked up and visually checked the position. 'Bingo!' exclaimed George. 'Exactly in the right place.' The modern marvels of electronic positioning were going to make life quite a lot easier for Captain George Penroy and his crew.

He went below. He would get lunch without interruption, check that John was still in one piece and put his feet up before the real voyage started. He wouldn't have much time to rest once they were out at sea. Time to read a chapter of his book before finding John. George was an avid reader and consumed novels at a rapid pace. At Bandar Mashur he even took his book on the bridge and read it when the tug was holding ships alongside whilst they made fast. The quartermaster would keep the tug on a steady course and George would sit in his pilot chair, with one ear on the radio, glancing up occasionally to see that all was going well.

He completed a chapter whilst lying horizontal on the settee in his day cabin. He didn't really think that people behaved as novels would have him believe. Would a young lady of high-class background part with her underwear and reputation as easily as the heroine? Not in George's experience. The ladies of the Hamburg and Amsterdam red light districts might happily dispense with both but in good old rural England it still only seemed to happen in the realms of fiction.

George's thoughts on novels reminded him that only that morning he had caught John in the act. 'Better go and check what he's been up to,' he thought. He heaved himself into a vertical position, slipped on his sandals and went out on to the deck. They were still in the river so he slid down the ladder to the lower deck and went into the saloon. No sign of John so he pushed open the chief engineer's cabin door and went in.

'Bloody hell, Henson,' he shouted. 'In your pit again. Too much bed and not enough sleep is your problem.'

John opened an eye.

'Give me a break, George. I'll miss lunch and kip through the afternoon, then I'll be up and about again when we're really on our way.'

'Just as well the engine room crew is on top of the job. I'll leave you in peace but I want a blow by blow description this evening.'

'No blowing, George, just the real thing. Now sod off and leave me be.'

George backed out quietly.

'I'll have my lunch now,' he said to the steward who was hovering nearby. 'And take the pilots some on the bridge, please.'

'I give pilots beer?'

'Okay,' agreed George. 'Two beers for the pilots and put it on my bill.'

The steward served George with the standard curry and hurried off to serve the pilots. George ate slowly. Time to finish lunch and have a cup of coffee before they reached the open sea.

When he went back on the bridge the tug and tow had left the Shatt al Arab estuary and was heading south into the Persian Gulf. The weather had deteriorated and a stiff northwesterly breeze was blowing, picking up sand from the desert and reducing the visibility to about three miles.

'Just what I need,' thought George, taking the readings from the dials of the Decca Navigator and transferring them to the chart. He marked the position. Only about another quarter of an hour and they would drop the pilot. He sent the quartermaster below to get the *Serang*, taking over the wheel himself whilst the helmsman was away.

'What's the forecast?' he asked the pilot.

'It should clear later this evening.'

'Thanks. Once you leave us I'll be taking the tow over the stern, so if you'll take us well clear of any other traffic it would be a help.'

'There's nothing due to arrive and you're the only sailing on this tide, so everything should be clear for you,' replied the senior pilot. 'When I go back to the pilot cutter I'll have a look on the radar and let you know if there is anything in sight.'

'Many thanks. It will make life a bit easier for me.'

The quartermaster returned with the *Serang* and George gave his instructions for taking up the tow. The old *Serang* nodded sagely and went to get the crew ready on the after deck. He had been at sea and working on tugs for many years and knew his job thoroughly. He smiled to himself, thinking that the job would go without a hitch as long as the captain *sahib* didn't make a pig's rear end of it.

The pilot stopped the tug about half a mile from the pilot station and handed over to George. Their boat bumped gently alongside and the two pilots scrambled aboard. They waved as the boat pulled away from the side but George was already busy transferring the tow from alongside to over the stern.

A crewmember climbed aboard the barge to let go the ropes and to make fast the main towrope. He crossed his arms above his head in the signal 'All fast' and leapt back aboard before the tug moved ahead. Slowly the coils of towing wire slipped over the stern as the tug pulled away from the barge. George stopped the tug's engines and let her drift slowly ahead until the last of the wire finally splashed over the stern and the manila rope hawser tightened over the towing arch and after bulwark. He pushed the telegraph to slow ahead and the towrope slowly lifted clear from the water. The barge started to move.

'Steer one three five,' said George, '*Exso, teen tally, pange.*'

He added the simple Hindustani numbers, one hundred, three tens, and five, to make sure that there would be no mistake.

'Steady on one three five,' called the quartermaster a few minutes later and George checked the compass. He chalked 135° on the board at the fore end of the wheelhouse and went back to the telegraph. He rang for half ahead and the tug slowly increased speed. The towrope occasionally dipped into the water and pulled taut again, dripping silvery drops of water back into the sea as the barge followed in the tug's wake.

'That'll do aft,' he shouted to the after deck and the crew stood down. The *Serang* came to the bridge with a sailor.

'Hamid Ali is your *pouri-wallah*, *sahib*.'

'Okay *Serang*. Does he know how to make coffee?'

The *Serang* questioned the sailor.

'Yes, *sahib*,' replied the sailor in singsong English, wobbling his head from side to side. 'Hamid make effing fine coffee.'

'Some kind soul has evidently taught him a few basic words of English,' thought George. 'He would probably eff and blind at the Seaman's Mission vicar's tea party, thinking his command of the language was effing brilliant.'

'Tell him coffee every hour,' said George, 'And every quarter hour he has to go aft and check that the tow rope is OK. He can go and take down the pilot flag now and put the towing signal up instead.'

The *Serang* left after passing on the orders and George rang the telegraph for full ahead. 'We'll see how the tow rides,' he thought, 'And ease her down again if necessary.'

The sailor returned rolling up the pilot flag and returning it to its position in the flag locker. He looked at George.

'Lookout,' said George and the man settled himself at the port side bridge window and gazed at the horizon. He would report anything he saw so George went to get a position on the chart. The Decca gave him a good reading and he marked it, along with the time, on the chart. He drew in the true course line of 135°. He would check what speed they were making after an hour and then step off the miles with his dividers to see when they could expect to sight anything. It wouldn't be for many hours yet. George settled down in the pilot chair. His four hour watch would be interrupted by dinner and later he would get a chance to relax and put his feet up again.

George regularly checked the tow and could see that the barge was rolling and pitching easily in the long swell that was coming from the north-west. Every few minutes the blunt bow of the barge would slap the water beneath it. Spray would fly and the towrope would vibrate for a few seconds. The towing hook on the tug would rattle before it settled down again to await the next large wave. He rang the telegraph for half ahead and then sent the sailor to find the Chief Engineer.

A few minutes later a bleary eyed John heaved his bulk up the bridge ladder.

'No peace for the wicked,' he moaned.

'At least I didn't blast you out of your bunk by blowing down the voice pipe.'

'Good thing too. What do you want?'

'Can you put the engine revs up to about mid point between half and full ahead, John?'

'Your wish is my command, master,' replied John, starting to wake up and find his sense of humour. 'I'll go and fix it now and order a couple of Shams while I'm at it. I take it we'll be splitting the bill?'

'Sure.'

John left, heading for the engine room. He made the necessary adjustments and after a shower and putting on clean clothes arrived back on the bridge with two icy green bottles of shams and two glasses. 'I'll keep lookout if you want to send the sailor for his *canna*,' he said. The sailor left, smiling his thanks and went aft to the galley, whilst John hauled a chair to the fore end of the bridge and kept a lookout ahead.

The barge was riding comfortably now and the towing hook quietly took the strain of the tow without complaint. George took another Decca reading and put the position on the chart. He would give it another hour, now that the tow had settled, before checking what speed they were making.

'I've told the steward we'll both eat on the bridge,' said John, and took another large gulp of his beer. 'I'm starting to feel human again,' he added.

'Was she worth it?'

'She certainly was, my boy. Don't know what she teaches the school children but she certainly taught me a few things last night.'

'You take care, sunshine,' replied George. 'She's one of McDougal's merry band of sinners. Mind you don't find the good Father round at your flat with a shotgun.'

'He's more likely to be round after my whisky,' retorted John. 'He can smell a cork coming out of a bottle at five miles range and has an automatic homing device under his cassock amongst other things.'

The steward arrived with a steaming tray of food and

laid it on the chart table. He dived down the ladder and returned with two more Shams, and John and George set too with gusto. The cook knew them both well by this time and always served large portions at every meal.

'I reckon that old cook must be well into his sixties,' said John, 'And he thinks of us as just a couple of growing boys.'

'Just as well,' replied George. 'I could eat a scabby dog.'

'In this place you probably will, sooner or later.'

'As long as it's well cooked it won't bother me.'

They worked their way happily through three courses, washed down with the continual Shams, and then ordered coffee to follow. George belched happily. 'Reckon I might have wind,' he commented, wiping a splurge of curry sauce from the chart table before it got on the chart.

'You're always full of wind. You could pass wind for England,' replied John, settling back in his chair.

'Reckon the visibility is improving a bit,' said George. 'It'll be getting dark soon, so that will make life a bit easier.' It was always easier to pick up a light at night than it was to see something in hazy daytime conditions. 'Reckon we'll be able to get Voice of the Desert on the radio soon. Might get some good music.'

Voice of the Desert was a radio station in Saudi Arabia, run by the Americans in the oil port at Ras Tannurah. All the latest pop music from America was pumped out over the airwaves, twenty-four hours a day and most ships in the area tuned in whenever they could.

'Pity the wind isn't from the South,' said George. 'For some reason the radio reception is much better then. Only trouble is that it gets really humid as well. See what stations you can get, John.'

John fiddled with the controls on the radio receiver and, sure enough, the strains of jazz music came through, loud and clear.

'I'm not in to jazz,' said John and after more atmospherics managed to find a Country and Western station. 'That'll do me,' he said. 'I'm surrounded by cowboys anyway.'

'Cheeky sod,' muttered George. 'I've wrung more water out of my socks than you've sailed over.'

They chatted quietly after that, whilst a lonesome cowboy on the radio yodelled about his lost horse and darkness gradually fell over the Gulf. The visibility had cleared completely now and they could see the dark line where the horizon met the sky all around them. The stars came out and shone brilliantly in the pollution free atmosphere. 'They look real pretty but I don't need them tonight. Not with Mister Decca's magic box of tricks,' said George.

He checked the position on the hour and worked out how far they had travelled. 'We're managing about eight knots. The tow has settled down at this speed, so we might as well carry on like this. We won't see any land during the night, so perhaps we'll be able to get a good night's sleep. I'll have to keep an eye on the Tindal during the eight to twelve watch, but hopefully I'll get a couple of hours before midnight.'

'Don't call me,' said John. 'My engine crew have strict instructions only to bother me in dire emergency. Fancy a game of cards after your watch?'

'Might as well. What are we playing for?'

'Better stick to match sticks or Kay will be on the warpath when you get home.'

'When the cat's away,' said George, tapping the side of his nose with a forefinger. 'Ten rials a hand.'

'Last of the big spenders,' said John. 'Get your lookout back up here for the last half hour and I'll go set up the cards.'

23

During that first night George didn't get very much rest. The *Tindal* came on watch at eight o'clock and he wasn't too sure of himself. George showed him how to take a position from the Decca Navigator but the man wasn't too confident when any other traffic showed up. The rank of *Serang* was equivalent to that of bosun in an English crew and *Tindal* equated to a bosun's mate. Such ranks would not normally be in charge of a navigational watch at sea. George had hoped that they would be experienced enough to leave on their own, but at first it wasn't to be.

George and John had not long settled down to their first hand of cards when there was a knock at the cabin door.

'*Sahib*, ship coming,' said the sailor. George went quickly up to the bridge to find that there was a light on the horizon, four points on the starboard bow. He focussed the binoculars on the light and the navigation lights of a ship were clearly visible. Two masthead lights and a green side light. George watched for a few moments until he was sure it was passing well clear.

'It's all clear, *Tindal*. No problem,' said George and he went below again.

Half an hour later the process was repeated, and this time the ship was right ahead. It was showing a starboard light again and crossing so once more it was no problem. George retreated to the cards once more, only to be interrupted again half an hour later.

'Holy shit,' he said to John, 'I'm going to be called out for every bloody ship in the Persian Gulf.'

'Shouldn't have joined if you can't take a joke,' said John as George wearily went back to the bridge.

This time there was a ship on a collision course, so George stayed on the bridge. The Narimand was clearly showing her towing lights so it was the duty of the approaching ship to alter course and avoid a collision. Sure enough the ship made a large alteration of course to starboard and then slowly passed down the port side of the tug. George went back below.

Things quietened down for a while after that and the cards flowed. A little heap of ten rial coins built up at George's side and he gloated every time the pile got bigger. They played till midnight when George once again went to the bridge, this time with a hundred rials in change clinking in his shorts pocket. The *Serang* was taking over from the *Tindal* and there was a midnight position on the chart. He checked it against the Decca readings and found it was correct. At least that part of the watch went well. They had made another 30 miles, which meant they were still making nearly eight knots. They were now over sixty miles south east of the mouth of the Shatt Al Arab River and well on their way. Away on the port bow there was a glow on the horizon from the flares on Kharg Island. The flares were over thirty miles away but still showed quite clearly.

George checked that the *Serang* was happy with the situation and went back to his cabin. He would be called again at four in the morning for his watch and he threw off his shirt and shorts and climbed into his bunk and under the covers.

Suddenly he was awake.

'*Sahib*,' came a voice from the darkness, 'Ship overtaking.'

'Ship overtaking?' It took George a few seconds for the words to register. He heaved himself out of his bunk, rubbing the sleep from his eyes, threw on a pair of shorts and a jersey and went up to the bridge.

'Where's the ship?' he asked, waiting for his night vision to take effect. He couldn't see a thing.

The *Serang* pointed out on the starboard quarter. 'Overtaking,' he repeated.

Suddenly George saw what he was talking about.

'It's our own bloody tow.'

The wind had shifted to the east and had pushed the barge well out on the starboard side and the towrope stretched tightly over the quarter of the tug. George had heard about this before but never experienced it. A tug and its tow could be different sizes, shapes and draft, and the wind could affect the tow in a different way to the tug. In extreme cases the tow could actually overtake the tug if no action was taken.

'Okay *Serang*,' said George. 'Go and get yourself a cup of *cha*. I'll watch her for a while.'

The *Serang* scuttled thankfully away while George carefully watched the tow. Every few minutes the towrope would slacken and then come taught again, giving the tug a jerky sideways motion that George wasn't happy with at all. 'Only one thing to do,' he thought checking the last Decca position to see they were well clear of land. 'We'll take a turn out of her and start again.'

He altered course ten degrees to port and when the tug had steadied again altered ten degrees more. After each alteration the tow dropped further astern and George repeated the process until a full three hundred and sixty degree turn had been made and the barge was right astern again. He was surprised how little time the turn took as the tug was already back on course when the *Serang* puffed his way back up the bridge ladder. 'All fixed, *Serang*,' said George, quietly heaving a sigh of relief. 'Let me know if there is any more trouble.' He went wearily back to his bed, only to find that he was wide awake. It took half an hour of reading his novel before his eyelids started to droop. He dropped his book over the side of the bunk and was asleep instantly.

It only seemed a few seconds later and a hand was shaking his shoulder. 'One bell,' intoned a doleful voice and George peered blearily at his watch. A quarter to four and time to get ready for duty. He pulled on his clothes. Trousers and a thick jersey this time as it could be quite cold during the early hours. Slowly he pulled himself up the bridge ladder and looked around.

'Coffee,' he croaked and a steaming mug was thrust into his hand. He took a deep draft. 'Christ!' He hastily went to the bulwark and spat the concoction over the side.

'Too hot?' asked the *Serang*.

'No bloody sugar,' said George 'And don't laugh,' he added seeing a pearly white grin spreading over the *Serang's* weathered, dark features. 'Bet you only did it to wake me up. Where are we?'

The *Serang* stubbed a broad, dusky coloured digit on the chart and George checked off the distance. His circular tour last night had dropped the average down to seven knots for the watch. Not too bad though. They must be nearly abeam of Bandar Bushire. George thought of One Eyed Ibrahim, the taxi driver. Bushire was Ibrahim's original home and he was always saving his taxi fares so that he could go back there and retire in style. 'Bet it's a right dung heap of a place,' thought George. As far as he knew there was little in Bushire other than a small fishing industry. George always automatically categorised any small town east of Calais as a dung heap unless he knew better.

The position also showed George that they had drifted slightly towards the Iranian side of the Gulf. He put a new position on the chart to make sure the *Serang* had got it right and then adjusted the course to bring the tug back on track.

'Steer one four five,' he told the quartermaster.

The helmsman brought the tug on to the new course.

'Steady, *sahib. Exso, chahar tally, pange,*' he called.

George settled into the pilot's chair, pushing his hands deep into his pockets and leaning back.

'Tell me if you see ships,' he ordered and closed his eyes. His chin kept hitting his chest when he really dropped off to sleep but he persevered with his rest, only fully waking when the sun rose over the eastern horizon in a red gold glare. He heaved himself to his feet and checked the compass before taking a Decca reading. There was no record of when the compass was last adjusted and no deviation card from which to work the compass error but the latest position indicated that the compass wasn't too far out. George would err on the side of safety and make sure that the tug didn't come anywhere near any shoals or rocks. Ten miles from any shore should be right.

'Keep good lookout,' he told the sailor on watch. 'I go below for half hour.'

He went below to his cabin, grabbed a towel and headed for the bathroom on the lower deck. A steaming shower revived him and when he went back to the cabin he put on a clean pair of shorts and a fresh shirt. He climbed the bridge ladder and put on the kettle. A cup of coffee would keep him going till the steward started work. George was looking forward to his breakfast.

At seven o'clock George was again putting a position on the chart when John appeared on the bridge. He was shaved and showered and looking a hundred percent better than he had the day before.

'Nothing like a good night's sleep,' he said.

'And I've certainly had nothing like one,' said George in reply.

'I'll keep an eye on things for an hour for you. Go and put your feet up for a while and then we'll pig out on a good breakfast at eight.'

'Good thinking. Can you work the Decca?'

'Is the Pope a Catholic?' asked John.

'Reckon he might be but I'm not so sure about his oppo, McDougal. He's a bit suspect.'

'Nothing wrong with McDougal that a good woman wouldn't put right. Or a bad one for that matter.'

George went down to his cabin and picked up his book from where it had landed on the deck last night. He lay on the settee and before he had finished reading the first paragraph he was asleep. However, no sooner was he asleep than he felt a hand shaking his shoulder. Wearily he opened his eyes to find John Henson grinning down at him.

'You looked so peaceful that I left you till nine. Now, why don't you get yourself another shower while I get the cook working on our breakfast? Say a quarter of an hour?'

It was the last thing George felt like but he struggled into a vertical position and dragged his shirt over his head. He threw it into a corner and grabbed his towel. 'Don't know if I'll live till breakfast,' he croaked as he went down the ladder towards the bathroom. The steaming rush of water from the shower completed his transformation back into the living world and he climbed the ladder back to his cabin feeling nearly half human. Breakfast completed the job and after a cigarette he went back to the bridge.

The crew had washed everything down whilst he ate and the decks steamed gently as they dried in the morning sun. The *Tindal* was on watch and had gained confidence now that it was daylight. George checked the position and watched the tow for a few minutes before going back below to his cabin. There he found John, shuffling the greasy deck of cards that they played with. As soon as he went through the door John started to deal.

'Time for revenge,' he said, putting a heap of ten rial coins on the table. 'Shake the moths out of your wallet,Penroy, and do your worst.'

'Deal them all from the top, Yorkie. If I've got a hand like a foot I'll know you've rigged the cards with your Liverpool shuffle.'

'That's fighting talk where I come from,' said John, 'Put your money where your mouth is.'

An hour later and George was a hundred rials richer. 'Last hand,' said John. 'Double or quits.'

'Okay, sucker.' George dealt another hand.

He won again, much to John's disgust and the pile of rials grew. 'Don't put them away. We'll have a return match tonight and it must be my turn to win.'

'Not against the superior brain power of the deck department, you won't,' boasted George. 'Get back down the black hole and do some work while I go and see what is happening in the real world. Curry for lunch at one. See you then.'

George went out on deck and sat in a deck chair. The sun was warm on his face and it wasn't long before he dozed off. When he woke his face was sore. Even at this time of year the sun was quite strong. He went into his cabin and looked in the mirror. He had two white circles around his eyes where his sunglasses had protected them from the sun. 'I look like a bemused panda,' he thought and he rubbed Vaseline from the medical kit on his face. Not as good as sun tan lotion or calamine but better than nothing.

At noon he went back on the bridge to check the position. They had averaged seven and a half knots since leaving the Shatt and were now a hundred and fifty miles into their voyage. Off on the port side he could see the foothills of Iran over twenty miles away. He was glad that Captain Robinson had arranged for the Decca Navigator to be on board. He could check that they weren't making any leeway and getting too close to the land at any time. It made life so much easier and took away a lot of worry.

He went below for his lunch to find John already opening two cold Shams beers. 'Get that down you, George. You look as if you need it.'

'Reckon I do,' said George, helping himself to a large plate of curry and rice and ladling mango chutney on top of it. He attacked the pile of food with great energy, washing it down with mouthfuls of Shams.

'Trouble with curry is that it makes me fart,' he said conversationally.

'Everything makes you fart. Have you been to Dubai before?'

'Sure have,' replied George. 'Went there in fifty seven when there was sod all there but desert, a creek and a few mud huts next to the fort.'

'They say it's built up a lot since then.'

'I hope so. They've been making a mint since they discovered oil there. I hear they are building as fast as they can go and that most of the stuff in the bazaar there is duty free.'

'Don't let them discharge the cargo too fast then, George. We want to get ashore and recharge the old batteries whilst we're there.'

'I might look like a cabbage but I'm not really that green,' laughed George. 'I've got to find something for the kids and for Kay as well, or I'll be in trouble. We'll be there for a couple of days. You can arrange a few engine repairs and extend our stay if necessary. That will solve the problem.'

'Means you can blame it on me when Robinson asks what took you so long,' complained John.

'He isn't going to ask. As long as he gets his new deep freeze in one piece he isn't going to bother us. Anyway, we can always say we had to wait for delivery of the deep freeze.'

'You're not as daft as you look, young George.'

'Softly, softly catchee monkey,' replied George with a wink, tapping the side of his nose with a forefinger.

George finished his curry and polished the plate with a piece of *chupatti*. 'Tell the cook that was very good,' he said to the steward. 'Coffee for me at quarter to four,' he added. 'I'm heading for my pit for the afternoon. It's alright for those who don't have to keep watch.'

John laughed. 'Think I might do the same even if I don't have to keep watch. See you later, George.'

24

George went on watch again at four and took over from the *Serang*. Both the *Serang* and *Tindal* were becoming used to dealing with the shipping traffic that passed and George was getting called to the bridge less often. He had slept for most of the afternoon and was feeling much refreshed.

They had been at sea for twenty-four hours and George looked at the last position on the chart with interest. The sturdy old Narimand was puffing along quite happily with her tow and she had averaged seven and a half knots for the voyage so far. He looked ahead with his binoculars, hoping to see the light float off Ras Mutaf Island. It shouldn't be far away according to Mister Decca. He focussed the glasses on a spec on the horizon and, sure enough, the light float showed up clearly. An hour later George marked the time and position on the chart as they came abeam of the navigation mark. His visual fix agreed exactly with the electronic position. All was well in the navigation department.

George looked out on the port side to where the foothills of Bushire Province showed clearly above the horizon. 'If you could just walk due East from here, ' thought George, 'You would cross the mountains into Pakistan, then through India and on into China before finally coming to the sea again at the Pacific Ocean.' Idly he tried to calculate how many miles that would be but gave it up in favour of drinking his first cup of coffee of the watch.

There were plenty of ships around. The tug was on the route through the Gulf that large tankers took towards Kharg Island. They surged past either way, flying light on the way in and heavily laden on the way out. These days they were starting to call the ships VLCCs. That was short for Very Large Crude Carriers, which George thought was a particularly stupid thing to call a ship. He could see nothing wrong with the term that had formerly been used. 'Super tanker' was quite adequate in George's book and he could see no need for what he thought of as poncy initials.

Shortly after George had consumed his third coffee another large tanker was sighted on the horizon ahead. It had no sooner appeared when a signal lamp started flashing towards the tug. 'Some bored second mate with sod all better to do,' muttered George as he pulled the Aldis lamp from its box and plugged it in. He flashed the answering code and watched as the first word of the message was sent. 'W-h-a-t' he spelt out. He flashed again. 'S-h-i-p'.

He flashed again. It was the usual question and he flicked through the reply. 'Narimand. Abadan to Dubai.'

The tanker flashed back her name in reply. 'VLCC English Tradition. Rotterdam to Kharg Island.'

'Thanks. Bon voyage,' replied George and then ignored all further flashing. He was getting concerned that the tanker was going to pass rather close down his port side. 'Hope the stupid bugger can see our towing signal,' he thought as he altered his course twenty degrees to starboard to make sure that they could see the tow. 'Ugly great bastard could run over our barge without even feeling a bump.'

The tanker eventually passed about a quarter of a mile away and George could see the officer of the watch quite clearly through his binoculars. He waved to the figure that lounged over the bridge dodger and brought the tug back on its course as an answering wave came back. Better safe than sorry.

During that evening George was called to the bridge for another close encounter which worried him greatly. The Tindal was getting a little too confident and had not called George until a fast cargo ship was getting rather close to the Narimand's tow. The ship was overtaking and either had not seen the tug's towing lights, or didn't understand them. George took in the scene as he arrived on the bridge and swiftly plugged in the Aldis lamp again. He hurriedly trained it aft and flashed it, first on the barge and then on the bridge of the fast closing ship. It certainly did the trick. The sleek cargo boat hastily made a large alteration of course to starboard and swept past the barge and tug at high speed. It must have been doing more than twenty knots and the wash as it passed caused the tow and the tug to pitch frantically into the waves. George flashed his Aldis lamp once again as the ship passed, to show his displeasure and then broadcast a rude message on the VHF radio just for good measure. If the 'ignorant prick who doesn't keep a proper lookout and who has just narrowly missed a tug and tow' ever received the message, he didn't reply and the cargo ship rapidly pulled ahead and disappeared over the horizon.

Before leaving the bridge George checked the latest position. It looked as if the tug was slowing down a bit. He adjusted the course by a degree to bring the tug back on the track he had chosen and went below. As he went down the ladder he called to the *Tindal*.

'*Tindal*. Any more ship come bloody close, you tell me, *jaldi jaldi*.'

'*Atcha, sahib*.'

He would probably call George if a porpoise swam near in the future. George went back to his cabin where he was in the process of losing all his recent winnings, much to the delight of John.

'Bit too close for comfort, that was.'

'Don't worry about it, George. No harm done. Now get on and deal.'

'You don't understand what a lonely job it is, being in command,' said George, dolefully.

'Bollocks!' said John, picking up his cards. 'That's just bullshit put out by the deck department to make them feel important.'

'Five eighths fitter,' said George, contemptuously. 'Don't knock what you don't understand.'

He looked at his cards. 'What sort of a bloody hand is this?' he hissed, 'Can't you deal anything better?'

John laughed and proceeded to win the hand and take George's last ten rial piece. 'I've got no more coins,' he said, putting a hundred rial note on the table. 'Give me some change and we'll see who's in luck tonight.'

They chatted as they played and coins passed backwards and forwards between them as the game progressed. At ten o'clock George called a halt. 'I must go and see where we are and then kip out or I'll never make it for the four to eight in the morning.'

'Okay, sunshine. I'll go and get some magazines for you while you're on the bridge. Might give you a bit of a lift.'

'More dirty books, Henson? You'll go blind before you're forty.' He went up to the bridge and it wasn't long before he was back in his bunk flicking through the pages of the latest Playboy magazine. He dozed off with the light still on and the magazine over his face still open at the centrefold. He woke shortly after midnight, feeling cold, so he pulled on another blanket, put out the light and knew no more till he was called for his watch.

He automatically checked the position that the *Serang* had marked on the chart and found it to be accurate. Their average speed was down a little but George was happy with the progress. It also meant that they would probably arrive in a little over thirty-two hours which indicated that they would approach Dubai at around noon, in daylight. 'Good timing,' he thought. 'Have a quiet night ashore and then start the discharge the next day.'

The tug trundled on, slowly eating up the watery miles whilst George lounged in the pilot chair reading another of John's Playboy magazines. He cracked up at the jokes page and filed away the best ones in his mind for use when he got back to Abadan. He had an extremely retentive brain for jokes and was fast getting a reputation around town as having a hilarious story for any occasion. He was also quite adept at mimicking accents and could take off many of the other tug captains. He would often baffle the pilots in Mashur by copying someone else's tone and accent so that they couldn't work out who was working each tug. His talent also came in handy when the in crowd met and he could keep them entertained for hours.

Another day dawned and passed without incident. No more cargo ships with inattentive officers and the tankers still passed in orderly fashion. They were not far away from Lavan Island where the Iranian Oil Company had another crude oil terminal. The amount of oil that came out of the country never ceased to amaze George and he often wondered what was left underground when the millions of tons of black gold gushed out into the waiting tankers. Was there a great black hole into which the whole of the desert would disappear one day? Would the mountains and hills be sucked down and form valleys? He also wondered what became of all the oil. The tankers spewed it out into terminals in Japan, Europe and America where it was eventually turned into exhaust fumes by cars, lorries and trains. Somewhere in the atmosphere was the residue of what came out of the earth. How could that amount of carbon stay up there?

Although he occasionally pondered these things he didn't worry about them. He certainly didn't thirst for knowledge. For now he was content with his lot and provided that he could keep Kay and the children in relative comfort he required little else from life. He couldn't understand how people could get so tied up with something that they would become activists. Not only did he let sleeping dogs lie, he was quite happy to act like one.

The third night at sea also passed without incident and when George went on the bridge at midnight to check the position there was a pinprick of light four points on the port bow from Sirri Island. He adjusted the course and made sure that they would pass at least five miles off the island. The small offshore island belonged to Iran but according to the Admiralty Pilot book only a few Arabs lived there. 'There must be fresh water there,' thought George, and he wondered if anyone looked after the navigation light other than the peripatetic Persian Gulf Lighting Service that operated out of Bahrain. He knew they had a buoy laying and service ship called the Relume that called at most of the remote places in the Gulf. The crew regularly serviced the south light on Kharg Island and they were just as regularly arrested by the Iranian soldiers who took them to be an invasion force from their traditional foe, the Iraqis.

There were plenty of passing ships to be seen and George was kept busy checking that each one would pass clear. They were now only about a hundred miles from the Straits of Hormuz or as they were better known by sailors, the Quoins. The Quoins were islands in the strait and it was a popular estimate that a different ship passed them every minute of the day. All traffic in and out of the Gulf converged at this point and with the number of oil ports and the upsurge of building in the former Trucial States it was no wonder the place was busy. There would be no watch below for George. He would have to remain on or near the bridge for most of the time.

For most of the day, apart from meal times, George took over the watch from the *Tindal* and *Serang*. John joined him on the bridge and they chatted in desultory fashion as the time slowly passed. By mid-day there was a smudge on the horizon ahead. Somewhere in the distance there was land. George regularly checked the Decca Navigator, resetting it each hour to make sure that the readings were accurate. He was now using the large-scale chart for the approaches to Dubai and steadily they were closing in on their destination.

Gradually the dark line on the horizon hardened into irregular shapes and through the binoculars the first details of the shore could be seen. There were far more buildings to be seen than when George had been there in fifty-seven. The oil money had been turned into high rise bricks and mortar. George swung the engine telegraph to 'stand by' and waited for the answering ring from the engine room. It was time to slow down.

The tug gradually reduced speed in response to George's orders and the crew spilled out on to the after deck to take in the towrope. They heaved it shorter and shorter until the barge was just a few feet astern of the tug. A crewman leapt the short distance between the two craft and a heaving line snaked after him. He let go the towrope from the tug and it was quickly brought aboard, dripping water and seaweed onto the after deck around the seamen's feet. George manoeuvred the tug alongside the barge and ropes were quickly heaved taught and made fast. They would make the last few miles with the barge alongside where it was more easily controlled.

'Put the 'G' flag up,' George said to the sailor on watch on the bridge. He handed him the blue and yellow striped flag and the sailor hurried up to the monkey island where he quickly lashed the flag on to the halyard and hauled it aloft. It was the International Code Flag signifying that the tug required a pilot. George turned to the VHF radio and checked the volume control.

'Dubai Pilots, this is tug Narimand.'

The radio crackled with atmospherics but there was no reply. They were still half an hour away from Dubai Creek so George headed the tug towards the entrance at slow speed calling again on the radio every few minutes. They were soon in clear sight of the Creek and still no reply.

'Sod them,' said George to John. 'If they don't answer soon we'll just creep into the Creek by ourselves. It's fairly deep water as far as I remember.'

He had no sooner spoken than a small boat roared out of the Creek entrance. George trained the binoculars on it and was relieved to see the red and white pilot flag flying above the tiny wheelhouse. He stopped the tug and let it drift and the approaching boat swept in a great circle and neatly dropped alongside the tug. Two men jumped on board and were escorted to the bridge by the *Serang*.

'Afternoon, Captain,' said the first, who was a European dressed in navy slacks and a white uniform shirt with epaulettes. 'I'm your pilot. We're going to berth you at the Oil Exploration Company's berth.'

'Okay, pilot. She's all yours.'

George turned to greet the second person as the pilot rang the telegraph for slow ahead.

'Christ,' thought George, irreverently. The second visitor was a tall, longhaired apparition, wearing shorts, a khaki shirt and open sandals with dusty toes sticking out of them. He looked like an illustration of Jesus from a child's book of the New Testament and seemed to be carrying a large ladies handbag that was decorated with coloured beads.

'Good afternoon,' said George, warily.

'Afternoon, dear fellow,' came the reply in carefully modulated Oxford English tones. 'I'm your agent, Stuart, but call me Calum. Thought I'd better come aboard and show the flag, old boy. You'll be needing my services, no doubt.'

'Certainly will,' said George. 'Care for a drink?'

'Thought you'd never ask, old chap. Don't suppose you've got a snifter of brandy?'

'You don't suppose correctly,' said George. 'It's Iranian beer, Iranian beer or Iranian beer.'

'How about an Iranian beer then?' said Stuart, 'In a tall glass if possible, old fruit.'

'Our average toothbrush mug is about six inches high,' muttered George as he sent for the steward. 'What about you, pilot?'

'Same for me, please. It won't take us long to get along-side and then you can go ashore and get the real thing. Canned and exported all the way from England.'

'I'd better get the business finished first,' said George, watching Calum Stuart sink a whole glass of Shams at one go. His prominent Adam's Apple bobbed up and down with each gulp.

The pilot pointed ahead to a small berth in the creek. 'That's where we're going. You'd better take over and park the damn thing when we get closer. It's not often I get to handle any tugs and certainly not when they've got barges alongside.'

It suited George to do the last of the manoeuvre himself. He no longer liked to watch someone else handle his ship. With the minimum of fuss he took the barge alongside and the crew made it fast. The pilot leapt ashore and jumped into a waiting car, leaving George with Calum Stuart.

'Come on down to the cabin,' said George and they went below.

'Will the customs come aboard or will we have to go ashore to sign in?'

'Already done, old boy,' drawled Stuart. 'Thought I'd arrange it before you arrived. A little dash of Dirhams in the right dirty paw and anything is possible here.'

'Great, ' said George. 'What about the cargo.'

'We don't start the discharge until the day after tomorrow,' said Stuart. 'National Holiday tomorrow, old fruit, so you can take it easy. Are you coming ashore tonight?'

'We'll need some local cash,' said George, 'And so will my crew. They all want a sub.'

'Easily done, dear boy.'

Stuart opened the oversized, decorative handbag and tipped a huge wad of currency notes on to the table. 'How much did you want?'

George took out his list from the safe and laid it on the table. He made a few quick calculations once Stuart had given him the exchange rate and then signed for the amount in triplicate. He counted out the correct amount and put it in the safe whilst Stuart scooped the rest back into his voluminous handbag.

'Tell you what, old sport,' said Stuart languidly, 'I'll come back in a few hours and I'll take you and the Chief out on the town.'

He waved a limp wrist at George and disappeared shoreward.

'Wonder what we've let ourselves in for, John? Do you reckon he's AC/DC or just public school?'

'Don't worry about it, George. Even if he is a poofter there's two of us. We'll be okay. Happen the posh bugger will buy us a few drinks.'

George called the steward and arranged to give out the money to the crew. They would all want to go ashore too. When the *Serang* arrived to oversee things George gave him his instructions for the night.

'At least one man on watch on deck and one in the engine room too. I don't want any of our equipment disappearing ashore during the night, and don't sell off any of our stores either.'

It wouldn't be the first time that ships stores had been sold ashore by a ship's crew.

'*Atcha, sahib.*'

The crew lined up outside the cabin door and one by one the *Serang* let them in to sign for their money and pocket the cash. George took the usual thumbprints instead of signatures and was pleased when the balance of cash at the end tallied with what he had written on the paper. The rest would be shared between him and John.

'Right,' said George when the last of the crew had left. 'Let's get something to eat to line the stomach and then we'll head for the bright lights with JC Super Star. Wonder if he'll line up a good evening for us?'

'Let's hope so,' agreed John. 'Shouldn't think we can come to much harm here. It's a Muslim country so there won't be too many distractions.'

'Don't you believe it. You should have seen Basrah in the old days. That was in a Muslim country too.'

George made sure the safe was locked and also locked his cabin door when he went for his dinner. Sharia Law might recommend the amputation of a hand for stealing but he still wasn't going to take the chance of losing any of his possessions. And he didn't want to be involved with any court case in a foreign country. Better safe than sorry was a good precept to follow.

When dinner finished George and John headed for a shave, shower and shampoo before getting dressed in civvy clothes. George even went so far as putting on a tie, something he normally avoided like the plague. 'Stupidest thing in the world,' he would say. 'Tying something round your neck when you really need it unobstructed for ease of drinking.'

They sat on deck in the warmth of the evening and waited for Calum Stuart to return. The last rays of the evening sun were lighting the nearby buildings and the local mosque was winding up the volume of its amplifier to call the faithful to evening prayer. 'Good timing,' thought George to himself. 'Wonder when Stuart will turn up?'

They didn't have to wait long before a taxi pulled up at the gangway and Stuart decanted, resplendent in flowery shirt and slacks, with a cravat tied neatly around his scraggy neck.

'JC has got really dolled up,' said John.

'Looks like a flower power fairy to me,' muttered George, darkly. 'Bet he's into poetry and he smokes pot. I'll stick to my own fags tonight. Never know what whacky baccy he might have in his.'

They tumbled down the steep gangway and got into the back of the taxi whilst Calum got back into the front.

'Bring on the dancing girls,' said John while Calum spoke to the driver in Arabic and they roared away from the jetty.

25

Calum Stuart draped a casual arm over the back of his car seat and turned to George and John. 'Got a reservation to eat later but thought you might like to do a pub crawl to start with,' he drawled.

'Sounds good to us,' they agreed.

They sped along a three lane tarmac highway towards the town. Where once there had been single story Arab dwellings and the occasional wind tower, high rise complexes were growing out of the desert sand. There was construction everywhere. Oil money was clearly making Dubai into a city of some standing, and no one was wasting any time. In the past ten years Dubai had graduated from a nineteenth century sleepy Arab village into a twentieth century, cosmopolitan city.

The car pulled in to a hotel forecourt and swished to a halt. The three of them walked through automatic revolving doors into the air-conditioned comfort of a five star establishment. 'My god,' gasped George, gazing around at the expanse of marble floor the size of a football pitch. 'Can we afford to drink in a palace like this?'

'Don't worry, old fruit,' said Calum. 'Prices around here are at duty free levels and the meal later tonight is on the Oil Exploration Company. They wanted to show their gratitude for a safe delivery of cargo. No expense spared, so you can fill your boots.'

They sank into plush armchairs in the bar and ordered drinks. George and John settled for lager whilst Calum preferred a large brandy. When it arrived he swirled it around the balloon glass and sniffed appreciatively. 'First today,' he murmured softly. 'Chin, chin, chaps.'

The brandy wasn't savoured for long. Before the beers were half finished Stuart had upended his glass and with one large gulp he demolished the full measure. He dabbed carefully at his lips with a large red spotted handkerchief before signalling to a hovering waiter for a second round. It was evident that he was settling in for a long session.

Between the second and fifth brandies Calum Stuart filled them in with a little of his background. He had been born in pre-Second World War Edinburgh and was the youngest of three sons. His family came from an obscure branch of Scottish nobles but the Stuart line had fallen on hard times and lived a life of genteel poverty. He had passed the eleven plus examination to attend the local grammar school but luckily some long forgotten ancestor had left enough in trust for Calum Stuart to be further educated, privately, in an institution for the sons of minor aristocracy.

Much to the surprise of his father and pleasure of his doting mother he had obtained several passes in the Scottish Higher Certificate examinations. Upper class Queen's English had overlaid his natural Scots accent and he was well fitted for the life of a country gentleman. His elder brothers had, by this time, exhausted their parent's meagre savings and so the youngest Stuart was faced with the unwelcome task of finding some form of gainful employment.

During the early fifties the youthful Stuart gained a foothold on the lower rungs of commerce in a banking establishment. Sadly, he had blotted his copybook one evening when leaving one of Edinburgh's seedier drinking establishments. The local constabulary apprehended him in a Princes Street doorway whilst he was defiling the footpath and when asked what he thought he was doing, told the officer in time honoured fashion to 'Go forth and multiply.' The procurator fiscal had deemed such a heinous crime worthy of a five pound fine and had warned Stuart not to appear before him in the future. The bank, however, was made of much sterner stuff and had decided that they no longer required the services of such a hardened criminal. His father then called in a favour owed by a business friend and the errant Calum was apprenticed to the firm of Gray Mackenzie and Company as a tea planter in Assam.

He had been given a third class passage aboard a British India Company cargo ship to India and had then taken a train into the wilds of the interior where he started learning the basics of overseeing the growing, harvesting and marketing of tea. Whilst there he also gained a fair understanding of Hindustani, the virtue of the planter's eldest daughter and an oversized capacity for the consumption of pink gin. He would have happily stayed in India but the days of the Raj were long over, the planter was beginning to suspect his motives regarding his daughter and Gray Mackenzie had sold their tea plantations to the fledgling Indian state. They transferred young Stuart to a job as a shipping agent in the Persian Gulf. There he prospered and after working in most ports around the area he had finally settled to life in Dubai, where times were easy and most of his appetites could be indulged.

George had also discovered that Calum was still single, fancy-free and knew all the best nightspots in town. They settled their bar bill and, at John's prompting, moved on to a livelier venue. George didn't think he needed female company but nevertheless went along to see how the night progressed. He had a fair idea of where Calum and John might end up and was rather sure that he wouldn't be joining them.

Their taxi dropped them next at a nightclub. Above the door a large flashing neon sign advertised the 'Carioca Club' and below were advertisements for their top of the bill, internationally famous entertainment. George briefly wondered if the show would be from Rio but soon found that the shapely hostesses mainly came from Wolverhampton and would sit at your table and drink coloured water for an inflated price if asked. Calum and John seemed to find this an acceptable practice and were soon deeply in conversation with two scantily dressed Brummie ladies with remarkable figures and whose accents could have been cut with a knife. George settled for more lager and watched the goings-on with interest.

After about an hour they all decided it would be wise to get a little solid food and prepared to move on to their restaurant for dinner. In between the decision to move on and getting into the taxi George found that the two hostesses had changed and were joining them for the meal. George was banished to the front seat whilst Calum and John squashed into the back with the girls. Girlish giggles and the occasional protesting squeal came from the back seat and George steadfastly looked to the front.

'Is he a poof?' he heard one of the girls ask.

George bridled at the suggestion. 'No, he bloody well isn't,' he replied. 'He's just happily married.'

It seemed to satisfy their curiosity and before they could question him further the taxi drew up at another hotel. If anything it was more plushly decorated than the first and the car door was whipped open with a flourish by a uniformed doorman. 'Looks like a general in the Venezuelan Army in that uniform,' commented George.

They were ushered into the restaurant by an elegantly dressed Sikh waiter. It didn't seem to bother anyone that there were two extra guests and they were soon seated at an enormous round table. Calum called loudly for champagne and the first bottle was quickly brought and even more speedily despatched. A second bottle swiftly appeared but George declined any more and asked for a beer instead. 'No more fancy stuff for me,' he said. 'I'll stick with what I know.' They then studied the menus. George was horrified that there were no prices and asked again if the Oil Company would accept the bill.

'Don't you worry about it, old darling,' said Calum. 'It's all taken care of.'

George settled for Gulf prawns to start and then conservatively went for fillet steak to follow and they all chatted whilst they waited for their meal. George laughed at the Black Country accents of the girls who then became quite defensive about their origins. They were surprised when George eventually admitted that he had once had a Midlands accent as well.

'How did that happen?' asked the girls.

'I was evacuated to the Staffordshire during the war,' he explained. 'I even went to school there for a couple of years. When I got back to the civilised South Coast all the kids laughed at my accent and odd sayings. I soon lost them though. It wasn't a good idea to be different from the other kids where I went to school.'

The meal came and went and so did the drinks and it was well past midnight when George decided he would call it a day. 'I've been up since four this morning,' he complained. 'It's okay for engineers and agents who got a good nights sleep.'

Neither Calum nor John was ready to end the night and George left them to carry on with the celebrations with the girls whilst he went back to the tug in a taxi. He was met at the gangway by one of the quartermasters who then kept a wary eye on him as he weaved his way up the ladders to his cabin. They were well used to the *sahibs* coming back on board fully ballasted with an internal cargo of 'whisky-wine' and to seeing them suffering and unsteady from the effects of too many *chota pegs*. George threw off his clothes and, leaving them where they fell, climbed into his bunk. He wouldn't need any rocking.

The next morning he awoke feeling a minimum of at least two degrees under. He knew he had over indulged both the food and the drink. He stood under the shower for about a quarter of an hour turning the taps first to hot and then to cold and back again. When the hot water ran out he emerged feeling slightly better and then made further improvements by brushing half a ton of foul tasting fur from his teeth. Slowly he made his way to the saloon and sat down.

'Breakfast, *sahib*?' asked the ever attentive steward.

'Orange juice and then Cornflakes, please. Where's the Chief Engineer?'

'Not coming, *sahib*,' said the steward, so George left it at that and got on with his food. He would take it easy for the morning, have a rest in the afternoon and maybe go and have a look at the local bazaar in the early evening.

After breakfast he sat out on deck in the sun and read his book. The crew worked around the deck, touching up the paint work, cleaning the brass and generally tidying up. The tug shone in the morning sun and George was content with his life. It was nearly midday when a taxi pulled up at the gangway and the dishevelled figure of John Henson opened the door and fell out of the back seat. The taxi driver got out too and there was much shouting and waving of arms.

George went down the gangway and dragged John to his feet. He weaved unsteadily and his eyes didn't seem to be focussing too well. 'George,' he slurred, 'Got any maney for the toxi?'

George hastily went back on board and grabbed a fist full of Dirhams from the pocket of his slacks. He went back on shore and paid off the surly driver and then, with the help of the quartermaster, heaved John up the gangway and along to his cabin. John slumped into his chair and promptly started to slide towards the deck. George heaved him into a vertical position and he tottered towards his bunk and fell into it with his feet still dangling over the side.

'You smell like a cross between a brewery and a bag shanty,' said George, accusingly, lifting John's feet into the bunk. 'Where the hell have you been?'

A raucous snore was his only answer, so he pulled off John's shoes and left him to sleep it off. 'It will be some time before he sees the light of day again,' thought George and he went off to get an early lunch before he took his own siesta.

At five that afternoon there was still no sign of John recovering so George called himself a taxi on the jetty phone and went off to the local *souq*. It was nothing like the bazaar in Abadan. Rows and rows of identical lock up shops fronted paved roads and all were freshly painted. Most of the shop workers were from the Indian sub-continent whilst the Arab owners sat at the rear of the shop with the all important cash box. It wasn't long before George had bought two children's bicycles and had hired a porter to carry them whilst he looked for something to buy for Kay. Before long he arrived at the gold *souq*.

A line of shops stretched out for about a hundred yards, each one crammed to the hilt with the yellow metal. Bare electric bulbs hung over the stocks of bangles, brooches and necklaces and it all glittered brightly with millions of reflections. George had never seen so much gold and he thought that it must seriously rival the Crown Jewels in the Tower of London. And there wasn't a policeman or security guard in sight. Tentatively George started to look in the windows. At each shop he was invited to come inside but he hesitated, as he didn't know if he could afford even the smallest item. There was not a sign of a price tag anywhere.

Finally he plucked up courage and went inside one of the shops. He was greeted warmly by the assistant and given a chair and a glass of Coca-Cola to drink. He started to worry that they would get rather irate if he didn't make a purchase.

'What you like?' asked the smiling, dark faced assistant, showing several gold teeth. George looked around. He had seen a narrow gold bracelet that he thought might fit the bill. He pointed at it hesitantly.

'How much?' he asked.

The assistant took it from the display and popped it on to the shiny brass tray of a spring balance. He shuffled the weights around, took a measurement and then made a calculation on a small hand held calculator. He told George the price.

Quickly, George converted the sum into pounds. Surely it couldn't be that cheap. He held out his hand and asked for the calculator and did his own sums again. There was no mistake. Feeling bolder George pointed at a larger bracelet. Again the assistant went through the process of weighing and costing and again George held out his hand for the calculator. He could still afford the price.

'Okay,' he said, inwardly heaving a sigh of relief and the bracelet was reverently placed into a smartly decorated box and wrapped in gift paper. He paid the assistant who rushed to the back of the store to hand the cash to the owner. With due ceremony the notes were counted and transferred to the cash box and George pocketed his box and was bowed from the store by the assistant. 'I could get used to this,' he thought as his porter led him out of the souq to a nearby taxi rank.

Back on board the tug it was time for dinner. He looked in on John Henson to find that he hadn't moved and was still deeply asleep. He ate dinner alone and then went back to his cabin. He would finish reading the novel and get an early night. Work was due to start at seven in the morning and he would need to be up and about.

The steward called him at six the next morning and he felt really fresh after a full eight hours sleep. A quick shower and then breakfast and he was out on deck when the mobile crane arrived to start discharging the drums of lubricating oil from the barge. A flat bed truck followed it and the crane started work without any delay. Four sets of can hooks were connected to the hook of the crane and the drums were lifted ashore, four at a time. The truck driver and his mate chocked off the drums as they were landed and in no time at all the truck was loaded. The driver leapt into the cab and the truck ground away from the jetty in low gear. Quiet descended again on the tug and barge. George and the crew waited.

They were all sitting happily in the sun when John Henson appeared on the deck of the tug. He peered around, shading his eyes with a hand and finally his gaze fell on George. 'What day is it?' he called.

'Work day,' replied George. 'You've been in you pit for about twenty hours, you idle sod.' He climbed off the barge and went aboard the tug.

'Hells teeth,' muttered John. 'I was supposed to meet Calum Stuart and the girls again last night. Wonder if they missed me.'

'You're about to find out,' said George as a taxi pulled up near the tug and Stuart unwound himself from the front seat. He was dressed in his biblical gear again and waved when he saw George and John. He pranced up the gangway like a two-year-old, handbag swinging jauntily and climbed the ladder two rungs at a time .

'Couldn't stand the pace, Henson old boy,' he crowed. 'I had to look after both girls last night. Lucky for me they are pretty friendly and don't mind sharing. Any of that Iranian beer on offer.'

'I suppose the sun is over the yardarm,' said George, looking at his watch. 'It's nearly nine o'clock. I'm sticking to coffee though. It's too early for me.'

They went in to the Captain's cabin and George made room for them by pushing the two bicycles into the bedroom. 'The discharge is going okay.'

'Right you are, squire,' agreed Calum. 'Should finish by this afternoon. They're only working one truck. After the last load of drums they will bring back a crate to go back to Abadan. Where do you want it?'

'That'll be the Super's deep freeze. Put it in the middle of the barge. We'll cover it with a tarpaulin and lash it down.'

'Now,' said Stuart downing the last of a glass of Shams, 'What about tonight? Are you ready for round two?'

'I've got no cash left,' said George. 'I spent my last on your taxi yesterday, John.'

'I'm skint too,' said John. 'I don't remember coming back in a taxi.'

'Shouldn't think you do. What the hell did you get up to with the girls? You had so much booze aboard you couldn't have managed very much.'

'They didn't complain,' said Calum. 'And they're looking forward to seeing him again. Tell you what,' he continued. 'There's a bunkering service here and they would love to sell you enough fuel to top up your tanks. They would show their appreciation in the appropriate manner if you gave them the business.'

'Perhaps we should make sure we have a safe margin of fuel,' said George. 'What do you think, John?'

'A wise precaution.'

'Okay, Stuart. Make the arrangements.'

That afternoon the fuel was delivered by road tanker and later that evening the inevitable taxi arrived at the jetty complete with Stuart, resplendent in a purple blazer and yellow slacks.

'Lucky that Jacob didn't put his coat up for sale,' commented John. 'Stuart would have bloody bought it.'

Once again the evening followed the same pattern but when George called a halt the others said they would come back to the tug too. 'We want to see your ship,' said the girls and George didn't have the nerve to say no.

They all climbed aboard the tug and George led them into the saloon. It was the only place big enough for all five of them. They raided the pantry fridge and shared out the bottles of Shams.

'I want to see the Captain's cabin,' decided one of the girls, so George led the way and to his dismay found that only one girl had followed him. He left the door open when she followed him into the cabin.

'Show me where you sleep,' she said and George went through to the bedroom. He was totally unprepared when she threw her arms around his neck. 'Kiss me, Captain,' she demanded. George squirmed free of her embrace and darted for the door. He rushed back to the saloon.

'John, come and get this god-damned girl out of my cabin. She's got arms like a bloody octopus'

'What's up George. Did she frighten you?'

'Too bloody right, she did. I'd get my head in my hands if Kay ever got wind of this.'

'Don't worry so much,' said John. He disentangled himself from his companion and she immediately grabbed hold of Stuart. 'Look after her for me,' he said and followed George up the ladder.

They went into George's cabin. All was quiet. They went through to the bedroom to find a trail of female underclothes strewn on the deck and a naked form in his bunk. 'Get her out of here,' said George in a strangled gasp and John threw a blanket round her and lifted her from the bunk.

He carried her off, kicking and squealing and George stuffed her clothes into John's arms too. George locked the cabin door behind them and stood there, panting. He'd had a narrow escape and there was no way he was coming out again until the coast was clear in the morning.

26

There were five for breakfast the next morning and it didn't phase the steward or cook in the least. They cheerfully served George and John plus two exotically dressed ladies and the colourful Stuart. George refrained from asking the girls if they slept well and hurried through his bacon and eggs with his eyes firmly on his plate.

'I'll have coffee in my cabin,' he told the steward and escaped at the earliest moment.

He called for the *Serang* who appeared in the doorway a few minutes later. The *Serang* confirmed that all the crew were on board and that they were ready for the return voyage. 'All men buy plenty gold, Captain George,' he said with great satisfaction. It probably meant he had bought the largest share of all. George knew that they would have bought roughly finished gold rings and bracelets and that they would sell them immediately they reached Bombay at the end of their contract. It was illegal to take gold bullion into India, which is why they bought the roughly finished items. The bullion dealers in Bombay would soon melt down the jewellery into gold bars again. How they made a profit on such a transaction George neither knew nor cared, but he was glad that the crewmen were happy.

About half an hour later Calum Stuart appeared at the cabin door. 'All ready for the off, old fruit?' he asked.

'Certainly I am. Will you send a cable to Abadan to tell them we're on our way back and you'd better sign us out with your friends at the customs.'

'Sure thing. Don't suppose you'll let Bugger Lugs Henson take one of the girls with him?'

'You don't suppose right, Stewpot. I'd get thrown into the calaboose for bringing in illegal immigrants and big bad John would get his head in his hands when a certain school teacher found out.'

'Right then, I'd better get the jolly old harem ashore,' drawled Stuart. 'Come back and see us some time. Toodle pip, old son.'

He waved languidly as he went down the ladder and a few minutes later the three visitors stood on the dock. A taxi drew up and the same pilot that had brought them in to Dubai climbed aboard.

'I see Stuart is still up to his usual tricks,' he commented.

'Let's go,' called George as he went to the bridge and the sailors poured out onto the deck ready to make the barge fast alongside.

They quickly lashed the barge alongside the tug. The barge was riding much lighter now with only the one single crate lashed down in the middle of the deck.

'Let go fore and aft,' said George and then backed the tug and barge away from the jetty as the sailors heaved the ropes inboard.

'Okay, pilot, she's all yours.'

The pilot took over and soon Stuart and the two girls were just gaily coloured, rag doll like figures, waving in the distance. John Henson arrived on the bridge in time to wave a last farewell.

'If you've washed your hands since the girls went ashore you could put the kettle on,' said George.

'Nowt wrong with my hands,' said John, and made three cups of coffee.

They sailed slowly out of the Creek, sipping at their coffee. George sorted the charts into order and drew in some courses. 'Shouldn't take so long to get back. The wind will be against us but we've got rid of all that cargo.' A fresh breeze blew in through the bridge windows and the Narimand started to pitch gently into the sea. George was glad to be heading for home.

When the pilot left they once more changed to towing the barge from the stern and by lunchtime they were well on their way. Dubai was just a distant dark smudge on the horizon and they could settle back into their seagoing routine.

'We'd better get one thing settled,' said George over his customary, piled high plate of curry. 'None of these high jinks get reported back to Kay. We had a couple of quiet nights ashore and a few beers, but nothing else.'

John smiled to himself.

'Never mind bloody grinning,' said George. 'Any word gets out and I'll make sure that every single girl in Abadan thinks you're attending the social diseases clinic.'

'Keep your hair on, George. It's thin enough already. We'll just have to make sure our stories agree, won't we?'

They finished their lunch and lingered on, chatting and speculating as to whether either of the girls would manage to snare Calum Stuart on a permanent basis. Strangely enough they both finally agreed that neither girl had a bat in hell's chance. Calum was a loner of long standing and likely to remain that way.

George was wrong in his judgement that the return voyage would be faster. It soon became apparent that the strong North Westerly wind was going to slow them down considerably. A long rolling sea came from ahead and the Narimand would bury her nose in the water every so often, sending spray up over the bridge. It soon became difficult to see out of the salt rimmed bridge windows and the only solution was to reduce speed. The barge then rode comfortably astern and the spray was reduced but the average speed was down to around five knots. The homeward run was going to take quite a lot longer.

George's watch keepers were much more proficient by now and his presence on the bridge was not required quite so often. He still regularly kept an eye on the tow and what shipping was around as watch followed watch and meal followed meal. They slowly made their way northwards. Past Sirri Island, past Lavan and on to Ras Mutaf and beyond. George took whatever rest he could and concentrated on getting his revenge at cards. Slowly he was winning back his share of ten rial coins. By the time they got back to Abadan he could well have restored his fortunes.

Three days and sixteen hours after leaving Dubai the Narimand steamed up towards the Shatt al Arab pilot boat with the barge now lashed securely alongside. The old tug was still covered in dried salt spray but had puffed her way down the Gulf and back without a hitch and, like Mary's little lamb, the barge had followed surely behind her. She had averaged only a fraction over five knots on her return voyage. Those lads in the builder's yard back in World War Two had certainly done a good job. The old girl was still doing sterling service, even if she did rattle a bit, and even if she did leave a long smoky trail behind her.

George left the pilot on the bridge and went to find the *Serang*. 'How much fresh water have we got left?'

'Maybe two ton.'

'Get the sailors to give her a good wash down then. Let's make sure she's bright and shining when we get alongside, even if it will be dark when we get there. Captain Robinson is sure to be waiting when we arrive. We'll top up with water again once we get alongside at number eight jetty.'

'*Atcha, sahib,*' said the *Serang* cheerfully. They would all be glad to get back in to port, although the tug still had to be taken back to Bandar Mashur. 'How many days in Abadan.'

'Maybe two,' said George, hoping that the Super would let him have a day or two at home with Kay before sailing back to Bandar Mashur. The *Serang* smiled happily, thinking about the stock of duty free whisky and cigarettes that he'd bought in Dubai to sell to the Abadanis at great profit. He went off, shouting to the crew to get hoses, brushes and brass polish and slowly the old tug began to shine again in the last rays of the evening sun.

They crept up the river against the ebb tide and finally the lights of Abadan and the refinery shone in the distance. George went up to the bridge as they neared Al Wassiliyah and the pilot station.

'Thanks, Mister Pilot,' he said and handed him a carton of Camel cigarettes.

'Thank you, Captain, George,' replied the pilot, happily, heading towards his boat and the shore.

'That gets rid of those rotten Yankee fags,' thought George, remembering the usual British sailor's description for that particular brand. 'The only cigarettes with a picture of the maker on the packet.'

He was now back in familiar waters. The refinery lights twinkled across the dark waters of the Shatt and George headed for the berth as fast as the barge would let him. It was nearing midnight and the moon was dipping behind the palm trees of Iraq but when George trained his binoculars towards the shore he could see a familiar tubby figure at the front of a small knot of people on the jetty. The Superintendent intended to be the first aboard.

The barge dropped easily alongside the jetty and George's sailors swiftly sent mooring ropes ashore and made fast. The telegraph jangled loud and long as George thankfully rang 'Finished with Engines'. The crew pushed a gangway ashore from the barge and George went down to see the Super. It was Kay who met him at the bottom of the gangway.

'Hello, George,' she said, throwing her arms round his neck and kissing him soundly. 'Have you been behaving yourself?'

'Certainly have. What are you doing here?'

'Captain Robinson said you would be in tonight and suggested I came down. He's quite a nice man, really. Minouche is looking after the children so we can stay on board tonight, if you like.'

'Think I'd rather be in a double bed at home than crammed into the bunk here,' he said. 'Lets see if we can get finished up and get home by one.'

A mobile crane was already in position to get the crate ashore from the barge. The Super was waving his arms and directing the crew, so George left him to it.

'Reckon we can get a taxi at this time of night?' he asked Kay.

'Sure,' she said. 'One eyed Ibrahim is half expecting the call.'

'Let's call him then. Come and see what I've got to take home for the kids.'

They went up to George's cabin and he showed Kay the gleaming new bicycles. 'We'll leave them in their bedroom tonight,' she decided. 'That'll surprise them when they wake up. Two wheeled bikes complete with stabilisers. They'll think it's Christmas and Easter and *Now Ruz* all rolled into one.'

George put his dirty clothes into his holdall and they went out on deck with the bicycles. The quartermaster immediately took the bikes from them and lifted them ashore. Captain Robinson was now seeing that his deep freeze was secure on the back of a truck and was preparing to leave.

'See you in the morning, George. Come in around eleven and sign the tug in with customs.'

'Okay, sir,' said George, saluting like an American soldier and he and Kay went out of the dock gates in Ibrahim's taxi, with one bicycle in the boot and the other on the front seat next to Ibrahim.

'I saw Bushire, Ibrahim.'

'Very nice place,' said Ibrahim turning to face his passengers and swerving across two lanes that were luckily free of traffic. 'I make plenty money and go back one day.'

'If you live that bloody long,' said George as Ibrahim casually swerved back across the road.

They got home in one piece and crept quietly into the house. When they went into the children's room with the bikes they found Minouche curled up at the foot of their beds, covered in a blanket and fast asleep. Next to her the dog wagged his tail, lazily and went back to sleep too. They tiptoed quietly out and headed for their own bed. They had to make up for ten days of being apart.

As they climbed into bed George took a package from his pocket. 'Thought you might like something from Dubai,' he said, giving it to Kay.

'George, you shouldn't have.'

'Well, I did, so unless you want me to have it back you'd better open it.'

She tore open the paper and put it to one side. Carefully she opened the lid of the box.

'George! It's beautiful,' she gasped. 'It must have cost a fortune.'

She slipped the bracelet over her hand and looked at it as it shone in the glow from the bedside light. She put out the light and turned to George. 'Welcome home, sailor,' she whispered.

27

George would have liked to lie in bed for a while the next morning but he didn't get the chance. By half past six two excited voices could be heard from the children's room. George opened a bleary eye as two happy children rushed into the bedroom.

'Mum, come and see what we've got,' yelled Louise. 'Oh, hello, Dad.'

She rushed away and then John looked in.

'I've got a red bike,' he announced, solemnly, his eyes wide. He followed his sister.

'So much for me,' said George. 'I'm not sure they've missed me very much.'

'Oh, they most surely have. They get away with a lot less when I'm in charge.'

They threw back the covers and got out of bed, taking their dressing gowns from the back of the door. 'Let's go and see the fun.'

The children were already riding their new bicycles around the house, chased by the dog, who thought it was all for his benefit.

'Enough,' commanded Kay. 'Let's get some breakfast and then you can take the bikes out in the garden where there's a lot more room.'

The children reluctantly complied with the edict and rushed to the breakfast table. They didn't take long over eating that morning and before long were hurtling round the garden in circles as fast as they could go. 'Wonder how long it will be before the first traffic accident?' George thought.

'I'll go in to work early,' he told Kay. 'Hopefully I can get finished quickly and then I'll see if I can arrange another day off before I have to take the tug back to Bandar Mashur.'

'Okay. I must go and show the girls my bracelet. They'll be envious.'

George smiled to himself. 'Got myself a few Brownie points there,' he thought.

He called for the tug bus and Ali was soon at the door. 'See you later,' he called to the children but they were far too busy to notice. 'Number eight jetty, Ali.'

George went on board the tug which was gleaming and steaming in the sun where it had just been washed down. 'We'll take the barge back to Braim Creek when the Chief Engineer comes on board,' he told the *Serang*. 'Then you can have the rest of the day off.'

'*Atcha, sahib*,' smiled the *Serang*. 'All men going shoresides.'

George knew that this meant much of the loot from Dubai would be going to the bazaar that night to be sold for a handsome profit. The crew would all be very happy. The opportunities for business in Bandar Mashur were few and far between, so they enjoyed their stays in Abadan.

George went to his cabin and collected the ship's papers. No sign of John so he might as well go and sign the ship in at customs and also sign her out again for two days time, when they would go back round the coast to Mashur. He found Ali, the driver, drinking tea with the crew and they got back in the bus and went to find Maroonian, the agent. When they got to the office there was only one very junior office boy to be seen.

'Where's Maroonian?' asked George.

The boy shrugged his shoulders and tossed his head in typical Iranian style. '*Nehmidonam*,' he grunted in surly fashion. George now knew enough of the language to translate that as 'I don't know.'

'Sod it,' he said and climbed back into the bus. He gave Ali directions and they arrived at the customs office.

'Wait here, please,' he said to Ali, but Ali shook his head.

248

'I come,' he said, smiling. 'My brother, he here.' He confidently went into the customs office and greeted all and sundry with *Salaams* and hand shakes.

A tall customs man with a long drooping moustache approached. He threw his arms round Ali and kissed him. The spectacle of men kissing no longer made George feel uneasy. It was an Iranian custom and was often to be seen.

George soon did feel uneasy though as the man with the moustache then approached, took him by the hand and led him into an inner office. Holding hands was not on George's list of favourite things to do, but he suffered in silence as they skirted a desk piled high with papers and then greeted a senior customs officer.

Still holding George by the hand his companion snatched the tug's papers and thrust them at his boss. They were casually inspected, stamped and thrust back at George, who remembered enough Farsi to stammer, 'Thank you.' He quickly found himself back in the outer office, complete with signed papers and still with his wallet intact.

'You're a star, Ali,' he said, finally extricating his hand from the brother's greasy paw. 'Now let's get out of here before he wants to kiss me too.'

They were back at the tug within half an hour of leaving. Never before had the local bureaucracy been so easily dealt with. 'Get yourself some *chai*, Ali,' instructed George, 'And then go and get Mr John from his house.'

'Okay, Captain George,' said Ali cheerfully as he headed towards his favourite teashop in the bazaar.

George went back to his cabin to wait for John and called for coffee. The steward arrived at the same time as Captain Robinson who sat down on George's settee and wiped the sweat from his forehead.

'Got the papers sorted out yet, George?' he asked, casually taking George's coffee from the steward and drinking a large gulp.

'Already done. Just waiting for John to arrive and we'll take the barge back. To Braim Creek.'

'You've done a good job. When are you leaving for Mashur?'

'Thought we'd give the crew a rest and then go the day after tomorrow on the morning tide, if that's okay?'

'That'll be fine. Did you know there's a navigation warning out for navy exercises in the Northern Gulf?'

'No,' said George.

'Call at the office on your way home. I'll get you a copy of the Notice to Mariners. The Yanks are exercising some of their ships along with the Iranian Navy. You'd better keep well clear of them. They're likely to be roaring around all over the place.'

George had the usual merchant seaman's attitude towards the armed forces. 'Blasted maritime gunmen. They ought to keep out of the way of real sailors.'

'You just take it easy, young George. We don't want any trouble. You'll still be in territorial waters so don't start World War Three.'

'Don't worry, sir. Even I'm not that stupid and I hear the jails around here are none too pleasant.'

The Super changed the subject. 'Don't suppose you managed to find any malt whisky while you were on your travels?'

'I didn't,' replied George, 'But I just might know a man who did. Couple of bottles do?'

'Excellent.'

George went to find the *Serang* and then told him what was wanted. A few minutes later the *Serang* came to the cabin door with a large parcel. 'Two bottles best whisky wine, *sahib*.'

'How much?' asked the Super.

'Five pounds, *sahib*.'

The bottles changed hands and five English pounds went into the *Serang's* dusky palm and disappeared into a shirt pocket.

George now knew that the Super was in a good mood so he approached him again with his usual request.

'What about a transfer to working in Kharg Island?'

'I've been thinking about it, George, and you've got to be top of the list for the next position that comes up.'

'When's that likely to be?'

'Maybe sooner than you think, George. There are some big changes in the pipeline that I can't tell you of, yet. Stick it out at Mashur for a little while longer. It will all be worthwhile in the long run.'

He would answer no more questions and told George not to tell anyone else that changes were afoot. They went ashore and George collected a copy of the navigation warning notice before returning on board. John Henson had just arrived so once more they made fast to the now salt spattered barge and towed it away from the jetty.

They nosed into the scummy backwater of Braim Creek, disturbing a pack of pi-dogs that were foraging for food along the bank and nudged the barge towards its berth. The crew made it fast for the last time and they backed stern first out of the Creek into the fast flowing tide of the Shatt al Arab. Soon they were back at number eight jetty and were making fast. 'I'm off home,' announced George. 'We'll sail at ten o'clock on the day after tomorrow. Tidy up today, *Serang* and let the crew have a day off tomorrow.'

'*Atcha, sahib.*'

George went home to see how the children were getting on with their new bicycles. It wouldn't be long before Louise could ride without the stabilisers and once she could do it John wouldn't be far behind. He found that his garden was full of children and his house full with off duty tug men and their wives. His stock of Shams beer would be seriously depleted and likewise Kay's jars of coffee.

'The kids wanted to show off their bikes,' explained Kay. 'Everyone else seemed to just appear.'

'Oh, well. I've got tomorrow off, so if today is going to be one of those lost days, so be it.'

And so it was. The lunchtime session lasted till well into the afternoon when everyone left for a siesta. They re-gathered again that night and all ended up at the Hotel Khalij in Khorramshahr. It was a noisy night of celebration and George spent the following day nursing a sore head. He got little sympathy from Kay and the children hardly noticed at all. They were still preoccupied with two-wheeled transport.

28

The Narimand puffed its stately course past Al Wassiliyah and an Iraqi pilot climbed on board. George welcomed him aboard and then, as usual, went below. It was late afternoon and George was definitely not happy. He had called the pilot station that morning, only to find that there was no pilot available. He then requested permission to transit the river without a pilot and the request was abruptly denied.

George had wondered what it was all about and then gathered that there had been a minor diplomatic incident earlier that morning when two Iranian warships had left port to take part in the exercises in the Gulf. Relations between the adjoining countries had never run smoothly and every few months they would get extremely ruffled. Usually neither country let that interfere with the business of making a profit from oil and shipping, but today, for some reason, they did.

Somewhere in the dim distant past it had been decreed that the border between the two countries would be the Iranian shoreline, meaning that the Shatt al Arab River belonged to Iraq. Perhaps some misguided politician had thought that as Iran had the majority of the oil then Iraq should have control of the shipping. Anyway, the two Iranian warships had left that morning without politely informing the Iraqi authorities of their departure and had compounded their heinous crime by not flying the Iraqi ensign from their foremasts as a courtesy.

It had taken most of the day for the disagreement to be put right and several ships had been delayed alongside at Khorramshahr. George found that he was at the back of the queue for a pilot as they preferred the relative comfort of a fast cargo ship to that of the plodding Narimand. He had fumed over the delay, as it would mean another night away from home. It also meant a night passage across the northern gulf and little sleep for George on the way.

John Henson was not happy either. After his diversions in Dubai he had resumed the relationship with his friendly schoolteacher and was looking forward to a little light entertainment during the hours of darkness. 'Bloody ragheads,' he fumed, using the derogatory term for any Middle Eastern ethnic. 'They're upsetting my love life with their petty arguments.'

'Don't let the raghead pilot hear you,' warned George. 'You'll cause another diplomatic incident. Go and get the cards. The way your luck is going I could make a fortune during the trip.'

They played cards until it was time for dinner and then resumed afterwards. George was accumulating a vast pile of ten rial pieces and John was getting ever more fed up. 'The only way I'm going to get my fair share is to get married,' he complained. 'But at the rate I'm losing money to you I will never be able to afford it, anyway.'

'About time you got hitched, Henson. Perhaps the lady might even civilise you one day.'

'Typical married man,' snorted John. 'Misery always likes company.'

He lost the next hand too. George went back on to the bridge to find the pilot staring moodily out of the bridge window.

'All okay, pilot?' asked George.

'Not okay, Captain George. One day big trouble between Iraq and Iran.'

'I hope not, Mister Pilot. If everybody takes things easy we'll all make our fortunes. Be silly to upset the boat.'

'It's all religion Captain. They're all Shia and we're all Sunni. All same your Protestant and Catholics.'

George laughed. He would have to remember to tell Father McDougal that he was a Catholitic. 'Sounds like a cross between cathodic and cathartic, with a dash of carbolic thrown in,' he thought.

'Don't get like us with our Irish problem, Mister Pilot. Stay out of any arguments like that and you might live long enough to collect your pension.'

George re-set the Decca Navigator and checked the position. He would have to arrange for the equipment to be collected from Mashur and returned to Abadan. Captain Robinson had hired the machine for a month so George had suggested he kept it for the last leg of the voyage. It saved an awful lot of bother, knowing where you were at all times.

'Another two hours to Rooka Buoy, pilot?'

The pilot grunted his agreement and went back to his unhappy thoughts. George went below.

'Is everyone on board bloody miserable today?' he asked John. 'Break open the beer and see if that will cheer you up.'

'Sod it. I can't be bothered. Think I'll head for my bed. Don't rock the boat too much on the way across to the Khor Musa.'

'It's all right for some,' said George. 'I'll be up all bloody night working whilst you're in your rotten, steaming pit.'

George picked up his book and started reading. Before long his eyes drooped and he dozed in the chair until the quartermaster called him. 'Pilot station, *sahib*. Plenty ships coming.' George rubbed his eyes and dashed tepid water from the sink tap into his face. He would have a job keeping his eyes open tonight. He threw on a jersey to ward off the cool night air and made his way to the bridge.

The quartermaster was right. There were ships all over the place. 'What goes on?' he asked.

'Warships exercising,' replied the pilot. 'Get in every bugger's way.'

'Well put, pilot. Where's your boat?'

The pilot pointed into the darkness and George could see the small boat heading towards them. 'You like cigarettes or whisky, pilot?'

The pilot visibly cheered up. 'Whisky, please Captain.' George produced a bottle of Red Label from the chart room drawer and handed it over.

'Thanks, Captain.'

'That's okay,' replied George. 'Just remember. When you declare war, make sure I'm not in the middle on my tug.'

The pilot grinned and left and George sorted out a set of charts from the drawer.

'Steer oh-nine-oh,' he called, ringing full ahead on the telegraph. He laid off the course on the chart and measured the distance to the Khor Musa light. 'Thirty two miles. About three and a half hours run if we're lucky.'

He settled in to the pilot chair and watched the warships dash madly about. He kept a wary eye on their navigation lights to see that they were passing well clear of the tug. It wasn't long, however, before they started to take an interest in the Narimand.

A brilliant beam of light swept back and forth before focussing on the Narimand. George swore as the brightness destroyed his night vision for a minute or two. There were no navigation lights to be seen behind the searchlight but gradually the darkened ship loomed into sight. The searchlight flickered out and darkness returned. George peered through his binoculars at the sleek silhouette.

He grunted, sourly, as he recognised the shape of the destroyer that was fast approaching. It was the Imperial Iranian Navy Ship 'Admiral Bayandour', one of the miscreants from that morning in Abadan. A signal light started flashing, and George answered with the Aldis lamp. In answer to the usual question he replied, 'Narimand. Abadan to Bandar Mashur.' The destroyer came ever closer.

The bow wave of the destroyer showed clearly under the approaching bow but George kept the Narimand on course. He was ready to take avoiding action but at the last minute the destroyer heeled to starboard and swept past. George was sweating. He had missed by less than fifty yards and that was a lot too close for comfort. 'Eff off and play silly games somewhere else,' shouted George at the retreating warship and settled down to his lookout again and another cup of coffee.

Gradually the lights of the fleet of warships dropped astern and George called for another cup of coffee. It would help him to stay awake. He stirred from the chair and checked the position. Another couple of hours to the light float. Should start to see the light soon. He jumped out of his wits, spilling his coffee down his jersey, as a dark shape roared overhead and went screaming into the distance.

'Jesus H.' he exclaimed, brushing the coffee on to the deck.

He peered into the darkness. Another shape flashed noisily overhead with a trail of fire behind it. 'Didn't know the locals had anything that flew at night,' he thought. 'Must be the Yanks playing games with night fighters. Wonder where they're based?'

He went back to his chair and half an hour later the navigation light on the Khor Musa light float pierced the darkness ahead. George went to the VHF radio and checked the channel.

'Khor Musa pilots,' he called, 'This is the tug Narimand, bound for Bandar Mashur. Do you read?'

The atmospherics crackled and the reply came back clearly. 'Narimand. Khor Musa pilot boat. Go ahead.'

'We'll be with you in about one hour and require a pilot.'

'Negative, Narimand. No pilot available before oh-nine-hundred hours. Anchor close to the pilot vessel and wait.'

'Charming,' muttered George. 'Bloody charming.' Another half day wasted. 'Oh well,' he thought, 'At least I'll get a few hours sleep.'

They dropped anchor an hour later just as the first light of dawn was inching its way over the eastern horizon. George yawned and scratched and told the quartermaster to keep a good lookout.

'Call me for eight o'clock,' he instructed before going below and getting into his bunk. No point in getting undressed. He would shower and change before breakfast and then the pilot would be coming on board.

29

George dozed fitfully, hearing the creak of the old tug as it pulled gently at the anchor cable. The light was coming through the curtains at the porthole and he could hear the soft tread of the quartermaster on the bridge above him. He was too warm with his clothes on but too sleepy to get up and take them off.

His reverie was shattered by the noise of a jet engine roaring close overhead followed by a loud bang. He was immediately wide awake. 'Must have broken the sound barrier,' he thought and then sat upright as his cabin door burst open.

'*Sahib*, come quick.'

He jumped from his bunk, narrowly missing catching his scrotum on the bunk board and tumbled out of the door. He made for the bridge, rubbing his eyes and found the quartermaster with binoculars to his eyes looking to the South.

'Big noise,' said the quartermaster, pointing to the horizon. 'Big fire,' he added.

George snatched his binoculars from the man and readjusted them. He could see nothing.

'Maybe go in water,' insisted the quartermaster.

'Okay,' said George. 'Crew stand by and heave up anchor.'

He rang the engine room telegraph and went to the VHF. He called the pilot boat and eventually a sleepy voice replied.

'Tug Narimand,' George announced. 'Any news of an aeroplane in trouble?'

There was silence, so George tried again and again until finally a new voice replied. He repeated his query.

'No news here,' came the answer.

'I'm heading south to investigate,' replied George, wondering what to do next.

He went back to the radio and broadcast on channel sixteen.

'Pan-Pan-Pan, Pan-Pan-Pan, Pan-Pan-Pan. This is tug Narimand. Am investigating possible aircraft accident approximately ten miles south of Khor Musa light float.'

He listened for a reply but nothing came. He wondered where the warships from the night before had gone. Surely they couldn't be far away.

The fo'c'sle bell clanged as the anchor rattled into the hawse pipe and George set course due south at full speed. He sent for the *Serang* and also for John Henson. They both came to the bridge at the same time.

'*Serang*, put two men on the monkey island to keep lookout. If they see anything, give me a call. All other men stay on deck, ready for orders.'

'Where's the fire?' asked John.

'Don't even know if there is one, but the quartermaster reckoned that plane that came over was in trouble and has maybe ditched.'

'Holy shit,' said John. 'Is anyone else around?'

'Don't think so. Do you know how to make an urgency call on the radio?'

John didn't, so George repeated the call himself. There was still no answer.

'Make the same call for me every five minutes,' said George. 'I'm just going to make a couple of calculations to see how far we have to go.'

He went to the chart desk and started working out figures on a scrap sheet of paper, muttering to himself as he did so.

'Say six hundred miles and hour. That's six hundred divided by sixty miles in a minute. Roughly ten miles. If we go ten miles and then start a box search, we'll see what happens. What about if the plane made eight or nine hundred miles an hour? We'd be looking in the wrong place. Could be anywhere between five and fifteen miles away and we've only got a rough direction of travel.'

He laid off ten miles on the chart and then took a reading from the Decca Navigator. At least Mister Decca would tell them exactly where the tug was. The steward bustled onto the bridge with a tray of coffee. Breakfast, *sahib*?' he asked.

George looked at his watch. Still only six thirty in the morning but he was hungry. 'Fried egg and bacon sandwiches,' he decided.

'Same for me,' echoed John.

'Tell the *bandari* to have food sent up to the crew too,' said George and the steward hurried below to get everything arranged. 'Leave the radio for a while, John. See if you can get any more revs out of the old girl if you can.'

John went below and George settled in his pilot chair with his binoculars glued to his eyes. He wondered vaguely what he should look for. Nobody trained people for something like this. Men overboard and ships calling for assistance was one thing. Aircraft ditching was something else.

The old tug started to rattle and shake as the engine revs increased and a greasy black plume of smoke oozed out of the funnel. In contrast the wake boiled white astern of them as the bow bit deeply into the swell. 'Go, you old bastard,' shouted George, startling the quartermaster.

At seven fifteen George checked the position again and was surprised to see that they had already travelled ten miles. They must be doing nearly twelve knots. The old tug probably hadn't gone so fast since coming home from the D-Day landings having safely helped to deliver a Mulberry Harbour to Arromanches.

'She's flying,' he said to John who had returned to the bridge. 'Hope she doesn't bust a gut.'

They started their search and all eyes were looking seaward. Every pair of binoculars available scanned the waters as far as the horizon. When they had gone two miles further south George altered course due east and after a further mile, north. Two miles more and then two miles to the west. Two more miles south and one back to the east and they had completed the first box. They had seen nothing apart from an empty oil drum and a few bedraggled seagulls that bobbed gently past. The search had taken nearly another hour.

'What do you think, John? Shall we try further to the south, or shall we try a little further east or west?'

'Hobson's choice, mate. Lets go further south and take a bigger box. Maybe a four mile square.'

'It's as good an idea as any,' said George. 'Steer one-eight oh.'

John went back to the radio and put out another Pan call but there was still no answer. Normally the VHF was full of chatter but today there was an ominous silence. No one else was going to help.

It took them nearly two more hours to complete a four mile box search and when it was finished they had still seen nothing. They had heard nothing on the radio either so at ten thirty George decided it was time to call a halt. It would take them till at least noon to get back to the pilot station and he considered that, under the circumstances, they had done what they could. There was still no confirmation that a plane was missing and nobody else had joined the search.

George hurriedly took a position from the Decca and transferred it to the chart. 'Steer three-five-five,' he called and the tug heeled over as the quartermaster swung the wheel.

'Steady on three-five-five, *sahib*.'

George settled back in his chair once more and John leaned on the bulwark nearby. 'The buggers will never believe us when we tell them,' he said. 'They'll think we anchored up and went on the piss.'

'Let them,' grunted George. He was now feeling decidedly tired and fed up. This trip hadn't gone quite according to plan. He heaved himself out of his chair and went up the ladder to the monkey island. 'All finish,' he said to the two lookouts, and they gratefully went below. It was not the easiest job in the world to keep a proper lookout at sea.

George went back to the bridge to find John in the pilot's chair. 'Jump in my bloody grave if I didn't move fast enough. No, don't get up. I'm going for a pony and trap.'

He made his way down to the officer's toilet and gratefully sat back on the seat. 'Better not take long,' he thought. 'I'll drop off to sleep if I don't get on with it.'

He washed his hands thoughtfully and went back up the ladders. He would stop off at his cabin and get a fresh packet of cigarettes. His mouth was like a gorillas armpit so he would clean his teeth whilst there. A few minutes later, feeling refreshed, he went back out on deck and as he closed the cabin door he turned to go up the ladder and from the corner of his eye he saw a flash of orange in the distance.

He rushed up the ladder and grabbed his binoculars from a startled John. 'There's something out there on the starboard side. Bring her round to oh-nine oh.'

The quartermaster swung the wheel and steadied the tug on her new course and George shouted for more lookouts to come to the bridge. He swept the area to starboard with his binoculars. Still nothing. After a few minutes he turned the tug towards the south again, all the time looking to starboard. Nothing.

He was about to give up when one of the lookouts shouted and pointed, four points on the bow. George rang for dead slow ahead and altered course in the direction the lookout pointed. Suddenly he saw it. An orange flash in the waves ahead. He stopped the engine and focussed his glasses again and the orange mass flickered into his view. The tug drifted nearer. 'Keep it in sight and point the direction,' he called to the lookout. The man pointed.

'Dead slow ahead, John,' said George watching the look-out. John swung the telegraph. 'Starboard easy...... steady now.' The tug crept forward. 'Stop engines.'

George focussed his glasses again and suddenly in clear view was an orange life jacket and an arm waving tiredly above it. 'Get the men on deck, starboard side,' George called to the *Serang*. 'Have a lifebuoy and lines ready.'

'Dead slow ahead. Steady as she goes.' George leaned out of the bridge window, watching as they got closer. 'Stop engines.' They drifted closer again.

'Once more with the engines, John and I reckon we'll be able to get close enough to him.'

'Okay, George. Say when.'

'Dead slow ahead. Starboard easy..........Mid-ships.......... Stop and dead slow astern.'

The tug shuddered gently as the propeller bit astern. 'Get a line to him, *Serang*.'

A lifebuoy and line snaked out from the side and splashed into the water close to the airman. He slowly paddled towards it with tired strokes.

'Stop engines. Come on, John. Let's go and see what we've found.'

They jostled each other down the ladders and on to the after deck. The starboard bulwark doors were open and the *Serang* and crew were gently heaving the lifebuoy back towards the tug. As it came alongside two crewmembers lay on the deck and reached over the side to the man in the water. He raised his arms and they held on to them and then pulled him gently up on to the deck where he lay, face down, gasping for breath.

George helped him to turn over and looked down at him. His grey flying suit was torn and he looked up with hollow eyes. 'I thought you would never come,' he gasped, in heavily accented American English.

'Who are you,' asked George.

'Flight Lieutenant Mahmoud Mohsenifar. Imperial Iranian Air Force.'

'Are you the only aircrew?'

'Yes. Single seater F5-A fighter plane.'

'What happened to the plane?'

'I don't know. I was on a flight to Bushire and supposed to rendezvous with an American flight for exercises. We only came south from Mehrabad yesterday. Anyway, my engine suddenly exploded and I hit the ejector. Didn't even have time to send a Mayday.'

'We'll see if we can let someone know,' said George, 'But we haven't been able to contact anyone by VHF all morning. Are you hurt?'

'No. Just tired from trying to keep my head above the waves.'

'Help him up to my cabin,' said George. 'Let's see if we can find him some dry clothes.'

The crew helped the pilot up the ladders and in to George's cabin where George found a clean boiler suit. 'You'd better have a shower and change into that. Show him where to go, John, and I'll get the show on the road again.'

He went up to the bridge and checked the position. He drew a new course line on the chart and rang for full ahead. 'Steer three-five-three.' It would be another hour and a half before they got near the pilot boat again. He went to the VHF radio again.

'Saycuritay, saycuritay, saycuritay. This is tug Narimand. Cancel previous message. Have picked up survivor from air accident and am proceeding to Bandar Mah Shahr.'

This time an answer came back immediately, loud and clear.

'Pilot boat to Narimand. Message received. A pilot will be available on arrival. I will inform the authorities of your message.'

Half an hour later John and the air force pilot joined George on the bridge. The pilot was freshly showered and was wearing George's boiler suit.

'You look a bit better, Mahmoud.'

'Sure thing, pal. Thanks to you and your crew.'

'Where did you get that Yankee accent?'

'I spent two years in the States. One was with a training squadron and the second with Northrop. They made the plane that I flew.'

'I think they should have made a better job of it,' said George to himself. 'Do you feel like some lunch? You must have missed out on breakfast.'

They were served lunch on the bridge and between the three of them they did justice to a large tureen of curry. By the time it was finished they were in sight of the pilot boat, and George was looking forward to an afternoon of sleep before arriving off Bandar Shahpour.

The pilot was soon aboard and after a few minutes talking with their rescued aviator, he settled to taking the ship in to the Khor Musa. George and John lay on their bunks while Mahmoud made himself comfortable on George's settee. 'Three hours sleep before you can get ashore at Shahpour,' George told Mahmoud.

The quartermaster woke them ten minutes before they arrived at Bandar Shahpour and they were all on the bridge as the pilot boat arrived. There seemed to be a lot of people on board the boat, many of them resplendent in military uniform.

'You've got a reception committee, Mahmoud. I hope you aren't deep in the brown stuff.'

A sailor brought all the visitors to the bridge and the one who seemed to be the most senior stepped forward. He looked around the bridge and when he spoke his tones were definitely those of Oxford English.

'Who is the Captain, please?'

George stepped forward.

'I'm Captain Penroy. What can I do for you?'

The officer looked at George and then offered his hand.

'You have already done the Imperial Iranian Air Force a great service, Captain. On behalf of the Commander in Chief I thank you.' He bowed and shook George's hand at the same time and was followed by all the other officers who thanked George effusively. The senior man then turned to Mahmoud Mohsenifar, who sprang to attention and saluted. After a short conversation in Farsi the whole party bowed again and headed down the ladder, followed by Mahmoud.

George and John peered over the side as they climbed back aboard the pilot boat and waved languidly as the boat pulled away from the side.

'Not a bad swap,' said George. 'He's gone off with my old boiler suit but I've got his flying gear. Now, let's get to Mashur before anything else happens.'

Within half an hour the tug was safely moored to its buoy at the head of the harbour. 'We might as well stay on board tonight,' decided George. 'We'll go home in the morning after they've taken the Decca Navigator ashore.'

'Good idea. Last one down below buys the first Shams.'

They fought for the ladder, laughing and pushing and glad to be back in harbour.

30

Two days later George reported to the Superintendents office first thing in the morning. He was well rested. He had returned across the desert from Bandar Mashur with John Henson the morning before and had been relaxing at home ever since. He had regaled Kay with the story of the rescue and she had shown him a small piece in the local English language newspaper. The Tehran Journal told of a plane crash in the Gulf but, much to George's disgust, there had been no mention of the rescue.

'Morning, Penroy.' Captain Robinson beamed over his half glasses and offered George a chair. 'You did well with the rescue. You'll probably be hearing from the company when I've put my monthly report in.'

'Just lucky, really,' said George, modestly. 'We'd actually given up searching and were on our way back when we spotted the survivor.'

'Well, I've got some news for you that you'll be pleased to hear. We've had some trouble with one of the wives in Kharg and she's no longer welcome on the island. That means transferring her husband back here, so there's a place for you on the Kharg roster from next week. You'll fit into the shift in his place.'

'It's got to be Big Mike,' guessed George. 'What's April been up to this time?'

'Never you mind, young George. That's for me to know and you to guess. Just be glad you've got the job. You can have the rest of the week off as you've been working so well. Don't get under Kay's feet too much. I don't want to get any complaints from her.'

'Shouldn't think you will. She'll be glad of the help with the children.'

'Now, before you go I've got some more information for you. You've done extremely well lately and deserve to know what is going on. It's strictly between you and me and mustn't go any further at this stage.'

George nodded his agreement, crossed his legs and sat back in his chair.

'There are going to be big changes here. All the tug men will soon be seconded to the Iranian Oil Company for a start and we're going to have to train Iranians as officers and crew. They will gradually take over from the Europeans.'

George's face fell. He had anticipated a job for life. Now he was going to train local staff to take his place.

'Don't look so downhearted, George. Those tug men who work at Kharg Island will be given the chance to transfer into the pilotage. They need more people there with Masters tickets to pilot the ships in to port and there is a lot of expansion going on. They're going to build a lot more jetties and export a lot more oil.'

'When does all this happen?'

'Not for a couple of months yet and, as I've said, keep it strictly under your hat. I don't want any rumours circulating round the bazaar next week. You're the only one that knows so far.'

'I won't say a word.'

'One further thing I need to know. What do you know about Voith Schneider?'

'Sod all, unless he was one of Hitler's boys.'

'You can be a daft bugger sometimes, George. I meant the Voith Schneider method of ship propulsion. It's a sort of marine version of an upside down helicopter in principle.'

'Like I said,' said George, 'I've never heard of it.'

'Well, you're going to hear plenty and very soon. It's a specialised German thing that is highly efficient for tugs and the locals have asked us to have a couple built for operations at Kharg. We're going to need to have someone trained to operate them so there's a chance to go to Bremen on a course. It would be combined with your next leave and would mean two or three weeks over there, all expenses paid.'

'Sounds pretty good to me,' said George. 'It's also to be kept quiet, I suppose.'

'Got it in one, George.'

George went home with all sorts of thoughts chasing each other around his head. There was one person he was going to discuss it all with. Kay. She would have to know what was going on but could be relied upon to keep it quiet. 'Reckon I must be flavour of the month with the Super,' he thought as Ibrahim took the last corner on two wheels. He paid Ibrahim a handsome tip and rushed inside. He would have to wait to share his news though as Liz Longford and her children were visiting.

'Hello, George,' said Liz. 'What's biting you. You look like the cat that got the cream.'

'Just that I'm transferring to Kharg,' said George. 'I'll be working the same shift as Peter.'

'It's what you've been wanting for a long time,' said Kay. 'Maybe you'll be a bit happier and more settled now.'

'Didn't know I'd been unhappy,' replied George.

'Well, I've certainly noticed,' said Kay, laughing as she passed George a steaming cup of coffee. 'Perhaps you'll find the aeroplane flight to Kharg a bit better than that taxi ride across the desert.'

Later, when they were alone, George passed on the rest of the news. She was astonished at the proposed changes but, as she said to George, it might open more opportunities. 'If it doesn't work out you can always get transferred back to the parent company and go back to sea,' she said.

'Don't even think it,' said George. 'After the last couple of years living ashore there's no way I'm going back to sea again.'

George impressed on Kay the need for secrecy and stressed that she hadn't even to mention it to any of the other wives. 'I'm the only one who knows anything about it,' he said, 'So if it gets back to Robinson on the grape vine he'll know it came from me.'

It was difficult for them both. Time and again they had to resist the temptation to pass the hot news on to the Longford clan. They would both have dearly liked to discuss the pros and cons of the changes with someone else but somehow they managed to keep quiet.

George started his shifts on Kharg Island and was soon used to the flights to and from the island. He was working with Al Faraday again and was also getting used to the modern diesel tugs once more. The work was so much more varied than at Mashur and there was so much of it. It wasn't uncommon to be working for the best part of the twenty-four hours on duty. It meant being very tired at the end of the shift and George's cigarette consumption was well into two packets at the end of it. It was just as well that he could still get a carton of cigarettes for a pound from his crew of veteran smugglers.

George also carried quite a lot of money back and forth to the Island. His crew would give him thousands of Iranian rials and George would get them changed into American dollars by the Abadan money changers. He was becoming an integral part of the smuggling business and would take the dollars back to Kharg on his next duty day. The dollars would then be converted into liquor and cigarettes from the visiting ships and these in turn would be sold to the traders on Kharg for a good profit in Iranian rials. George would then repeat the process all over again. It ensured a continuing supply of cheap cigarettes and booze for George and kept his crew happily in business. It also meant George was regularly in the bazaar and Kay was only too happy to go along too. She was now totally at home in the marketplace and was fast becoming adept at bargaining with the tradesmen in their own language.

Some six weeks later all of the tug men were called to the office once more and finally Captain Robinson let all of them know what George had been keeping under his hat with such great difficulty. George sat smugly listening as the others all asked the questions to which he had long since worked out the answers. Surprisingly, some of the masters didn't want to become pilots and were asking what would become of them when local staff took over. George mentally crossed them off his list and worked out where he would stand in the order of seniority. At least he was now established as working in Kharg Island. He would automatically be considered for pilotage duties before those who still worked in Bandar Mashur. He made a note to thank Captain Robinson once more when an opportune moment arose.

When everyone left the office there was still a buzz of excitement. Everyone was invited to continue the meeting at the Longford's house, so George collected Kay from home and went round to see what conclusions they would all come to. He needn't have bothered. Apart from reducing Peter's stock of beer to zero nothing new came up.

George and Kay later walked home. They were glad that they no longer had to keep secrets from the others. 'Of course,' said Kay to George, 'You realise that if you want to stay in Iran and become a pilot it will mean two things for sure.'

'What are they?'

'Well, firstly we'll have to send the children to boarding school in England one day.'

'I suppose we will,' agreed George. 'What do you think about that?'

'We'd get used to it, I suppose. Wonder what the kids would think of it?'

'Don't know,' said George. 'What's the second thing?'

'Think about it, George. We'd have to move from Abadan to the Island.'

George thought about it.

'I suppose it wouldn't be too bad.'

'If you think so, George.'

He thought about it some more. Would he really like to live on a tropical desert island surrounded by a coral reef? Would he really like to be a pilot and get paid extremely well?

For a nanosecond he thought about the alternatives.

'Let's do it,' he said.

'Why not?' agreed Kay and they linked arms and went off home.

THE EPILOGUE

The evening breeze rustled the drooping fronds of the stately old palm trees a hundred foot above them and the bullfrogs croaked hoarsely in the nearby *nullah*. In the distance a lonely pi-dog howled. The breezes were still balmy after a long day of tropical sunshine and George carried his suit jacket over his shoulder. Beside him walked Kay, in evening dress, complemented with a sequinned purse and light stole. It would be cool inside the company club with the air conditioning still going at full speed.

One eyed Ibrahim had dropped them off in the main square as they had been early and they strolled, arm in arm, towards the nearby complex of buildings. George felt stifled in his starched collar and tie but he was still pleased that they had received the printed invitation card from Captain Robinson. He had requested the pleasure of Captain and Mrs Penroy at a function to be held in the ballroom of the club. It would be a formal affair and all the refinery managers were due to attend. George wondered why he had been selected out of all the tug officers but supposed that his recent exploits had made his name known amongst the top brass.

'Have you got plenty of cash, George?' asked Kay.

'You know me,' he replied. 'Never go out without a wad big enough to choke a scabby donkey. Last of the big spenders.'

'Peasant,' remarked Kay, smiling. 'I've a sneaking feeling this may be a charity type evening. Donations to the *Sheer-e-Khorshid*.'

'The who? Sounds like an Iranian pop group to me.'

'The Red Lion and Sun,' explained Kay. 'Equivalent of our Red Cross as far as I can tell.'

'No. It can't be. That's the Red Crescent over here.'

'Oh! Full of local knowledge these days, aren't we, George?'

'I do pick up a few pearls of wisdom on my travels. Just need to find more swine to cast them before.'

They were now nearing the entrance to the club and could see the guard on the gate. Nobody else seemed to be arriving.

'Wonder if we're first to arrive?' muttered George. 'We have got the right day, haven't we?'

'Yes, we have. Have you got the invitation?'

George fished in the inside pocket of his jacket and brought out the gold edged card. He shrugged his arms into the jacket and buttoned it.

'Right day, right time,' he confirmed, 'How do I look?

'You'll do if you brush your hair down at the back.'

George licked his hand and stuck the wayward strands of hair in place. 'I've got thick hair,' he commented quietly. 'It's just widely spaced.'

He showed the invitation to the guard and was surprised when the man said, 'You wait here.' He looked quizzically at Kay, who raised her eyebrows questioningly. This was a bit unusual. The guard hurried back, followed by Captain Robinson.

'Good evening Kay. Evening George. Come with me.'

'Don't always get met at the door by the Super,' commented George. 'Must say the service around here is improving.'

They followed Captain Robinson who led them into the ballroom. They stopped just inside the door. The room was packed with well dressed people, all of whom were on their feet. George was about to ask what was going on when the whole crowd began clapping. He looked about, wildly. 'What goes on?' he hissed at the Superintendent.

'Just walk to the front and meet the Governor of Khuzestan, George. And you, Kay.'

He pulled George forward, so they did as they were

asked. The applause died down. The Governor was dressed in evening dress with a purple sash over his dinner jacket. He shook hands with George and then Kay and then addressed the assembly in English.

'Ladies and gentlemen, it gives me great pleasure to present Captain George Penroy with the Order of Homayoon, fifth class, in appreciation of his fine work, rescuing a member of the Imperial Iranian Air Force from the sea.'

He stepped close to George and pinned a large shiny medal to the lapel of his jacket. He then shook his hand again and presented him with a large scroll of paper, written in Farsi. The crowd clapped once more and then fell silent. 'Say something, George,' whispered the Super.

George cleared his throat. 'What could he say?' He thought, quickly.

'Your Excellency, Ladies and gentlemen, thank you for this honour. I will wear it with pride on behalf of all the crew of the tug Narimand, without whom the rescue would not have been possible. Thank you.'

There was another ripple of applause. 'Okay, George,' said Captain Robinson. 'We'll all go through to the dining room now. They've laid on a meal.'

'Shit!' muttered George, under his breath.

'We've already eaten once tonight,' said Kay. 'You should have warned us.'

'If I'd have warned you, your dearly beloved would probably have refused to come,' said the Super. 'Just forget the diet for one night. It's a buffet, so you can get away with only eating a little.'

They eased their way through a crowd of people who were jostling for position around the buffet. The Iranian code of courtesy didn't extend to food and there was always an unseemly rush when a meal was announced. George and Kay finally got plates and eased nearer to the food. It was then that George spied the waiter, standing in an oasis of calm amongst the turmoil. He was dressed in evening dress and was holding an immense oval serving dish of rice.

'Might as well start with the basics,' said George to Kay and taking the spoon from the dish commenced transferring rice onto his plate.

'Do you mind? That's mine.'

'Oh,' stuttered George, pushing the rice back on to the plate. 'I beg your pardon.'

He beat a hasty retreat followed closely by Kay. As soon as they were out of earshot they burst into uncontrollable laughter. 'You might be a hero to some, George, but to others you're just someone who would take the food from their plate.'

'Well,' said George, 'It's been quite an evening, so far. To hell with the buffet, let's see if we can get ourselves a drink.'

They found the bar and also Captain Robinson who was propping it up.

'Waste of time trying to get food. What are you having?'

'Beer for me and a soft drink for Kay, please. How long do you think before we can safely escape?'

'Better give it a while yet. You are the guest of honour, after all.'

'How long have you known about this little jaunt?' asked Kay.

'Oh, about three weeks. The company had to approve George getting a foreign decoration. They said it was fine and when you are home on leave they want you to go to head office so they can do an article for the house magazine.'

'Bloody hell, do I have to?' asked George, plaintively. 'I'm not too keen on being plastered all over the magazine.'

'Yes, you have to. You're flavour of the month and it won't do any harm at all for your face to be known in the office. Play your cards right, young George, and you could go far.'

'Kharg Island will be far enough for me. A pilots job will suit me fine, for now.'

'You're on the list but in the meantime you'd better come and see me in the office soon. We've got to get you on leave, then to the office and then to Bremen to learn about Voith Schneiders. He's going to be a busy boy, Kay. You'd better look after him.'

It was late when George and Kay finally left the club and George was rather unsteady on his legs. Kay held on to his arm as they went out to find a taxi and gently removed his medal from one clenched hand. He waved his scroll at a passing car hoping it was a taxi. Kay put the medal in her purse and gently took the scroll from his sweaty grasp.

'I'll look after these for you, sailor. You're likely to give your medal to the taxi driver as payment, the state that you're in.'

An aged black and white Opel taxi drew up next to them and Ibrahim looked at them through the open window with his one sparkling good eye.

'Taxi, Captain George?'

'Sure thing, you bloody old bandit. More loot for your retirement fund.' said George, cheerfully.

'Where you go, Captain?'

George thought carefully for a while.

'Take us home, Ibrahim,' he said, finally, and he realised that home was no longer a semi-detached in Southern England. Home was a flat roofed bungalow in Abadan, Iran.

THE END